George Gilbert Ramsay

Latin Prose Versions

George Gilbert Ramsay

Latin Prose Versions

ISBN/EAN: 9783337366766

Printed in Europe, USA, Canada, Australia, Japan

Cover: Foto ©Andreas Hilbeck / pixelio.de

More available books at **www.hansebooks.com**

LATIN PROSE VERSIONS

CONTRIBUTED BY VARIOUS SCHOLARS

EDITED BY

GEORGE G. RAMSAY,

M.A., LL.D., LITT. D.

PROFESSOR OF HUMANITY IN THE UNIVERSITY OF GLASGOW
AUTHOR OF 'LATIN PROSE COMPOSITION,' VOLS. I, II
EDITOR OF 'SELECTIONS FROM TIBULLUS AND PROPERTIUS'

Oxford

AT THE CLARENDON PRESS

M DCCC XCIV

EDITOR'S NOTE

Dr. Johnson thus defines Latin: 'An exercise practised by schoolboys who turn English into Latin.' Without accepting the limitations implied in this Johnsonian definition, teachers of classics will probably agree that the practice of Latin Prose Composition supplies them with their most effective instrument for teaching clearness of thought and purity of style. It has been thought, therefore, that a collection of specimens of work done in this department of scholarship by those who either are, or have been, teachers in our great schools and Universities, cannot fail to be of interest to all friends of classical education. It is hoped that the names to be found in the list of contributors to this volume will be a guarantee that it is fairly representative of the best Latin scholarship of this country at the present day.

The spelling adopted in the Latin Versions contained in this volume is as nearly as possible

uniform.   Where two spellings are found, if one particular form is held to be distinctly better than another, that form has been adopted throughout; where the usage of the best writers of the best period seems to have varied (as between *tanquam* and *tamquam, quidquid* and *quicquid*), the spelling preferred by each contributor has been retained. The numbers enclosed in brackets at the foot of many of the English passages refer to the number of the passage as given in *Ramsay's Latin Prose Composition, Vol. II*; where the letters *F. C.* occur, the reference is to *Foliorum Centuriae*.

As specimens of a different style of Latin, some of the Complimentary Addresses sent to Trinity College, Dublin, on the occasion of the recent Tercentenary have been appended.

I have to give my warm thanks to all the Contributors for the kindness with which they have placed at my disposal materials from which the versions which follow have been selected; and I have especially to thank Mr. Montague J. Rendall, and my Assistant Mr. John Brown, M.A., late Scholar of Worcester College, Oxford, for valuable help given in the editing of this volume.

G. G. R.

UNIVERSITY OF GLASGOW,
March 1, 1894.

LIST OF CONTRIBUTORS

Initials.	Authors of Latin Versions.	Pages
E. A.	Evelyn Abbott, Esq., M.A., LL.D., Fellow and Tutor of Balliol College, Oxford.	99, 109, 319.
A. T. B.	Alfred T. Barton, Esq., M.A., Fellow and Tutor of Pembroke College, Oxford.	49, 175 243, 293.
E. W. B.	His Grace the Archbishop of Canterbury, D.D., &c., &c., formerly Headmaster of Wellington College, and Fellow of Trinity College, Cambridge.	3, 45, 119, 131, 167, 287.
H. B.	Henry Broadbent, Esq., M.A., Assistant Master at Eton College; late Fellow of Exeter College, Oxford.	23, 127, 161, 163, 281.
S. H. B.	Samuel H. Butcher, Esq., M.A., LL.D., Litt. D., Professor of Greek in the University of Edinburgh, late Fellow of Trinity College, Cambridge.	5, 25, 35, 125, 205, 211, 303, 337.
W. H. B.	Rev. William Haig Brown, M.A., LL.D., Headmaster of Charterhouse, late Fellow and Tutor of Pembroke College, Cambridge.	53, 275, 283.
A. H. C.	Rev. Alfred H. Cruickshank, M.A., Assistant Master at Harrow School, Fellow of New College, Oxford.	29, 155, 167, 301, 357.

Initials.	Authors of Latin Versions.	Pages
J. C.	The late JOHN CONINGTON, Esq., M.A., late Professor of Latin Literature in the University of Oxford and Fellow of Corpus Christi College; formerly Fellow of University College.	51, 75, 141, 151, 313.
J. D. D.	JAMES D. DUFF, Esq., M.A., Fellow of Trinity College, Cambridge, and Lecturer in Classics.	111.
R. E.	ROBINSON ELLIS, Esq., M.A., LL.D., Professor of Latin Literature in the University of Oxford, late Vice-President and Lecturer, Trinity College; formerly Professor of Latin in University College, London.	89, 135, 161, 237.
T. S. E.	The late REV. THOMAS S. EVANS, M.A., D.D., late Professor of Greek in the University of Durham, and formerly Assistant Master at Rugby School.	79, 85, 95, 171, 183.
H. C. G.	HARRY C. GOODHART, Esq., M.A., Professor of Humanity in the University of Edinburgh, formerly Fellow and Lecturer of Trinity College, Cambridge.	73, 343, 373.
W. D. G.	SIR WILLIAM D. GEDDES, LL.D., Vice-Chancellor and Principal of the University of Aberdeen; formerly Professor of Greek.	372.
J. H.	JOHN HARROWER, Esq., M.A., Professor of Greek in the University of Aberdeen; late scholar of Pembroke College, Oxford.	15, 61, 65, 67, 69.
W. R. H.	WILLIAM R. HARDIE, Esq., M.A., Fellow and Tutor of Balliol College, Oxford.	187, 219, 225, 309, 315.

Initials.	Authors of Latin Versions.	Pages
D. S. M.	David S. Margoliouth, Esq., M.A., F.R.S., Sub-Warden, Fellow and Lecturer of New College, Oxford, and Laudian Professor of Arabic in the University.	137, 193, 233, 241, 279.
E. D. A. M.	Edmund D. A. Morshead, Esq., M.A., Assistant Master at Winchester College, late Fellow of New College, Oxford.	9, 101, 157, 177, 273, 321, 325, 351.
F. D. M.	Rev. Francis D. Morice, M.A., Fellow of Queen's College, Oxford, Assistant Master at Rugby School.	11, 21, 27, 33, 107, 195, 197, 267, 341, 345.
W. W. M.	Rev. William W. Merry, D.D., Public Orator of the University of Oxford, and Rector of Lincoln College.	364.
H. N.	The late Henry Nettleship, Esq., M.A., late Professor of Latin Literature in the University of Oxford, and Fellow of Corpus Christi College ; formerly Fellow of Lincoln College.	105, 133, 263, 277, 289, 349.
J. P. P.	John P. Postgate, Esq., M.A., Litt.D., Professor of Comparative Philology in University College, London, and Fellow of Trinity College, Cambridge.	121.
G. G. R.	The Editor.	17, 45, 97, 147, 181, 197, 215, 231, 370.
G. H. R.	Gerald H. Rendall, Esq., M.A., Vice-Chancellor of the Victoria University, Principal of University College, Liverpool ; late Fellow of Trinity College, Cambridge.	113, 233, 239, 249, 267, 291, 311, 375.
M. J. R.	Montague J. Rendall, Esq., M.A., Assistant Master at Winchester College, late Fellow of Trinity College, Cambridge.	13, 59, 129, 247, 259, 359.

Initials.	Authors of Latin Versions.	Pages
J. S. R.	JAMES S. REID, Esq., M.A., Litt.D., Fellow of Gonville and Caius College, late Fellow of Christ's College, Cambridge.	7, 79, 85, 117, 149, 189, 209, 251, 269, 323, 329, 339, 353.
A. S.	ARTHUR SIDGWICK, Esq., M.A., Fellow and Tutor of Corpus Christi College. Oxford, and Greek Reader in the University; late Fellow of Trinity College, Cambridge.	37, 41, 137, 173, 179, 203, 219, 229, 235, 257, 327, 335.
J. E. S.	JOHN E. SANDYS, Esq., M.A., Litt.D., Public Orator of the University of Cambridge; Fellow, Tutor and Lecturer of St. John's College.	95, 366, 368.
R. S.	The late REV. RICHARD SHILLETO, M.A., Classical Lecturer at King's College, Cambridge, and formerly Fellow of St. Peter's College.	57, 71, 91, 145, 201, 215, 223.
E. C. W.	THE VERY REV. EDWARD C. WICKHAM, M.A., Dean of Lincoln, late Headmaster of Wellington College, and formerly Fellow of New College, Oxford.	19, 123, 185, 191, 299, 305, 333.
W. W.	WILLIAM WYSE, Esq., M.A., Professor of Greek in University College, London; late Fellow and Tutor of Trinity College, Cambridge.	81, 255, 295.

LIST OF AUTHORS OF ENGLISH PASSAGES

The numbers refer to the pages.

ERRATA

Page vii, col. 3, line 6, *omit* 23

,, viii, ,, 3, *omit* line 2

,, viii, ,, 3, line 4, *insert* 151

,, viii, ,, 3, ,, 10, *insert* 23

,, x, *insert*

| J. Y. S. | J. YOUNG SARGENT, Esq., M.A., Fellow of Hertford College, Oxford. | 313 |

,, 23, last line, for *H.* read *J. H.*

,, 46, line 21, *for* progress *read* prowess

,, 46, last line, for *J. R. Green* read *Hume*

,, 69, line 14, *for* honestium *read* honestum

,, 153, last line, for *J. C.* read *R. E.*

,, 197, line 4, *for* praestes *read* praesta

,, 231, ,, 11, *for* gentibus *read* gentes

,, 315, ,, 9, for *J. C.* read *J. Y. S.*

Latin Prose Versions (quarto edition)

LATIN PROSE VERSIONS

OVER and above the raging epidemic, they had just gone over Attica and ascertained the devastations committed throughout all the territory (except the Marathonian Tetrapolis and Dekeleia districts spared, as we are told, through indulgence founded on an ancient legendary sympathy) during their long stay of forty days. The rich had found their comfortable mansions and farms, the poor their modest cottages, in the various demes, torn and ruined. Death, sickness, loss of property, and despair of the future, now rendered the Athenians angry and intractable to the last degree; and they vented their feelings against Pericles, as the cause, not merely of the war, but also of all that they were now enduring. Either with or without his consent, they sent envoys to Sparta to open negotiations for peace, but the Spartans turned a deaf ear to the proposition. This new disappointment rendered them still more furious against Pericles, whose long-standing political enemies now doubtless found strong sympathy in their denunciations of his character and policy. That unshaken and majestic firmness which ranked first among his many eminent qualities, was never more imperiously required, and never more effectively manifested.

[No. 258.]　　　　　　　　　　　　*Grote.*

PESTI quae adhuc grassabatur accessit quod Attica perlustrata regressi cognouerant tandem quantum agro uniuerso iniuriae per quadraginta iam dies hostis intulisset. Scilicet non nisi a Marathonensium quattuor uicis ac Decelea, ex gratia quadam uetustis ut ferebatur fabulis conciliata, temperatum. Diuitibus uillarum deliciae ac fundi, pauperibus praediola, singulis in pagis indigne euersa atque diruta. Amicorum, ualetudinis, rerum iactura, futuri denique desperatione, irae populares adeo exstimulatae, ut nulli parerent, unum Periclem incusarent quasi non belli modo sed et omnium quibus opprimerentur malorum auctor fuisset. Ergo, suadente ipso necne incertum, Spartam legatos qui de pace agerent misere: qui cum re infecta rediissent, hac quoque spe deiecti in Periclem ira accendi, ut inimicis in mores domesticos pariter ac ciuilia consilia iam diu inuehentibus multi consenserint fautores. Cuius quidem firmitatem magnitudinemque animi, quae tot inter praestantissimas ingenii dotes praecipue eminebat, nunquam alias maior aut occasio postulauit aut euentus comprobauit.

E. W. B.

BUT the prospect at home was not over-clouded merely; it was the very deepest darkness of misery. It has been well said that long periods of general suffering make far less impression on our minds than the sharp short struggle in which a few distinguished individuals perish; not that we over-estimate the horror and the guilt of times of open blood-shedding, but we are much too patient of the greater misery and greater sin of periods of quiet legalised oppression; of that most deadly of all evils, when law, and even religion herself, are false to their divine origin and purpose, and their voice is no longer the voice of God, but of his enemy. In such cases the evil derives advantage, in a manner, from the very amount of its own enormity. No pen can record, no volume can contain, the details of the daily and hourly sufferings of a whole people, endured without intermission, through the whole life of man, from the cradle to the grave. The mind itself can scarcely comprehend the wide range of the mischief.

[No. 223.]   *Dr. Arnold.*

DOMI interea non minacia tantum omnia, sed, ut in perditis rebus, nihil dispici poterat. Haud insipienter illud quidem dictum est, non tam diuturna uniuersorum miseria animos moueri, quam iis dimicantium furoribus qui cum singulorum et inlustrium interitu sint coniuncti. Non quo ea, quae in manifestis caedibus atrociter ac nefarie fiunt, aequo grauiora esse uideantur, sed quia parum indignamur quotiens maiore cum calamitate et scelere, ne legibus quidem reclamantibus, uexantur ciues; cum eo res recidit ut saluis legibus ac religionibus, quarum uis et origo peruertatur, fas et nefas misceantur. Quo in genere sua ipsius immanitate malum quodammodo alitur: nam quid sit in uniuerso populo cotidiana dolorum adsiduitas, nullo temporum aut aetatum interuallo, usque ad extremum spiritum continuata, neque memoriae prodi neque scriptis contineri potest; idque malum quam late pateat ne cogitando quidem satis comprehendimus.

S. H. B.

HIS Majesty being dead, the Duke, now K. James II, went immediately to Council, and before entering into any business, passionately declaring his sorrow, told their Lordships that since the succession had fallen to him, he would endeavour to follow the example of his predecessor in his clemency and tenderness to his people, that however he had been misrepresented as affecting arbitrary power, they should find the contrary, for that the laws of England had made the king as great a monarch as he could desire; that he would endeavour to maintain the government both in Church and State, as by Law established, its principles being so firm for Monarchy, and the members of it showing themselves so good and loyal subjects, and that as he would never depart from the just rights and prerogatives of the Crown, so would he never invade any man's property; but as he had often adventured his life in defence of the nation, so he would still proceed and preserve it in all its lawful rights and liberties. This being the substance of what he said, the Lords desired it might be published, as containing matter of great satisfaction to a jealous people upon this change, which his Majesty consented to.

[F. C. 45.]   *Evelyn.*

DECESSERAT iam imperator et frater in imperium ascitus extemplo senatum adit. Neque ullam rem prius rettulit quam dolorem esset flagrantissime testatus. Scirent patres se qui in principatum successisset, exemplo diui Caroli indulgentiam in populum misericordiamque adhibiturum. Nimirum esse qui dominationem quaeri criminarentur; ceterum alia omnia euentura. Quippe ipsius rei publicae leges principi tantum tribuisse quantum fas esset optari; destinasse igitur se maiorum cum caerimonias tum instituta conseruare, praesertim cum ista tanto opere unius imperio fauerent, ipsique ciues et uirtute et obsequio praestarent. Se quidem, ut nihil de iure imperatorio et auctoritate detrahi passurum, ita nullius bona inuasurum; immo et saepius antea dimicantem pro patria in periculum uitae uenisse, et nunc in eodem consilio perseueraturum, ut iura ciuitatis libertatemque uindicaret. Quae in hanc fere sententiam dixisset, patres edicenda censuere, quasi ad populum, ut in rerum mutatione arrectum, pergrata futura; neque ipse recusauit.

J. S. R.

WHEN the remnant of the Old Guard gave way, and Bulow's Prussians marched up from the valley to the chaussée, they found the main body of the French flying in utter disorder along the road and across the fields. The great high road was choked up by the fugitives; the very efforts of the pursuers were obstructed by the chaos into which they plunged. Arms were thrown down, packs cast off, guns abandoned. The British and the Prussians, con-verging upon the Charleroi road between La Belle Alliance and Rossomme, forced all they did not take or slay into the fields or the main road. Darkness had settled over the field; the masses, moving through the obscurity, hurtled against each other, and more than once friends were mistaken for foes. But in the gloom of that summer evening, lighted only by a rising moon, there was such exultation as men can feel only when, by fortitude and skill, they have snatched a brilliant victory from the very jaws of destruction. As the Prussians came up from the bloodstained village of Planchenoit, their bands played 'God save the King,' and the heroic British infantry in the van answered with true British cheers.

[No. 232.]   *Hooper.*

IAM cedentibus qui supererant Gallorum ueteranis, Germanorum dux suos e ualle in stratam pauimento uiam erigere et promouere; quo cum uenissent, Gallos effusa fuga aut uiam occupare aut agros transcurrere conspexerunt; ipsa uia, ut lata erat, ita fugientibus conferta; nec ipsi qui insectabantur, corpore et armis nisi, confusam uirorum turbam aut penetrare aut propellere poterant, adeo abiectis armis et sarcinis undique obsaepiebantur. Iam Britanni et Germani inter duo praedia in unum coeuntes quidquid Gallorum nec ceperant nec occiderant aut in agros aut in magnam uiam compulerunt: inde, noctis umbris campo incumbentibus, uictores inter caliginem sibi obuiam facti nonnumquam ignari ignaris ut hostibus concurrebant: uerum inter tenebras aestiui uesperis, oriente luna parum distinctas, ea emicabat inter sociatos laetitia quae iis tantum conceditur qui inter summa pericula, imminente exitio, uictoriam uirtute et consilio arripuerint. Ita Germanis iam praeter uicum strage et sanguine fluentem progressis et patrio Britannorum more uictoriam canentibus, qui peditis nostri prouectiores erant, longa dimicatione insignem famam meriti, Martio clamore et salutatione responderunt.

E. D. A. M.

IN the invasion of France, many years after, some Polish regiments in the service of Russia passed through the village where this exiled patriot then lived. Some pillaging of the inhabitants brought Kosciusko from his cottage. 'When I was a Polish soldier,' said he, addressing the plunderers, 'the property of the peaceful citizen was respected.' 'And who art thou?' said an officer, 'who addressest us with a tone of authority?' 'I am Kosciusko.' There was magic in the word. It ran from corps to corps. The march was suspended. They gathered round him, and gazed with astonishment and awe upon the mighty ruin he presented. 'Could it indeed be their hero, whose fame was identified with that of their country?' A thousand interesting reflections burst upon their minds; they remembered his patriotism, his devotion to liberty, his triumphs, and his glorious fall. Their iron hearts were softened; the tears trickled down their faces as they grieved in idle indignation over their country's shameful doom, nor is it difficult to conceive what would be the feelings of the hero himself in such a scene.

[No. 241.]   *Percy Anecdotes.*

MVLTIS postea annis cohortes aliquae Polonicae, dum secutae Russorum signa Galliam inuadunt, paganis apud quos tum Coscius exulabat spoliatis, e tugurio rustico ipsum exciuerunt. Qui praedantes allocutus, Me uero, inquit, uobiscum militante, ciuium quietorum bonis temperabatur. Tum roganti tribuno alicui, quis tam imperiosa uoce milites corriperet, respondit ille Coscium se esse. Quod dictum cum per exercitum totum cito celebratum mentes omnium obstupefecisset, statim omisso itinere milites undique congregati uiri tanti quasi umbram et reliquias timide mirantur. Huncne illum esse, cuius laudes Poloniam honestauissent? cui non succurrere multa eius et praeclara facta? quantum in eo patriae, quantum libertatis amorem fuisse: denique post tot tantasque uictorias quam splendide cecidisse. Recordantibus haec animi praeter solitum molliuntur: effusi in lacrimas funus dedecusque patriae frustra detestantur. Neque difficile est coniectu quomodo affectus ipse maerentem coetum circumspexerit.

F. D. M.

HERE, therefore, we are to enter upon one of the grand scenes of history; a solemn battle fought out to the death, yet fought without ferocity, by the champions of rival principles. Heroic men had fallen, and were still fast falling, for what was called heresy; and now those who had inflicted death on others were called upon to bear the same witness to their own sincerity. England became the theatre of a war between two armies of martyrs, to be waged, not upon the open field, in open action, but on the stake and on the scaffold, with the nobler weapons of passive endurance. Each party were ready to give their own blood; each party were ready to shed the blood of their antagonists; and the sword was to single out its victims in the rival ranks, not, as in peace, among those whose crimes made them dangerous to society, but as on the field of battle, where the most conspicuous courage most challenges the aim of the enemy. It was war though under the form of peace; and if we would understand the true spirit of the time, we must regard Catholics and Protestants as gallant soldiers, whose deaths, when they fall, are not painful, but glorious; and whose devotion we are equally able to admire, even where we cannot equally approve their cause.

[No. 255.]   *Froude.*

ATTINGIMVS igitur annalibus nostris mag-
nificam rerum speciem, ubi partium inter se
aemulantium uindices proelium augustum nullis
induciis, nulla tamen impotentia committebant.
Nam ut mira constantia, nouandae scilicet religionis
crimine, caesi erant ad multos et caedebantur, ita
qui alios morte mulctauerant, fidem ipsi suam pari
supplicio testarentur necesse erat. In Britannia
cruentum praebituri erant exercitus duo spectaculum proelii non collatis signis, non aperto
campo, sed ad palum crucemque commissi, cum se
nullis armis, sed, quod praestantius erat, uirtute
omnes ac patientia defenderent. Itaque, et his et
illis uel suum praebere uel hostium haurire
sanguinem paratis, ferro destinabantur utrimque
non qui, quae pacis ratio, facinoribus rei publicae
periculosi, sed ut in acie, ubi Mars fortissimum
quemque pignerari solet. Cum igitur specie pacis
bellum gereretur, debemus, si rerum rationem
recte perspiciemus, et fautoribus Papae et aduer-
sariis militum tribuere uirtutem; et fata utrorum-
que admirati potius quam lamentati, etsi consilia
pariter comprobare non possumus, constantiam
saltem laudabimus.

M. J. R.

FOR two centuries the history of British possessions in India was the history of accumulated successes. Dangers there had been, and difficulties ; but each onward movement, with here and there a fluctuation, ended in a triumph which the fluctuation enhanced. There is no record of so many and such prosperous struggles leading to such a supremacy in the previous annals of any people save of the Romans alone. Here, too, as there, the empire seemed to grow by the very necessity of the case. ᛁ New contracts brought new collisions. The sagacity of the civilized race, the steadfastness of the disciplined host, here by negotiation, there by the shock of armies, widened the circle of a conquest. There was nothing which could be called a reverse to shade the bright outline except that one instance which invested with horror the name of Sooraj-ud-Dowlah. The memory of disasters is lost in the keener recollection of disgrace. We boast no longer that the flag of Britain in India is free from the soil of dishonour. Rome had her Furcae Caudinae. On the page of the English historian will stand out for ever a blot unerased— the tale of the Khyber Pass.

PER annos ducentos fines imperii Britannis apud Indos propagantibus uictoriae uictorias deinceps exceperunt. Multa quidem pericula et labores obeunda erant; quotienscumque tamen longius pergebant arma nostra, totiens res prospere ad postremum euenerunt, eoque faustius quod aliquando anceps fuerat fortuna. Tantum uero imperium nullam aliam gentem audiuimus praeter ipsos Romanos tot et tam prosperis certaminibus esse consecutam. Namque ut illorum sic nostra res tamquam ipsa necessitate augeri uidebatur. Cum enim e nouis foederibus noua orirentur certamina, Britanni, ut qui cum hoste rudi contenderent, et sollerter res agendo et constanti militum in dimicando disciplina imperii fines semper promouebant. Nec quicquam sane acceptum est incommodi quod tantam nostram claritudinem obscuraret praeter unam illam cladem quae nomen Soraeodolii infestum reddidit. Iam uero rerum aduersarum memoriam pudor exsuperat; neque posthac iactare possumus uexilla Britannorum nullum in India dedecus suscepisse: ut Romanis dolendae erant Furcae illae Caudinae, sic nostris ex annalibus cladis illius labes ad fauces acceptae Khybernias numquam eluetur.

J. H.

WHERE was there ever such peace, such tranquillity, such justice, such honours paid to virtue, such rewards distributed to the good and punishments to the bad; when was ever the state so wisely guided, as in the time when the world had obtained one head, and that head Rome? the very time wherein God deigned to be born of a Virgin and to dwell upon earth. To every single body there has been given a head; the whole world therefore also, which is called by the poet a great body, ought to be content with one temporal head. For every two-headed animal is monstrous; how much more horrible and hideous a portent must be a creature with a thousand different heads, biting and fighting against one another! If, however, it is necessary that there be more heads than one, it is nevertheless evident that there ought to be one to restrain all and preside over all, so that the peace of the whole body may abide unshaken. Assuredly both in heaven and in earth the sovereignty of one has always been best.

[No. 205.]

ET quando fuit usquam in terris tanta pacis, otii, tranquillitatis diuturnitas? Quando in tanto honore uirtus? Quando tam digna bonis improbisque uel laudis uel poenae distributio? Quando umquam tanta in gerendis rebus sapientia, quanta eo fuit tempore cum Roma quasi caput toti terrarum orbi praefuit, Deusque ipse, natus e Virgine, inter homines uersari dignabatur? Nam ut corporibus omnibus caput unum est natura constitutum, ita et ipsi terrarum orbi, quod quasi immensum corpus esse poeta quidam finxit, unum modo caput ad dirigenda omnia imponi oportet. Quippe corpora ea quibus bina sunt capita pro monstris habentur: quanto immanius et foedius portentum illud cui mille sint capita, quae inter se pugnantia sese inuicem mordicus dilanient? Quod si capita existant plura necesse est, apparet tamen unum saltem ita esse oportere ut praesit ceteris, pacemque omnibus imperio confirmet. Nam ut ab uno dirigantur omnia, id semper apud deos hominesque optimum esse existimatum est.

G. G. R.

SUCH will be the impotent condition of those men of great hereditary estates who indeed dislike the designs that are carried on, but whose dislike is rather that of spectators than of parties that may be concerned in the catastrophe of the piece. But riches do not in all cases secure an inert and passive resistance. There are always in that description men whose fortunes, when their minds are once vibrated by passion or evil principle, are by no means a security from their actually taking their part against the public tranquillity. We see to what low and despicable passions of all kinds many men in that class are ready to sacrifice the patrimonial estates which might be perpetuated in their families, with splendour and with the fame of hereditary benefactors of mankind, from generation to generation. Do we not see how lightly people treat their fortunes, when under the influence of the passion of gaming? The game of ambition or resentment will be played by many of the rich and great as desperately and with as much blindness to the consequences as any other game.

[No. 274.]

TANTA erit eorum imbecillitas qui in ueteri dignitate fortunaque nati consilia ista oderint, ita tamen oderint quasi spectatores sint otiosi potius quam ii ipsi quorum res agatur. Ac ne id quidem semper praestant diuitiae ut segniter saltem et timide nouis rebus resistatur. Sunt enim semper in hoc genere quibus, cum animi semel ira aut libidine aliqua corrupti sint, nihil per fortunas obstet quominus ipsi consilia ineant reipublicae conturbandae. Videmus profecto in quam uiles abiectasque libidines plurimi huiusmodi patrimonia soleant effundere, quae posteris legata splendorem nominis cum hereditaria quadam publicae utilitatis gloria per longam nepotum seriem continuare potuissent. Vidimus nimirum quam parui fortunas homines aestimare soleant cum aleae studio flagrauerint. Erunt uero e diuitibus qui si ambitioni uel irae se dederint non minus inconsiderata dementique temeritate res agant quam qui alea ludunt.

E. C W.

SOME time after, the people discovered their sentiments in such a manner as was sufficient to prognosticate to the priests the fate which was awaiting them. It was usual on the festival of St. Giles, the tutelar saint of Edinburgh, to carry in procession the image of that saint; but the Protestants, in order to prevent the ceremony, found means, on the eve of the festival, to purloin the statue from the church; and they pleased themselves with imagining the surprise and disappointment of his votaries. The clergy, however, framed hastily a new image, which, in derision, was called by the people young St. Giles; and they carried it through the streets, attended by all the ecclesiastics in the town and neighbourhood. The multitude abstained from violence so long as the queen-regent con-tinued a spectator, but the moment she retired, they invaded the idol, threw it in the mire, and broke it in pieces. The flight and terror of the priests and friars, who, it was remarked, deserted, in his greatest distress, the object of their worship, was the source of universal mockery and laughter.

[No. 247.]   *Hume.*

POSTEA aliquanto plebes, quae in animo haberet, facinore tali indicauit, ut facile esset sacerdotibus diuinare, quis exitus ipsos maneret. Forte enim, cum mos esset ut stato die effigies Diui Aegidii, quem praecipue uenerabantur Edinenses, per urbem in pompa ferretur, eam tum effigiem, ne sollemne fieret, homines quidam sacerdotibus aduersarii e templo pridie illius diei auferendam curant: inopinatum id scilicet et luctuosum religionis cultoribus fore, eoque magis sibi ipsis laetum. Sacerdotes autem fabricantur propere effigiem nouam, quam plebeii irridentes *Aegidiolum* uocant. Ferebatur tamen per plateas, comitantibus quodcunque sacerdotum aut in urbe ipsa aut in uicinia erat. Quae dum regina spectabat, tantisper manus plebes continebat: postquam recessit, statim, impetu facto, effigiem deiectam et in luto prostratam confregerunt. Ac fugati et pauentes pontifices ceterique sacerdotes uulgo deridentur; quippe qui proprium illum suum et quasi peculiarem Diuum in extremo discrimine ac periculo destituissent.

F. D. M.

I T was scarcely possible that the eyes of contemporaries should discover in the public
felicity the latent causes of decay. This long
peace and the uniform government of the Romans
introduced a slow and secret poison into the vitals
of the empire. The minds of men were gradually
reduced to the same level, the fire of genius was
extinguished, and even the military spirit evapo-
rated. The natives of Europe were brave and
robust; Spain, Gaul, Britain, and Illyricum supplied the legions with excellent soldiers, and
constituted the real strength of the monarchy.
Their personal valour remained, but they no
longer possessed that public courage which is
nourished by the love of independence, the
presence of danger, and the habit of command.
They received laws and governors from the will
of their sovereign, and trusted for their defence to
a mercenary army. The posterity of their boldest
leaders was contented with the rank of citizens
and subjects. The most aspiring spirits resorted
to the court or standard of the emperors; and the
deserted provinces, deprived of political strength or
union, insensibly sunk into the languid indifference
of private life.

[No. 259.]   *Gibbon.*

VIX quidem fieri potuit ut ab iis qui illorum temporum essent aequales futuri semina exitii discernerentur quae sub tanta omnium felicitate latebant. Attamen tamquam lene et occultum uenenum pax illa diuturna tenorque perpetuus dicionis Romanae in medullas imperii ac uiscera instillabant. Paullatim enim factum est ut, restinctis ingenii igniculis, nulli inter ciues ob indolem eminerent, exolesceretque etiam studium militare. Prouinciarum ex incolis, fortitudine ualidisque corporibus militiae aptissimis, explebantur legiones, quod uerum imperii erat tutamentum. Ciuibus quidem singulis non deerat animus, euanuerat tamen illa uirtus quae in tota ciuitate amore libertatis, periculo communi, usuque imperandi nutritur. Imperatoris ex arbitrio et leges et praefectos acceperunt; armis mercenariis suam salutem committebant. Atque adeo iam loco ciuium priuatorum contenti fuerunt qui originem a ductoribus fortissimis traxerunt; gloriae si quis erat studiosior, ad aulam aut uexilla imperatoris se contulit. Itaque cum provinciis, desertis et inter se disiunctis, nihil uirium esset relictum, apud ciues qui in rebus priuatis uersabantur hebescebat cura rei publicae.

H.

A T such times society, distracted by the conflict of individual wills, and unable to attain
by their free concurrence to a general will, which
might unite and hold them in subjection, feels an
ardent desire for a sovereign power, to which all
individuals must submit; and as soon as any
institution presents itself which bears any of the
characteristics of legitimate sovereignty, society
rallies round it with eagerness; as people under
proscription take refuge in the sanctuary of
a church. This is what has taken place in the
wild and disorderly youth of nations, such as
those we have just described. Monarchy is won-
derfully suited to those times of strong and fruitful
anarchy, if I may so speak, in which society is
striving to form and regulate itself, but is unable
to do so by the free concurrence of individual
wills. There are other times when monarchy,
though from a contrary cause, has the same merit.
Why did the Roman world, so near dissolution at
the end of the republic, still subsist for more than
fifteen centuries under the name of an empire,
which, after all, was nothing but a lingering
decay, a protracted death-struggle? Monarchy
only could produce such an effect.

[No. 224.]

EIVSMODI temporibus, cum singulis inter se dissentientibus discordat ciuitas, neque possunt ciues ita conspirare ut ad uniuersi populi uoluntatem et arbitrium res publica reuocetur, uulgo homines imperium quo singuli coerceantur expetunt; itaque primum quidque amplectuntur quod iure aliquo id sibi adrogare uideatur; huc, sicut in aram proscripti confugiunt, omnium se studia conferunt. Quod quidem in ciuitatibus nondum adultis, et in ea, quam commemoraui, morum licentia iam saepe euenit: tum enim cum incondita adhuc est libertas, cum inchoata multa sunt, perfectum nihil, cum homines id agunt ut instituatur et informetur ciuitas, neque singulorum consensu id fieri potest, nihil tam conuenit quam penes unum esse summam rerum. Iam uero diuersam ob causam est ubi eadem fere regni uis sit. Rem quidem Romanam stante adhuc re publica paene dissolutam, quid in milesimum quingentesimum annum seruauit, ita tamen ut specie imperii consenesceret et interiret aliquando? Nempe id in regno omne positum est.

S. H. B.

NO sooner was the king alone, than his temper, more cautious than sanguine, suggested very different views of the matter, and represented every difficulty and danger which could occur. He reflected that, however the world might pardon this folly of youth in the prince, they would never forgive himself, who, at his years, and after his experience, could entrust his only son, the heir of his crown, the prop of his age, to the discretion of foreigners, without so much as providing the frail security of a safe conduct in his favour ; that if the Spanish monarch were sincere in his professions, a few months must finish the treaty of marriage, and bring the Infanta into England; if he were not sincere, the folly was still more egregious of committing the prince into his hands; that Philip, when possessed of so invaluable a pledge, might well rise in his demands, and impose harder conditions of treaty; and that the temerity of the enterprise was so apparent, that the event, how prosperous soever, could not justify it ; and if disastrous, it would render himself infamous to his people, and ridiculous to all posterity.

[No. 243.]   *Hume.*

HIS egressis, continuo rex, ut erat semper ad cauendum quam ad spem propensior, longe aliter rem spectare ; quicquid difficultatis, quicquid periculi habere poterat, omnia iam animo praecipiebat. Posse quidem in filio suo adolescentulo ferendam uideri audaciam : se uero apud neminem unquam excusatum iri, qui id aetatis, tot res expertus, filium suum unicum, haeredem regni, senectutis tutelam ac praesidium, peregrinorum in fidem traderet, ne hoc quidem ante cauto, in quo quantulum defensionis esse, ut redeundi libertas promitteretur. Quae professus esset rex Hispanus, ea si uera essent, ratum futurum esse intra paucos menses foedus de filiae eius matrimonio, ipsamque simul in Angliam uenturam ; si falsa, eo stultius sese agere, qui peieranti filium committeret. Exspectandum esse etiam, ut accepto tanto pignore Philippus plura expeteret, et in foedere faciendo duriora stipularetur. Consilium denique tam aperte temerarium euentum nullum, ne felicissimum quidem, commendare posse. Sin male uertisset, se ideo et apud ciues infamem, et posteris ludibrio futurum.

F. D. M.

WHEN they were introduced into his presence, they declared, perhaps in a more lofty style than became their abject condition, that the Romans were resolved to maintain their dignity, either in peace or war; and that, if Alaric refused them a fair and honourable capitulation, he might sound his trumpets and prepare to give battle to an innumerable people, exercised in arms, and animated by despair. 'The thicker the hay, the easier it is mowed,' was the concise reply of the Barbarian; and this rustic metaphor was accompanied by a loud and insulting laugh, expressive of his contempt for the menaces of an unwarlike populace, enervated by luxury before they were emaciated by famine. He then condescended to fix the ransom which he would accept as the price of his retreat from the walls of Rome; all the gold and silver in the city, whether it were the property of the state or of individuals; all the rich and precious moveables; and all the slaves who could prove their title to the name of Barbarians. The ministers of the senate presumed to ask, in a modest and suppliant tone, 'If such, O king, are your demands, what do you intend to leave us?' 'YOUR LIVES,' replied the haughty conqueror: they trembled and retired.

[F .C. No. 344.]   *Gibbon.*

AD regem adducti asseuerabant superbius
fortasse quam afflictos decebat, se statuisse
dignitatem suam uel in Marte uel in pace tueri;
proinde, si condiciones aequas et honestas recu-
saret, bellicum caneret, et decertare cum populo
pararet innumerabili, assueto armis, spe deposita
securo. Quibus rex barbarus breuiter respondit
quo densius faenum eo facilius demeti, adiecto
sententiae tam agresti cachinno contumelioso quo
significabat quantum minas hominum ignauorum
sperneret, non modo fame confectorum sed luxu
iam antea diffluentium. Tum demum ei placuit
pretium constituere quo expenso urbem relinqueret: omne scilicet aurum et argentum quod
in urbe esset, et publicum et priuatum, supellec-
tilem omnem pretiosam et diuitem, seruos denique
omnes qui barbarorum originem sibi asserere
possent. Tum legati a senatu uoce demissa et
supplici rogare ausi, quid sibi tot tantisque rebus
exactis relinqueret. Ille autem, 'Vitas,' inquit,
'uestras': nec plura superbiens. Illi tremebundi
facessere.

A. H. C.

THE road, all down the long descent, and through the plain to the banks of the river, was lined, mile after mile, with spectators. From the West Gate to the Cathedral Close the pressing and shouting on each side was such as reminded Londoners of the crowds on Lord Mayor's Day. Doors, windows, balconies, and roofs were thronged with gazers. An eye accustomed to the pomp of war would have found much to criticize in the spectacle. For several toilsome marches in the rain, through roads where one who travelled on foot sank at every step up to the ancles in clay, had not improved the appearance of men or their accoutrements. But the people of Devonshire, altogether unused to the splendour of well-ordered camps, were overwhelmed with delight and awe. Descriptions of the martial pageant were circulated all over the kingdom. They contained much that was well-fitted to gratify the vulgar appetite for the marvellous. For the Dutch army, composed of men who had been born in various climates, and had served under various standards, presented an aspect at once grotesque, gorgeous, and terrible to islanders, who had, in general, a very indistinct notion of foreign countries.

[No. 213.]   *Macaulay.*

DESCENDENTIBVS per tam longum cliuum et inde per campum ad ripas fluuii continuata utrimque ingens series spectantium. Ab occidentali porta usque ad aedem maximam ornatae ut in festo domus, confertae intuentibus ianuae, fenestrae, tecta, porticus. Et erant quae reprehenderet si cui usitatior bellorum apparatus. Deformarat militum armorumque speciem repetitus per imbres labor itinerum, dum per uias proficiscuntur ubi ut quisque pedes ibat singulis passibus crurum tenus caeno mergebatur. Sed Deuonienses, quibus insolitus castrorum is decor et disciplina, cum gaudio metuque omnia prospiciebant. Increbrescere ubique fama tanti apparatus: nec sane deerant quibus auidum mirabilium uulgus caperetur. Quippe Batauorum exercitus, homines qui aliis alii regionibus nati diuersa tulerant stipendia, speciem praestabant ut ludicram magnificamque, ita insulam colentibus terribilem: qui incerta plerumque de peregrinis intellegerent.

THE pirates called themselves Cilicians; in fact their vessels were the rendezvous of desperadoes and adventurers from all countries—discharged mercenaries from the recruiting-grounds of Crete, burgesses from the destroyed townships of Italy, Spain, and Asia, soldiers and officers from the armies of Fimbria and Sertorius, in a word the ruined men of all nations, the hunted refugees of all vanquished parties, every one that was wretched and daring—and where was there not misery and violence in this unhappy age? It was no longer a gang of robbers who had flocked together, but a compact soldier-state, in which the freemasonry of exile and crime took the place of nationality, and within which crime redeemed itself, as it so often does in its own eyes, by displaying the most generous public spirit. If the banner of this state was inscribed with vengeance against the civil society which, rightly or wrongly, had ejected its members, it might be a question whether this device was much worse than those of the Italian oligarchy and the Oriental sultanship which seemed in the course of dividing the world between them.

[No. 251.]

CILICES se praedones appellabant, cum re uera ex omnibus potius oris in naues eorum conuenissent desperati homines rerumque nouarum cupidi. Alii Cretenses erant, conducti olim mercede ad militandum, posteaque dimissi; alii, municipales quondam, ex oppidis bello dirutis eodem confluxerant, Itali, Hispani, Asiani: fecerant alii cum Fimbria uel Sertorio stipendia, ordinesue duxerant. Adeo ex omnibus gentibus congregati erant perditi omnes; omnes post partium suarum ruinas expulsi ac fugientes; denique quicquid miserorum hominum, quicquid audacium usquam erat: quis autem usquam per illos annos locus aut miseriis aut facinoribus uacabat? Verum ex latronibus casu et temere congregatis factus erat exercitus, ut ita dicam, ac paene res publica ciuium inter se non cognatione quidem, sed tamen communitate aliqua exilii scelerisque coniunctorum; quorum praeterea scelera—id quod scelerati fieri saepe confidunt— maximis in commune meritis compensabantur. At societati generis humani, unde siue iure siue iniuria expulsi erant, bellum indixerunt. Indixerint: sed nescio an honestius bellauerint quam Romani illi optimates Asianusque rex, qui tum inter se partituri iam esse terras omnes uidebantur.

F. D. M.

O N the whole comparison there can be little doubt that the balance of advantage lies in favour of the modern system of large states. The small republic indeed develops its individual citizens to a pitch which in the large kingdom is utterly impossible. But it so develops them at the cost of bitter political strife within, and of almost constant warfare without. It may even be doubted whether the highest form of the city-commonwealth does not require slavery as a condition of its most perfect development. The days of glory of such a commonwealth are indeed glorious beyond comparison; but it is a glory which is too brilliant to last, and in proportion to the short splendour of its prime is too often the unutterable wretchedness of its long old age. The republics of Greece seem to have been shown to the world for a moment, like some model of glorified humanity, from which all may draw the highest of lessons, but which none may hope to reproduce in its perfection. As the literature of Greece is the groundwork of all later literature, as the art of Greece is the groundwork of all later art, so in the great democracy of Athens we recognize the parent state of law and justice and freedom, the wonder and the example of every later age. But it is an example which we can no

HAEC rei publicae genera in uniuersum aestimanti non dubium est quin paullo maiores sicut hodie constitutae sunt ciuitates potiores habendae sint. Singuli sane ciues in minima quaque re publica tantis uirtutibus instruuntur quantis non alias instrui possunt; ita tamen ut domi acerrima sit inter ipsos discordia, foris bella prope sempiterna. Et nescio an sublatis seruorum ministeriis ea urbs, quae et ipsa sit ciuitas, perfecta et absoluta existere non queat. Florente quidem eiusmodi re publica auream fere aetatem dixeris; tanta tamen laus per se breuis est, ut et cito deflorescat et consenescentem aetatem uexare soleat omnium malorum diuturnitas. Exstiterunt quidem illae Graecorum res publicae, semel exstiterunt, tanquam diuinum quoddam exemplum hominibus oblatum, cuius hodie quoque permultum ualeat cognitio, uera et expressa effigies reuocari possit nulla. Sicut enim a Graecorum litteris, Graecorum artibus, ceterarum quae postea fuerunt initia repetenda sunt, ita Atheniensium illam rem publicam legum et iuris et libertatis inuentricem dixeris, quam laudant posteri et sequuntur. Ita tamen sequuntur ut adsequi non liceat; sicut ne Homeri quidem reuocari potest quasi diuinus ille spiritus, Phidiae plus quam humana artificia, ingenium Thucydidis et sapientia. Illorum similes

more reproduce than we can call back again the
inspiration of the Homeric singer, the more than
human skill of Pheidias, or the untaught and
inborn wisdom of Thucydides. We can never be
like them, if only because they have gone before.

[No. 273.]   *Freeman.*

ON the promontory of Misenus is yet standing
the mansion of Cornelia, mother of the
Gracchi; and, whether from the reverence of
her virtues and exalted name, or that the gods
preserve it as a monument of womanhood, its
exterior is yet unchanged. Here she resided
many years, and never would be induced to re-
visit Rome after the murder of her younger son.
She cultivated a variety of flowers, and naturalized
several plants, and brought together trees from
vale and mountain, trees unproductive of fruit
but affording her in their superintendence and
management a tranquil and expectant pleasure.
We read that the Babylonians and Persians were
formerly much addicted to similar places of re-
creation. I have no knowledge in these matters;
and the first time I went thither I asked many
questions of the gardener's boy, a child about nine

uel idcirco esse non possumus, quod illi antea
uixerunt.

S. H. B.

EXSTARE adhuc in Miseni promontorio
domum uidi Corneliae, Gracchorum matris;
et species eius—seu ob tantam uirtutem et in-
signe nomen homines, seu monimento eximiae
pro femina firmitatis Di seruauerunt—hodie etiam
immutata est. Ibi multos annos ipsa egit, nec
ei umquam post filii minoris necem ut Romam
rediret persuaderi potuit. Varia florum genera
colebat, et nonnulla etiam ex Oriente illata in-
serenda et solo assuefacienda curabat; nec non
arbores diuersi generis de montibus et campo con-
ferebat, quae ut frugiferae omnino non erant, ita
curanti et fouenti tranquillam quandam patientiae
et expectationis uoluptatem praebebant. Istius
modi hortos audiuimus Babylonios et Persas
otii causa plurimum excoluisse; ipse uero, cum talia
ignorarem, multa illuc primum profectus puerum
quendam, topiarii filium, nouem circa annos natum,

years old. He thought me still more ignorant than I was, and said among other such remarks, ' I do not know what they call this plant at Rome, or whether they have it there ; but it is among the commonest here, beautiful as it is, and we call it cytisus.' 'Thank you, child,' said I smiling ; and pointing towards two cypresses, 'pray what do you call these high and gloomy trees, at the extremity of the avenue, just above the precipice ?' 'Others like them,' replied he, 'are called cypresses ; but these, I know not why, have always been called Tiberius and Caius.'

   [No. 250.]   *W. S. Landor.*

THE town is most pleasantly seated, having a very good wall with round and square bulwarks, after the old manner of fortifications. We came thither in the night, and indeed were very much distressed by sore and tempestuous wind and rain. After a long march, we knew not well how to dispose of ourselves ; but finding an old abbey in the suburbs, and some cabins and poor houses, we got into them, and had opportunity to send the garrison a summons. They shot at my trumpeter, and would not listen to him

percontatus sum. Qui me nil omnino ratus scire, inter alia et similia hoc dixit: 'Hic utrum apud uos flos inueniatur, non didici, nec quo nomine Romae appelletur: apud nos uero ut pulcherrimus est, ita omnino non rarus; et nomen ei cytiso ponimus.' At ego arridens, 'Benigne, puer,' respondi: tum, duabus cupressis digito indicatis, 'Quo tandem nomine,' inquam, 'arbores celsas illas et funebres, in fine xysti super praecipiti pendentes cliuo, appellas?' 'At istius generis arbores,' respondit, 'cupressos; duarum uero, quas indicasti, illa apud nos Tiberius, haec Caius appellatur; sed ratio in obscuro est.'

E. D. A. M.

OPPIDVM amoeno iacet situ, firmis moenibus munitum, turribusque ueteri more et rotundis et quadratis. Quo cum noctu uenissemus, uento pluuiaque nimia confecti et longo itinere laborantes, non erat ubi pernoctaremus, nisi templum casulasque extra moenia repperissemus. Huc receptis copiis obsessos extemplo se dedere iubebam. Qui quidem nuntium et sagittis petebant et diu se negabant admissuros: itaque missis quos norant legatis certiores feci ducem adesse cum magna parte exercitus. Nostri omnino telis

for an hour's space; but having some officers in our party whom they knew, I sent them to let them know I was there with a good part of the army. We shot not a shot at them; but they were very angry, and fired very earnestly upon us, telling us it was not a time of night to send a summons. But yet in the end the governor was willing to send out two commissioners,—I think rather to see whether there was a force sufficient to force him, than to any other end. After almost a whole night spent in treaty, the town was delivered to me the next morning, upon terms which we usually call honourable; which I was the willinger to give, because I had little above two hundred foot, and neither ladders nor guns, nor anything else to force them.

[No. 207.]   *Cromwell.*

IN the great lottery of civil war the prizes are enormous, and when such prizes may be obtained by a course of action which is profoundly injurious to the State, the deterrent influence of severe penalties is especially necessary. In the great majority of cases, the broad distinction which it is now the fashion to draw between political and other crimes, is both pernicious and

abstinere : illi succensi intentius in nos conicere, tam inopportunam increpantes legationem. Deni-que duo milites remisit imperator, eo potissimum ut uidebatur consilio ut cognosceret an satis adesset copiarum ad uim adhibendam. Tota ferme nocte legationibus consumpta, deditum postridie oppidum aequa (ut uisum) condicione : cui eo facilius assentiebar, quod uix CC habui milites, nec scalas nec tormenta quibus expug-narem.

A. S.

CVM ciuilis belli auctores maxima, si pro-spere gesserint, praemia consequantur, ita tamen possint gerere ut ciuitati penitus noceant, necesse sane est ut poenis non minoribus de-terreantur. Praua ergo plerumque et exitiosa est eorum sententia, qui facinora condemnant ceterorum, res nouantium solent excusare. Vbi enim facilius, ubi perniciosius malae hominum

untrue. There is no sphere in which the worst
passions of human nature may operate more easily
or more dangerously than in the sphere of politics.
There is no criminal of a deeper dye than the
adventurer who is gambling for power with the
lives of men. There are no crimes which produce
vaster and more enduring sufferings than those
which sap the great pillars of order in the State,
and destroy that respect for life, for property, and
for law, on which all true progress depends. So
far the rebellion had been not only severely but
mercilessly suppressed. Scores of wretched
peasants, who were much more deserving of
pity than of blame, had been shot down. Over
great tracts of country every rebel's cottage had
been burnt to cinders. Men had been hanged
who, although they had been compelled or induced
to take a leading part in the rebellion, had so com-
ported themselves as to establish the strongest
claims to the clemency of the Government. But
what inconsistency, what injustice, it was asked,
could be more flagrant, than at this time to select as special objects of that clemency, the very
men who were the authors and the organizers
of the rebellion—the very men who, if it had succeeded, would have reaped its greatest rewards ?

[No. 276.]   *Lecky.*

conflantur cupidines, quam in ciuili dissensione ?
quis illo magis nefarius, qui ut ipse rebus potiatur
alios in uitae uocat discrimen ? quis ciuibus uel
grauius nocet uel diutius, quam qui publicam
salutem labefactat, eamque legum, uitae, bonorum
euertit incolumitatem, sine qua non uere potest
florere res publica ? Hic autem tumultus non seuere
modo sed atrociter erat compressus.   Permulti
agricolae, misericordia quam culpa digniores, tru-
cidati : per latas regiones seditiosorum omnes casae
incensae.   Nonnulli supplicio affecti, qui duces
quidem, uel coacti uel exorati, fuerant tumultus,
ita tamen se gesserant ut senatui summa digni
uiderentur clementia.   Quid ergo iniustius esse,
quid insanius, quam ut illis potissimum parceretur,
qui rem totam et concitassent et gessissent, et
si modo prospere euenisset, ipsi praecipua essent
praemia lucraturi ?

A. S.

AFTER reading I entered upon my exhortation, which was rather calculated at first to amuse them than to reprove. I previously observed that no other motive but their welfare could induce me to this; that I was their fellow-prisoner, and now got nothing by preaching. I was sorry, I said, to hear them so very profane; because they got nothing by it, but might lose a great deal; 'for be assured, my friends,' cried I, '—for you are my friends, however the world may disclaim your friendship,—though you swore twelve thousand oaths in a day, it would not put one penny in your purse. Then what signifies calling every moment upon the devil, and courting his friendship, since you find how scurvily he uses you? He has given you nothing here, you find, but a mouthful of oaths and an empty belly; and, by the best accounts I have of him, he will give you nothing that's good hereafter.'

[No. 196.] *Goldsmith.*

THE English and Normans now prepared themselves for this important decision. But the aspect of things, on the night before the battle, was very different in the two camps. The

FINITA recitatione comites adloqui incepi, ita tamen ut oblectarem potius quam obiur-garem; praefatusque me id modo agere ut pro-dessem iis—quippe qui et ipse captiuus essem, neque lucri quicquam ex oratione percepturus—inuitum me tot impie dicta audiisse dixi, unde boni nihil profecto, damni fortasse aliquid euen-turum. 'Scitote enim, amici,' inquam,—'nam amici mihi re uera estis, quantumuis a ceteris con-tempti—si uos impia atque nefasta totum usque per diem imprecemini, ne minimo quidem nummo uos inde ditiores fore. Quid prodest igitur Satanam istum identidem inuocare, eiusque aucu-pari gratiam, qui uobis tam inique usus sit? Nam uiuis profecto nihil nisi maledicere cum inedia donauit; neque mortuis, si quid ego ueri auguror, boni quicquam largietur.'

G. G. R.

QVO in discrimine rem uerti postquam uter-que uiderat exercitus, diuersa erat facies binorum inter apparatus castrorum pridie quam pugnatum est. Noctem Angli cum strepitu, comis-

English spent the time in riot, and jollity, and disorder; the Normans in silence and prayer, and in the functions of their religion. On the morning, the duke called together the most considerable of his chieftains, and made them a speech suitable to the occasion. He represented to them that the event which they and he had long wished for was approaching, and the whole fortune of the war now depended on their sword, and would be decided in a single action; that never army had greater motives for exerting a vigorous courage, whether they considered the prize which would attend their victory, or the inevitable destruction which must ensue upon their discomfiture; that if their martial and veteran bands could once break those raw soldiers, who had rashly dared to approach them, they conquered a kingdom at one blow, and were justly entitled to all their possessions as the reward of their prosperous valour; that, on the contrary, if they remitted in the least their wonted progress, an enraged enemy hung upon their rear, the sea met them in their retreat, and an ignominious death was the certain punishment of their imprudent cowardice.

[No. 208.]   *J. R. Green.*

satione, turbis ducere, Normanni inter silentium ac sacra. Dux mane principibus suorum conuocatis contionem habuit quae tempus deceret. Quem ipse, quem illi sibi tam diu expectassent diem adesse; totam in manibus belli fortunam stare; uno proelio decertatum iri; quem unquam exercitum animis intentis operae alacrius incumbere oportuisse? Quippe quod uincendi foret praemium, quippe quanta uictis clades subeunda, contemplarentur. Qui si forti ac ueterano suo milite temerarios tirones satis in se audacter aggressos profligassent, fore ut uno ictu gentem debellarent, iustissimis autem virtutis fortunaeque nominibus omnes eorundem possessiones promererentur. Si solitis uiribus defecissent, ultro iratos sibi a tergo imminere hostes, fugientibus pontum obiacere, tantam imprudentiam, tantam infirmitatem animi uno necis atque infamiae piaculo uindicatum iri.

E. W. B.

THE oracle of Delphi had fallen into oblivion or contempt in the general decay of faith, or on the discovery of its profligate corruption. Whatever credit might still attach to their pretensions to divine inspiration, its hierophants were no longer the confederates or the creatures of the statesman. Alarmed and bewildered, they sought to disclaim the invidious responsibility: 'The destinies of Rome,' they said, 'were recorded once for all in the verses of the Sybil: the conflagration of their temple by the Gauls had choked the cave with cinders, and stifled the voice of the god: he who spurned from his shrine the profane and unrighteous, found none to address in these degenerate days.' But all these evasions were vain. Appius demanded the event of the war, and pertinaciously claimed a reply. The priestess took her seat on the fatal tripod, inhaled the intoxicating vapours, and at last delivered the response which her prompters deemed the most likely to gratify the intruder: 'Thou, Appius, hast no part in the civil wars: thou shalt possess the hollow of Euboea.' The proconsul was satisfied. He determined to abandon all active measures for the party which had entrusted the province to him, and fondly hoped that, in retiring to the deep recesses of the Euripus, where the sea

ORACVLVM Delphis, seu obsolescente in deos pietate, seu uenale repertum, in obliuionem et contemptum uenerat, ministrique eius, de afflatu isto diuino quodcunque adhuc crederetur, desierant certe conscii regum aut instrumenta esse. Pauidi igitur turbatique detrectant tantum inuidiae: fata Romae libris Sibyllinis semel esse condita; templum autem Galli cum incendissent, oppleto cineribus antro fatidicae uoci interclusum iter; nec deum, qui procul a se profanos impiosque habeat, degeneri in aeuo inuenire quibus ora soluat. Sed frustra erat ea fraus proconsule responsa ac sortem belli efflagitante. Tum Pythia fatali in tripode consedit, haustuque uaporum furibunda id demum responsi edit quod auctores eius credidere molesto homini laetum: 'Bellorum, Appi, ciuilium expers es, tu cauam Euboeam possidebis.' Satis Appio id uisum. Mota pro iis arma qui sibi prouinciam credidissent omittere statuit et in sinu Euripi subsidere, qua Aulim inter et Chalcida angustum mare rapitur,

rushes through the gorge between Aulis and Chalcis, the waves of civil war would pass by him, and leave him in undisturbed possession of his island sovereignty. But he had scarcely reached the spot when he was seized with fever, and the oracle was triumphantly fulfilled by his death and burial on the rock-bound shore.

Merivale.

NEW Carthage is situate near the middle of the coast of Spain, upon a gulph that looks towards the south-west, and which contains in length about twenty stadia, and about ten stadia in breadth at the first entrance. The whole of this gulph is a perfect harbour. For an island lying at the mouth of it, and which leaves on either side a very narrow passage, receives all the waves of the sea, so that the gulph remains entirely calm; except only that its waters are sometimes agitated by the south-west winds blow-ing through those passages. All the other winds are intercepted by the land, which encloses it on every side. In the inmost part of the gulph stands a mountain in form of a peninsula, upon which the city is built. It is surrounded by the

spe captus fore ut belli quoque fluctus se prae-
terirent imperium insulae tuto obtinentem. Sed
statim illuc uectus febri correptus est, et saxoso
in littore exstinctus sepultusque fata Delphica
impleuit.

A. T. B.

SITA est Carthago Noua media fere Hispaniae
ora in sinu ad Africum uentum opposito,
qui in longitudinem patet circiter uiginti stadia,
in latitudinem intrantibus prope decem. Totus
sinus portui quam maxime idoneus est. Quippe
insula in ostio iacens, angustissimo utrimque
introitu, omnes ab alto fluctus accipit, ita ut
sinus omnino tranquillus maneat, nisi quod Africo
introitus perflante nonnunquam agitatur. Ceteros omnes uentos intercipit terra qua sinus undique circumcluditur. In intimo sinu stat tumulus
in modum peninsulae, ubi sita est urbs. Hunc
ab oriente et meridie claudit mare, ab occasu
lacus, adeo etiam ad septentrionem diffusus, ut
terra quae eum a mari diuidit, urbem autem con-
tinenti coniungit, duo tantum stadia latitudine

sea, upon the east and south; and on the west
by a lake, which is extended also so far towards
the north, that the rest of the space, which lies
between the lake and the sea, and which joins
the city to the continent, contains only two stadia
in breadth. The middle part of the city is flat;
and has a level approach to it from the sea, on the
side towards the south. The other parts are
surrounded by hills, two of which are very high
and rough; and the other three, though much
less lofty, are full of cavities and difficult of
approach.

   [F. C. 50.]   *R. Southey.*

IT was vacation-time, and that gave me a
loose from my business at the bar; for it was
the season after the summer's heat, when Autumn
promised fair and put on the face of temperate.
We set out, therefore, in the morning early, and
as we were walking upon the sea-shore, and a
kindly breeze fanned and refreshed our limbs, and
the yielding sand softly submitted to our feet and
made it delicious travelling, Caecilius on a sudden
espied the statue of Serapis, and according to the
vulgar mode of superstition, raised his hand to
his mouth and paid his adoration in kisses. Upon

contineat. Media urbs in aequo est: facilis per planum aditus ex meridiana parte a mari ascendentibus. Ceteras partes cingunt quinque colles, quorum duo magnae et praeruptae sunt altitudinis. Reliqui tres multo quidem humiliores, sed cauorum pleni et paene inaccessi.

J. C.

IAM uero ludi Romani rerum forensium intermissionem attulerant. Tum enim temporis, ui caloris remissa, auctumnus speciem tepidae tempestatis prae se ferebat. Multo igitur mane profecti secundum litus ambulauimus, aura mitissima membra uentilante ac reficiente; tum harena mollis, quae lente uestigiis cedebat, uiam praebebat gratissimam. Mox autem Caecilius, imagine Serapis conspecta, de solito uenerandi more manu sublata et osculis iactis adorauit. Itaque Octauius ad me conuersus, 'Haud bene facis, Marce frater,' inquit, 'quod sodalem coniunctissimum uulgari

which Octavius, addressing himself to me, said,—
' It is not well done, my brother Marcus, thus to
leave your inseparable companion in the depth of
vulgar darkness, and to suffer him, in so clear a
day, to stumble upon stones ; stones, indeed, of
figure and anointed with oil and crowned; but
stones, however, still they are ;—for you cannot
but be sensible that your permitting so foul an
error in your friend redounds no less to your
disgrace than his.'   This discourse of his held us
through half the city ; and now we began to find
ourselves upon the free and open shore.   There
the gently washing waves had spread the extremest
sands into the order of an artificial walk ; and as
the sea always expresses some roughness in his
looks, even when the winds are still, although he
did not roll in foam and angry surges to the shore,
yet were we much delighted, as we walked upon
the edges of the water, to see the crisping, frizzly
waves glide in snaky folds, one while playing
against our feet, and then again retiring and lost
in the devouring ocean.   Softly, then, and calmly
as the sea about us, we travelled on and kept
upon the brim of the gently declining shore, be-
guiling the way with our stories.

H. W. Longfellow, translated from *Minucius Felix.*
[*F. C.* 310.]

obscuritate relinquis obuolutum, eumque sinis die tam clare lucente pedem in lapides offendere, sculptos illos quidem oleoque inunctos et coronatos, lapides tamen. Neque enim te fallere potest, quod tibi, qui tam foedo amici errori ueniam concedas, haud minus quam illi uitio dandum est.' Tali sermone nos usque per dimidiam urbis partem tenemur; uentum denique ad latum patulumque litus. Ibi fluctus leniter allisi extremas ipsas harenas in ambulationem quasi manu factam complanauerant. Vt autem mare, uentis etiam compositis, semper aliquid saeuitiae praefert, nec tamen spumas fluctusue iracundos tum ad litus aduoluebat, nos multum iuuabat propter litus ambulantes undas crispas et cristatas anguium more sinuatas intueri, tum pedibus nostris alludentes, tum autem reductas atque in ponti uoraginem absorptas; itaque leniter ut ipsum mare secundum mollem litoris decliuitatem uiam sermone fallebamus.

W. H. B.

H IS success in this scheme for reducing the power of the nobility encouraged him to attempt a diminution of their possessions, which were no less exorbitant. During the contest and disorder inseparable from the feudal government, the nobles, ever attentive to their own interests, and taking advantage of the weakness and distress of their monarchs, had seized some parts of the royal demesne, obtained grants of others, and having gradually wrested almost the whole out of the hands of the princes, had annexed them to their own estates. The titles by which most of the grandees held their lands were extremely defective: it was from some successful usurpation, which the crown had been too feeble to dispute, that many derived their only claim to possession. An inquiry carried back to the origin of these encroachments, which were almost coeval with the feudal system, was impracticable; as it would have stripped every nobleman in Spain of great part of his lands, it must have excited a general revolt. Such a step was too bold even for the enterprising spirit of Ximenes. He confined himself to the reign of Ferdinand; and beginning with the pensions granted during that time, refused to make any further payment, because all right to them expired with his life. He

ITA feliciter, uti diximus, immunita nimia optimatium auctoritas eo Ximenem impulit ut
possessiones aeque et ipsas immodicas recidere
conaretur. Nam inter tumultus contentionesque
feodali quod uocant imperio proprias sui semper
tenacissimi nobiles, regumque angustiis aut imbe-
cillitate usi, agrum regium partim ui raptum
partim dono concessum, uniuersum fere principi
e manibus extorserant, suisque ipsi praediis
continuauerant. Sed plerisque parum ualida
possidendi auctoritas, cum complures eo demum
iure niterentur, quod principem inferiorem quam
ut obsisteret despoliassent. Quarum tamen occu-
pationum in initium ipsi ferme imperio aequalium
non potuit fieri inquisitio ; quae cum nobilissimum
quemque per Hispanias magna agrorum parte
praedatura esset, uerendum erat ne in uniuersum
conflaretur seditio. Periculosius hoc consilium
quam pro audaci ipsius Ximenis ingenio. Itaque
intra Fernandi regnum stetit ; orsusque a pecuniis
annuis eo rege donatis negauit se quidquam ultra
soluturum : rege enim mortuo periisse etiam ius
accipiendi. Dein ab iis repetebat si quis eodem
tempore agrum regium usurpasset, quidquid idem
alieni iuris fecisset ilico reuocato. Ceterum ea
res ad plerosque optimatium pertinebat; Fernan-
dus enim ceteroqui parum liberalis, cum tamen et

then called to account such as had acquired crown-
lands under the administration of that monarch,
and at once resumed whatever he had alienated.
The effects of this revocation extended to many
persons of high rank, for, though Ferdinand was
a prince of little generosity, yet he and Isabella
having been raised to the throne of Castile by
a powerful faction of the nobles, they were
obliged to reward the zeal of their adherents
with great liberality, and the royal demesnes
were their only fund for that purpose.

   [No. 217, 218.]   *Robertson.*

I NTO the heart of this mysterious Africa I wish
   to take you with me now. And let me magnify
my subject by saying at once that it is a wonderful
thing to see. It is a wonderful thing to start from
the civilization of Europe, pass up these mighty
rivers and work your way into that unknown land,
—work your way alone and on foot, mile after mile,
month after month, among strange birds and
beasts and plants and insects, meeting tribes which
have no name, speaking tongues which no man
can interpret, till you have reached its secret heart
and stood where white man has never trod before.

ipse et Isabella coniunx ualida nobilium factione
freti regno Castiliensi potiti essent, studia partium
summa munificentia augere cogebantur; neque
aliud suppetebat nisi ager regius.

R. S.

ILLVD igitur mihi proposui ut uos in ipsos
Africae huius recessus et quasi mysteria
sermone meo comites deducam, loca certe, ut
ab initio consilium amplificem, omni admiratione
digna. Quis enim non obstupescat, qui ab Europa
excultisque populis profectus, traiectis ingentium
fluuiorum spatiis, multa milia passuum menses
multos in ignotam istam regionem solus ac pedes
uiam moliatur, qui per sescenta uolucrum, ferarum,
herbarum, insectorum miracula, gentibus offensis,
quae neque nomen ullum habeant, neque intellecta
cuiquam utantur lingua, quasi in intima terrae

It is a wonderful thing to look at this weird world of human beings—half animal, half children, wholly savage and wholly heathen; and to turn and come back again to civilization before the impressions have had time to faint, and while the myriad problems of so strange a spectacle are still seething in the mind. It is an education to see this sight, an education in the meaning and history of man. To have been here is to have lived before Menes. It is to have watched the dawn of evolution. It is to have the great moral and social problems of life, of anthropology, of ethnology and even of theology, brought home to the imagination in a new and startling light.

[No. 253.]   *H. Drummond.*

THE beginning of the following year saw the revolt of Mytilene. The news was received at first with incredulity by the Athenians who were all but crushed by the recent plague and harassed by the repeated invasions of the Spartans. But when confirmation of the tidings left no room

penetralia progressus ibi tandem constiterit, ubi Europaeorum antea nemo? Illud etiam plane miraculo est, cum tot et tam miras hominum gentes, paene dixerim animalium uel infantium, humanitatis omnis deorumque cultus expertes exploraueris, impresso adhuc animo recentibus rerum uestigiis, et inter mille spectacula ac cogitationes titubante, in nostram hanc uitam ac consuetudinem extemplo reuerti. Didicit enim, qui haec uidit, unde profecti sint homines et quorsum creati. Vixit, ut ita dicam, qui hic uersatus est, ante bellum Troianum, ipsique rerum humanarum origini interfuit: quid fas et nefas, quid ciuium societates sibi uelint, quae sit hominis ipsius ratio, quae gentium, immo quae deorum, haec omnia insolita illa mirabilique rerum specie plane coactus est ut animo contempletur.

M. J. R.

I NEVNTE proximo anno descierunt Mytilenaei ab Atheniensibus. Adlato nuntio primum uix credebant ciues, iàm recenti paene fracti pestilentia, crebrisque Spartanorum incursionibus conflictati. Cum tamen, re confirmata, haud diutius dubitare possent quin nouum et inopinatum

for doubt that the state was threatened by a new and unexpected danger, a blaze of indignation ensued. Athens had never subjected Mytilene to harsh or overbearing rule: when almost every other state in the confederacy had been reduced to a position of dependence, Mytilene had enjoyed equal rights and had been treated with marked distinction, paying no tribute and retaining its fortifications and its navy. Now on the flimsy pretext that they had no assurance of safety in the future, and were unwilling to go hand in hand with the Athenians in their schemes for the sub-jugation of the whole of Greece, their allies had seized the moment when they fancied Athens was tottering to its fall to revolt to the enemy. If this example were followed, if Athens were stripped one by one of the supports on which it leant, what hope of success remained? How could the state continue the struggle against overwhelming odds when it was already plunged in such difficulties? Exasperated as much by the insolence as by the treachery of their ally, the Athenians determined to prove that their power was not at so low an ebb as was imagined, and accordingly equipped a powerful fleet and despatched it to blockade Mytilene.

[No. 233.]   *Adapted from Grote.*

periculum urbi immineret, summa indignatione
exarserunt animi. Numquam enim Mytilenaeis aut
crudeliter aut superbe a se imperitatum esse:
cum omnes fere aliae e ciuitatibus foederatis
stipendiariae factae essent, eos pari iuris condicione usos, praecipuoque in honore habitos nulla
pendere tributa et moenia nauesque longas
retinere. Nunc tamen cum uanam interposuis-
sent causam quod nullam haberent fiduciam
futurae salutis, nollentque secum participes esse
consiliorum totius subiugandae Graeciae, arrepta
occasione qua labare iam crederent res Athenienses, ad hostes defecisse socios. Quid? eorum
exemplum si alii imitati essent, si deinceps
illis tamquam adminiculis quibus adniterentur
essent exuti, quam spem rei prospere gerendae
esse relictam? Quomodo enim ciuitatem uiribus
imparibus in certamine perstare posse iam in
tantas delapsam angustias? Et contumacia et perfidia sociorum irritati Athenienses, cum ostendere
statuissent nondum opes adeo comminutas esse,
magnam classem ornatam miserunt quae Mytilenaeos obsideret.

J. H.

DISAPPOINTED at length in their hopes of assistance from the Spartans, and reduced to utter despair by the growing pressure of famine, the Mytilenaean authorities determined on arming the populace and making a sortie against the blockading force. But the result of this step was different from their expectations. The starving citizens who had never been in sympathy with the revolt no sooner found themselves possessed of weapons than they declined to face so perilous an enterprise. Secret complaint and discontent changed to open menace and abuse of their masters. The cry was raised, invariable at such a moment, that the authorities had stored up great quantities of food which they shared with the rich, while the poor were dying of starvation. Unless they brought the contents of their granaries into the light of day and distributed them at large, immediate surrender was threatened. Well aware that this meant their own certain destruction, the magistrates preferred themselves to take the initiative in this movement, and opened negotiations with the Athenian general, the result being that the town was conditionally made over to him, while an embassy was despatched to Athens to sue for pardon.

[No. 234.] *Do.*

TANDEM deiecti spe auxilii Spartanorum, et ingrauescente fame ad ultimam adducti desperationem, Mytilenaei magistratus consilium armandi plebem et in obsidentes hostes ex urbe erumpendi inierunt. Quod tamen aliter euenit atque expectauerant. Ciues enim fame paene confecti, simul atque in manus ceperunt arma, recusauerunt ne tantis periculis se opponerent, utpote qui numquam ab Atheniensibus deficere uoluissent. Iam non per secretas querimonias et inuidiam agitabatur: minae et conuicia propalam in principes iactari. Etiam clamitabant, id quod semper tali in discrimine fieri solet, magistratus magnam uim frumenti coaceruatam cum diuitibus partiri dum pauperes inopia enecarentur: quod nisi omnium in conspectum elata ea quae horreis condidissent uulgo uellent distribuere, urbem se extemplo dedituros esse. Magistratus tamen cum non ignorarent si quae minarentur exsecuti essent ciues, id sibi certo fore exitio, auctores ipsi huius incepti esse maluerunt, et de deditione cum Atheniensium duce agebant; unde factum est ut condicionibus ratis urbs ei concederetur, legatique Athenas ueniam petendi causa mitterentur.

J. H.

THE exultation at Athens was unbounded. At last the opportunity had come for wreaking vengeance on the Mitylenaeans. In the blind resentment of the moment all prayers for mercy were rejected, and it was resolved to put to death the whole male population of military age, and to sell the women and children as slaves. This frightful decision was taken mainly on the advice of Cleon, a man of low extraction, who at that time commanded most influence with the populace. But hardly had the assembly broken up before the citizens began to repent of their headlong haste. Reflexion showed them that it was a piece of monstrous cruelty to cut off a whole population at a blow: their anger would fall on innocent and guilty alike, and the honour of Athens would be seriously compromised. In this state of public feeling, Diodotus and others who were advocates of milder measures succeeded with little difficulty in getting the magistrates to call a second meeting on the morrow for the purpose of giving the whole question fresh consideration.

[No. 235.]　　　　　　　　　　　　　*Do.*

ATHENIENSES, laetitiae impotentes, quod iam tandem oblata esset occasio Mytilenaeos ulciscendi, iraque occaecati, preces misericordiam implorantium auersabantur, omnesque homines qui militari essent aetate interfici, mulieres liberosque uenum dari iusserunt. Cuius sententiae atrocissimae praecipuus auctor Cleon erat, homo ignobilis, qui tum maxime apud plebem ualebat. Vix tamen dimissa contione ciues consilii raptim praecipitati paenituit. Videbatur enim reputantibus infandae esse crudelitatis totum populum uno ictu interimere : sic et in nocentes et insontes saeuitum iri, quod ciuitati summo dedecori futurum. Cum talia sentirent fere omnes, Diodoto aliisque qui mitiora suadebant haud grauate a magistratibus concessum est ut proximo die mane iterum conuocaretur concilium totam rem de integro deliberandi causa.

J. H.

NEXT day in the assembly Cleon violently attacked the populace for the inconstancy they had displayed, warning them at the same time that it was the height of madness for a people with such imperial responsibilities as theirs to give way to unwise tenderness of heart. The Mytilenaeans had inflicted on them grievous injury without provocation, and unless stern justice were meted out, there would be fresh outbreaks of these troubles in the not distant future. They ought to adhere to their former decision and turn a deaf ear to politicians whose prime aim was not the commonwealth but self. On the other hand Diodotus argued the folly of deciding a matter of such moment under the influence of strong passion. Even if considerations of expediency weighed more with them than those of honour, some mitigation of their harsh sentence was called for. It would not prevent any other of the allied states from revolting if a fair chance of success appeared ; and beyond all question a revolted ally would resort to the most desperate measures rather than fall into the hands of so pitiless a foe. Happily for Mitylene the party of mercy carried the day, and messengers were at once despatched with orders for the Athenian general to spare the vanquished city.

[No. 236.]　　　　　　　　　　　　　　　　*Do.*

POSTERO die, contione habita, Cleon ue-hementer plebem incusat quod adeo uacillas-sent animi, monetque summae esse dementiae, cum tantum imperium Atheniensium esset, stultae indulgere clementiae. Nisi enim in Mytilenaeos ob iniurias grauissimas quas ultro attulissent, acerrime animaduerterent, fore ut perbreui haec mala recrudescerent. Priore igitur starent sententia, neue iis obedirent oratoribus qui ipsorum, non communi commodo studerent. Contra Diodotus contendit non esse prudentium rem tantae grauitatis, dum flagrarent ira animi, decernere. Etiamsi antiquius illis quod utile quam quod honestum esset, aliquid de seueritate illius poenae remittendum esse, quippe quae alii nulli e ciuitatibus foederatis obici foret quominus defi-ceret, si modo adstaret occasio rei bene gerendae speciosa; nec dubium esse quin extrema omnia experiri mallent si qui socii defecissent, quam hostium tam saeuorum uenire in potestatem. Mytilenaeis bene euenit ut uincerent mitiorum auctores consiliorum, statimque missi sunt qui ducem Atheniensium uictae urbi parcere iuberent.

J. H.

AFTER his departure everything tended to the wildest anarchy. Faction and discontent had often risen so high among the old settlers that they could hardly be kept within bounds. The spirit of the new-comers was too ungovernable to bear any restraint. Several among them of better rank were such dissipated, hopeless young men as their friends were glad to send out in quest of whatever fortune might betide them in a foreign land. Of the lower order, many were so profligate or desperate that their country was happy to throw them out as nuisances to society. Such persons were little capable of the regular subordination, the strict economy, and persevering industry, which their situation required. The Indians, observing their misconduct, and that every precaution for sustenance or safety was neglected, not only withheld the supplies of provisions which they were accustomed to furnish, but also harassed them with continual hostilities. All their subsistence was derived from the stores which they had brought from England; these were soon consumed; then the domestic animals sent out to breed in the country were devoured; and by this inconsiderate waste they were reduced to such extremity of famine, as not only to eat the most nauseous and unwholesome roots and

SIMVL discessum est a colonia, et omnia in effrenatam licentiam retro ruere. Nam et antiquis colonis prauitas et discordia saepe eo usque flagrauerat, ut sisti non posset: et qui proxime adscripti sunt, iis animus impotentior et coercentium impatiens. Quorum qui loco meliore nati erant, perditos plerosque adolescentes et nulla spe boni qualemcunque fortunam in alieno experturos haud inuiti relegauerant propinqui. Vulgus autem improbissimum genus et flagitiosissimum lubenter patria tamquam communem hominum pestem euomuerat. Hi parum idonei uidebantur qui pro necessitate loci aut apte parerent imperio, aut parsimoniae consulerent, aut grauiter et strenue agerent. Quos cum Indi male rem gerere, neque salutis neque cibariorum rationem iam habere animaduerterent, non modo solitos commeatus intercipere, sed continuis proeliis lacessere. Vtensilia suppetebant nulla nisi quae secum ex Anglia apportauerant, quibus breui absumptis carne bestiarum mansuetarum quae feturae causa domo emissae erant uescebantur; donec inconsulte prodigi eo famis redacti sunt ut non solum baccae et radices teterrimae et maxime pestiferae, sed Indorum quoque caesorum cadauera et ipsorum comitum quos tam multiplex calamitas confecerat, uictum necessarium

berries, but to feed on the bodies of the Indians whom they slew, and even on those of their companions who sank under the oppression of such complicated distresses. In less than six months, of five hundred persons whom Smith left in Virginia, only sixty remained: and they so feeble and dejected that they could not have survived for ten days if succour had not arrived from a quarter whence they did not expect it.

   [No. 220.]   *Robertson.*

THUS supported upon his crutch and upon the shoulder of William of Orange, the Emperor proceeded to address the States. He reviewed rapidly the progress of events from his seventeenth year up to that day. He sketched his various wars, victories and treaties of peace, assuring his hearers that the welfare of his subjects and the security of religion had ever been the leading objects of his life. As long as God had granted him health, he continued, only enemies could have regretted that Charles was living and reigning; but now that his strength was but vanity, and his life fast ebbing away, his affection for his subjects, and his regard for their interests,

praeberent. Intra sex menses ex quingentis hominibus, is enim numerus erat ante legati decessum Virginiensis, uix sexaginta supererant fessi et fracti animo, neque in diem decimum uitam sustentaturi ni ex inopinato subuentum esset laborantibus.

R. S.

ITAQVE Caesar, simul baculo suo simul Batauorum Principis umero innixus, primores ciuitatum allocutus est. A septimo decimo aetatis suae anno exorsus, quae usque ad id temporis deinceps essent facta, omnia breuiter percensere. Bella, uictorias, foedera strictim percurrere, et audientibus confirmare nihil se unquam antiquius habuisse quam ut ciuium commoda et rerum diuinarum salutem pro sua parte tueretur. Olim cum, deorum beneficio, integra esset ualitudine, nec uiuere se nec regnare ulli nisi patriae hosti molestum fuisse. Nunc uero, infractis uiribus, et decrescente in dies quicquid uitae superesset, pro amore erga ciues quibus libentissime inseruiret

required his departure. Instead of a decrepit old man with one foot in the grave, he presented them with a sovereign in the prime of life and the vigour of health. Turning toward Philip he observed, that for a dying father to bequeath so magnificent an empire to his son was a deed worthy of gratitude; but that when the father thus descended to his grave before his time, and by an anticipated and living burial sought to provide for the welfare of his realms and the grandeur of his son, the benefit conferred was surely far greater. He added that the debt would be amply repaid to him, should Philip conduct himself in his administration of the provinces with a wise and affectionate regard for their true interests.

Motley.

IT was now broad day; the hurricane had abated nothing of its violence, and the sea appeared agitated with all the rage of which that destructive element is capable; all the ships on which alone the whole army knew that their safety and subsistence depended were driven from their anchors, some dashing against each other,

de imperio esse decedendum. Principem habi-
turos pro sene iuuenem, pro infirmo et iam mori-
bundo ualidum corpore et integra aetate florentem.
Deinde in Philippum conuersa oratione, gratias
dixit referendas esse si quis tam praeclarum imperium uel moriens filio legasset : quanto autem
melius eum promerere qui filii amplitudinem et
incolumitatem regni ita curae haberet, ut sic ante
diem in sepulcrum se conderet, et quasi exse-
quiis maturatis uiuus efferretur ?   Sed satis super-
que se pro meritis suis accepturum, si Philippus
in prouinciis administrandis eorum quibus prae-
esset saluti comiter ac sapienter prouideret.

H. C. G.

IAM multo die nihil remitti de procella : mare,
res natura saeuissima, affatim furere : naues
ruptis retinaculis, solum exercitus praesidium, aut
inter se collisas aut litori ui appulsas aut in
scopulos afflictas aut fluctibus submersas cerne-
bant. Deletae minus una hora naues longae
quindecim, onerariae centum et quadraginta,

some beat to pieces on the rocks, many forced
ashore, and not a few sinking in the waves. In
less than an hour, fifteen ships of war, and one
hundred and forty transports with eight thousand
men perished: and such of the unhappy crews
as escaped the fury of the sea, were murdered
without mercy by the Arabs, as soon as they
reached land. The Emperor stood in silent
anguish and astonishment, beholding the fatal
event which at once blasted all his hopes of
success, and buried in the depths the vast stores
which he had provided as well for annoying the
enemy as for subsisting his own troops . . . At last
the wind began to fall and to give some hopes
that as many ships might escape as would be
sufficient to save the army from perishing by
famine and transport them back to Europe. But
these were only hopes: the approach of evening
covered the sea with darkness: and it being
impossible for the officers aboard the ships which
had outlived the storm, to send any intelligence
to their companions who were ashore, they
remained during the night in all the anguish of
suspense and uncertainty.

[No. 244.]   *Robertson.*

uirorum octo milia. Quorum miserorum si qui maris rabiem effugissent terrae appulsos Arabes trucidabant. Stabat princeps tristis attonitusque qui una clade spes frangi, opes siue ad hostes lacessendos siue ad suos sustentandos collectas in alto sepeliri aspiciebat. Tandem cadente uento sperabatur tot naues euasuras esse quot satis forent ad exercitum fame haud dubie periturum in Europam transuehendum. ' Quae tamen spes nondum rata est: caligante enim sub aduentum uesperis mari, cum ducibus nauium superstitibus nulla esset consiliorum cum terrestribus facultas, nox summa anxietate transacta est.

J. C.

AFTER the mutual and repeated discharge of missile weapons, in which the archers of Scythia might signalize their superior dexterity, the cavalry and infantry of the two armies were furiously mingled in closer combat.   The Huns, who fought under the eyes of their king, pierced through the doubtful and feeble centre of the allies, separated their wings from each other, and wheeling with a rapid effort to the left, directed their whole force against the Visigoths. As Theodoric rode along the ranks, to animate his troops, he received a mortal wound from the javelin of Andages, a noble Ostrogoth, and immediately fell from his horse.   The wounded king was oppressed in the general disorder, and trampled under the feet of his own cavalry ; and this important death served to explain the ambiguous answer of the haruspices.

[No. 202.]   *Gibbon.*

THE cardinal, although virtuous and disinterested and capable of governing the kingdom with honour in times of tranquillity, possessed neither the courage nor the sagacity necessary at such a dangerous juncture.   Finding

MISSILIBVS crebris inuicem effusis quorum suum usum sagittarii Scythici prae se ferre possent, pedites equitesque utriusque exercitus collato gradu ferociter pugnant. Hunni, qui regis sub oculis dimicabant, mediam sociorum aciem inualidam incertamque perfregerunt; alarumque discidio facto, sinistrorsum celeriter conuersi, cuncti in Visigothos incubuere. Theodoricum, dum ordines perequitans militum erigit animos, ab Andage, Ostrogotho nobili, iaculo letaliter percussum, statim delapsum equo promiscuaque obrutum turba equites sui calcibus protriuere. Insignis ea clades ambiguo haruspicum uaticinio expediendo erat.

T. S. E.

PONTIFICI uero, sanctis moribus et citra ambitionem agenti, qui per otium rem publicam salua dignitate regere ualeret, deerat et fortitudo et prudentia qua tanta pericula euaderet. Cum facinora ante oculos patrata compescere ne-

himself unable to check these outrages committed under his own eye, he attempted to appease the people by protesting that Fonseca had exceeded his orders and had by his rash conduct offended him as much as he had injured them. This condescension, the effect of irresolution and timidity, rendered the malcontents bolder and more insolent; and the cardinal having soon after recalled Fonseca, and dismissed his troops, which he could no longer afford to pay, as the treasury, drained by the rapaciousness of the Flemish ministers, had received no supply from the great cities, the people were left at full liberty to act without control, and scarcely any shadow of power remained in his hands.

Robertson.

AS soon as the approach of the troops was announced, the Caesar went out to meet them, and ascended his tribunal, which had been erected in a plain before the gates of the city. After distinguishing the officers and soldiers who by their rank or merit deserved a peculiar atten-tion, Julian addressed himself in a studied oration to the surrounding multitude : he celebrated their

quisset, plebem studet mulcere, tamquam Fonseca inconsulte mandata egressus tantum ipsius animum laesisset quantum ciues temerasset. Turbulentis gliscere in dies audacia petulantia, comitatem in socordiam leuitatemque trahentibus. Mox pontifex exuit legatione Fonsecam, milites ex· auctorat; quippe stipendium iam non suppetere, neque quicquam subsidii e magnis ciuitatibus fisco ab auaris prouinciarum praetoribus exhausto. Inde penes ipsum ne imago quidem potestatis, populo quod libuisset agendi plena impunitas.

J. S. R.

AD nuntios iam propinquantis exercitus egres- sus in campum Caesar structo ante portas tribunali consedit. Ac primo, ut quisque cen- turionum et manipularium praecipua dignitate aut factis notabilis, id commendationibus insignitum : dein conuersus ad uulgum et circumfusos composi- tam iniit orationem, mixta rerum gestarum gratu- latione laudibusque, et adhortatus agnoscerent

exploits with grateful applause ; encouraged them to accept, with alacrity, the honour of serving under the eyes of a powerful and liberal monarch ; and admonished them that the commands of Augustus required an instant and cheerful obedi‑ ence. The soldiers, who were apprehensive of offending their general by an indecent clamour, or of belying their sentiments by false and venal acclamations, maintained an obstinate silence ; and after a short pause were dismissed to their quarters. The principal officers were entertained by the Caesar, who professed, in the warmest language of friendship, his desire and inability to reward, according to their deserts, the brave com‑ panions of his victories. They retired from the feast full of grief and perplexity ; and lamented the hardship of their fate, which tore them from their beloved general and their native country. The only expedient which could prevent their separation was boldly agitated and approved ; the popular resentment was insensibly moulded into a regular conspiracy ; their just reasons of com‑ plaint were heightened by passion, and their passions were inflamed by wine, as on the eve of their departure the troops were indulged in licen‑ tious festivity.

[No. 249.]   *Gibbon.*

alacres decus in commilitium asciti principi ualido
et liberali ; nec tarde aut segniter obtemperandum
iussis Augusti. Haec atque talia disserens per-
uicaci silentio exceptus, metu offensionum si
obturbassent, et ne plausus uenalis ludibrio
uoluntatem dissimularent : itaque breui spatio
in castra remittitur miles. Tribuni praefectique
ad epulas acciti : ubi Caesar in speciem flagrantis-
simi studii conquestus negatum uotis suis tam
forti, tot uictoriarum socio exercitui merita re-
pendere, dimisit conuiuas luctum inter metumque
trepidos, et fatum insectantes si a duce dilecto
patriaque diuellerentur. Atque unum iam huius
rei remedium palam sermonibus iactari, com-
probari : coalescere sensim in uim coniurationis
castrorum indignatio. Et iustas querimonias ira,
iram temulentia accendebat, concesso discedentibus
lasciuire.

W. W.

I T is not the purpose of this work to enter
into any minute descriptions of the Roman
exercises. We shall only remark that they com·
prehended whatever could add strength to the
body, activity to the limbs, or grace to the mo·
tions. The soldiers were diligently instructed to
march, to run, to leap, to swim, to carry heavy
burdens, to handle every species of arms that was
used either for offence or for defence, either in
distant engagement or in a closer onset; to form
a variety of evolutions; and to move to the sound
of flutes, in the Pyrrhic or martial dance. In the
midst of peace, the Roman troops familiarized
themselves with the practice of war; and it is
prettily remarked by an ancient historian who had
fought against them, that the effusion of blood
was the only circumstance which distinguished a
field of battle from a field of exercise.

[No. 221.]　　　　　　　　　　　　　*Gibbon.*

C HARNOCK held very different language.
He acknowledged that the plot in which
he had been engaged appeared, even to many
loyal subjects, highly criminal. They called him
assassin and murderer. Yet what had he done

NON huius est operis Romanorum exer-
citationes uerbis accuratius depingere, cui
satis erit consultum si quidquid corporis robori,
membrorum agilitati, motuum denique uenustati
promouendae inseruiat, id omnes eas complecti
dixero. Ad incedendum currendum saliendum
nandum milites informabantur; ferre onera atque
arma tractare discebant, secum portare si quid
usui esse posset, siue inferre arma, siue sese
defendere expediret, siue eminus siue cominus
pugnandum: quin et uarias conuersiones flexus-
que agminis quam plurimos facere, et ad tibi-
cinem saltatione Pyrrhica seu Martia moueri.
Ita factum est ut media in pace cotidiano usu et
consuetudine milites quasi bello interessent, neque
ineleganter a nescio quo scriptum est qui aduersus
eos ipse stipendia meruerat, non nisi effuso
sanguine exercentium prolusiones et uera proelia
dignosci.

T. S. E.

LENTVLVS uero alia omnia disserebat.
Non enim denegare quin illa in qua uersatus sit coniuratio multis etiam bonis uiris
facinerosissima uideretur. Sibi quidem caedem
et parricidium exprobrari. Quid tamen se ad-

more than had been done by Mucius Scaevola?
Nay, what had he done more than had been done
by everybody who had borne arms against the
Prince of Orange? If an army of twenty thousand
men had suddenly landed in England and surprised
the usurper, this would have been called legitimate
war. Did the difference between war and assassination depend on the number of persons engaged?
What then was the smallest number which could
lawfully surprise an enemy? Was it five thousand, or a thousand, or a hundred? Jonathan and
his armour-bearer were only two. Yet they made
a great slaughter of the Philistines. Was that
assassination? It cannot, said Charnock, be the
mere act, it must be the cause, which makes
killing assassination. It followed that it was not
assassination to kill one—and here the dying man
gave a loose to all his hatred—who had declared
a war of extermination against loyal subjects, who
hung, drew, and quartered every man who stood
up for the right, and who had laid waste England
to enrich the Dutch.

Macaulay.

misisse quod non antea Mucius ille Scaeuola
patrasset, immo quod non omnes qui contra
Batauorum imperatorem stipendia meruissent?
Si quis uiginti milia armatorum in Angliam
traiecisset ut nouicium illum regem ex improuiso
adoriretur, futurum sane fuisse ut istud iustum
bellum piumque haberetur. Bellumne sit an
parricidium ita scilicet discerni, si finitus aliquis
hominum numerus exsequendo facinori interesset.
Quot igitur esse eos qui, si uno pauciores adessent,
non iure possent hostes intercipere? Quinane
milia istos hominum esse, an mille, an centum
tantum? Iudaeum uero illum uno comite de-
pugnasse, et magnam Philistinorum stragem edidisse. Num istum igitur fuisse sicarium? Inde
colligi posse neminem idcirco tantum latrocinii
argui, quod hominem occiderit, sed crimen totum
in causa facinoris uerti. Hic autem Lentulus quasi
frenis immissis se totum in iracundiam praecipitare,
cum clamaret prorsus sibi liquere id minime fore
nefarium, si quis eum interficeret qui bellum contra
bonos ad internicionem gessisset, qui cunctos
bonarum rationum auctores enecasset cruciasset
lacerasset, qui Angliam uastasset ut Batauos
locupletaret.

J. S. R.

ITS stem is sometimes as thick as a man's thigh, and in the dense woods at Quiballa I have seen a considerable extent of forest festooned down to the ground, from tree to tree, in all directions with its thick stems, like great hawsers; above, the trees were nearly hidden by its large, bright, dark-green leaves, and studded with beautiful branches of pure white star-like flowers, most sweetly scented. Its fruit is the size of a large orange, of a yellow colour when ripe, and perfectly round, with a hard brittle shell; inside it is full of a soft reddish pulp in which the seeds are contained. This pulp is of a very agreeable acid flavour, and is much liked by the natives. The ripe fruit, when cleaned out, is employed by them to contain small quantities of oil, &c. It is not always easy to obtain ripe seeds, as this creeper is the favourite resort of a villainous, semi-transparent, long-legged red ant—with a stinging bite, like a red-hot needle—which is very fond of the pulp and seeds.

[No. 240.]   *Monteiro.*

THE Blacks ascend the trees by the aid of a ring formed of a stout piece of the stem

STIPITES his interdum humani feminis crassitudine: quorum ego grandibus thyrsis prope Quiballam, ubi densior tractus siluarum, uidi magna nemorum spatia ex arbore in arborem tamquam magnis funibus in humum usque dependentia, superne autem prope occultari arbores foliis amplis nitidisque et in nigrorem uirentibus, distinctas globis florum qui stellarum instar canderent, essent autem odoris gratissimi. Pomis magnitudo mali aurei amplioris, color flauus simul atque maturuerunt, rotunditas plena, folliculus durior fragiliorque: intus caro mollis ac rufescens, in qua semina. Carnis sapor acidae iucunditatis, gratissimus barbaris. Pomum adultum purgant, eoque tamquam uase ad olei parua pondera uel similium utuntur. Neque semper parabile maturum semen, cum fruticis maxima sit gratia inhabitantibus formicis: his inproba species, corpus prope dilucidum, longa crura, color rufus, morsus uix minus candefacta pungens acu: carnem et semina adamant.

R. E.

IN has Afri ut scandant anulos ex caudicibus efficiunt truncorum fruticis qui arboribus

of a creeper, which is excessively strong and
supple ; one end is tied into a loop, and the other
thrown round the tree is passed through the loop
and bent back: the end being secured forms a
ready and perfectly safe ring, which the operator
passes over his waist. The stumps of the fallen
leaves form projections which very much assist
him in getting up the tree. This is done by
taking hold of the ring with each hand, and by
a succession of jerks the climber is soon up at
the top, with his empty gourds hung round his
neck. With a pointed instrument he taps the
tree at the crown, and attaches the mouth of
a gourd to the aperture, or he takes advantage
of the grooved stem of a leaf cut off short to use
as a channel for the sap to flow into the gourd
suspended below.

[No. 239.]   *Monteiro.*

IN far different plight, and with far other
feelings than those with which they had
entered the pass of Caudium, did the Roman
army issue out from it again upon the plain of
Campania. Defeated and disarmed, they knew
not what reception they might meet with from
their Campanian allies : it was possible that

durissimus ac lentissimus circumligatur. Huius
alteram oram in nodum constringunt, alteram
circumiectam arbori atque inde per nodum trans-
ditam flectunt retro : sic adstricta ora anulus fit
subiti usus et tutissimi. Hunc qui in eo opere est
circumdat lateri suo : sed et deciduae frondis
stili prominent, auxilia scandentibus. Adscensus
fit utrisque manibus correpto anulo : hoc modo et
se iterum iterumque iaculans cito in summum
peruenit, uacuis cucurbitis circum collum depen-
dentibus. Tum terebra aperit arboris uerticem,
foramini os cucurbitae applicat : interdum in usum
sibi aduocat scapum praesectae frondis cuius per
cauaturam tamquam per canaliculum umor in
cucurbitam infra dependentem influat.

R. E.

L ONGE aliter affecti et animo et corpore
qui nuper Furculas Caudinas intrauerant
in Campanum agrum euaserunt. Victos et inermes
quanam fide se recepturi essent Campani socii
anquirebant : posse et oppidanos occlusis portis
ultro in uictoris partes transire. Sed Cam-
panis nec fides nec benignitas defuit : arma

Capua might shut her gates against them, and
go over to the victorious enemy. But the Cam-
panians behaved faithfully and generously ; they
sent supplies of arms, of clothing, and of provisions, to meet the Romans even before they
arrived at Capua ; they sent new cloaks, and the
lictors and fasces of their own magistrates, to
enable the consuls to resume their fitting state ;
and when the army approached their city, the
Senate and people went out to meet them, and
welcomed them both individually and publicly
with the greatest kindness. No attentions, however, could soothe the wounded pride of the
Romans : they could not bear to raise their eyes
from the ground, nor to speak to anyone. Full
of shame they continued their march to Rome ;
when they came near to it, all those soldiers who
had a home in the country dispersed, and escaped
to their several homes singly and silently : whilst
those who lived in Rome lingered without the
walls till the sun was set, and stole to their
homes under cover of the darkness. The consuls
were obliged to enter the city publicly and in the
light of day, but they looked upon themselves as no
longer worthy to be the chief magistrates of Rome,
and they shut themselves up at home in privacy.

[No. 203.]   *Dr. Arnold.*

uestimenta commeatus exercitui appropinquanti
mittunt : consulibus noua paludamenta, suorum
magistratuum fasces, prout dignitas postulabat,
suppeditant: et uenientibus Capuam cunctus
senatus populusque obuiam egressi iustis omnibus hospitalibus priuatisque et publicis funguntur
officiis. Nulla tamen comitate Romanorum
ignominia et indignitas leniri : neque oculos
attollere, nec quemquam alloqui : pudor omnium
implere animos ad urbem proficiscentium : ubi
iam propius moenia aduentum est, quibus ruri
praedia erant suam quisque in domum singuli
ac silentes dilabebantur : qui in urbe habitabant
diu extra morati sero domum post obortas
tenebras intra tecta sese abdiderunt. Consules
autem quibus palam intranda erat urbs et
interdiu, rati se haudquaquam dignos qui primi
Populi Romani magistratus haberentur, domi se
tamquam priuati clauserunt.

R. S.

FROM the hill on which this villa stood the spectator surveyed a wide and various prospect, rich at once in natural beauty and historic associations. The plain at his feet was the battle-field of the Roman kings and of the infant commonwealth; it was strewn with the marble sepulchres of patricians and consulars; across it stretched the long straight lines of the military ways which transported the ensigns of conquest to Parthia and Arabia. On the right, over meadow and woodland, lucid with rivulets, he beheld the white turrets of Tibur, Aesula, Praeneste, strung like a row of pearls on the bosom of the Sabine mountains; on the left, the glistening waves of Alba sunk in their green crater, the towering cone of the Latin Jupiter, the oaks of Aricia and the pines of Laurentum, and the sea bearing sails of every nation to the strand of Ostia.

[No. 245.]   *Merivale.*

STRANGE and delusive destiny of man! The pope was at his villa of Malliana when he received intelligence that his party had triumphantly entered Milan: he abandoned himself

E COLLE in quo positum erat Ciceronis Tusculanum spectanti, late patebat multiplex uariusque prospectus, tum ipsa regionis amoenitate, tum rerum ibi gestarum memoria egregius. Subter pedes enim iacebat campus ubi decertauerant olim reges Romani et iam nascens res publica; sternebantur undique marmorea patriciorum et consularium sepulcra; trans ipsum recto limite longe tendebant militares uiae, per quas uictrices Romanorum aquilae usque ad Parthos Arabesque ferebantur. Dextra autem, ultra siluas et prata, riuulis collucentia, uideres candidas Tiburis, Aesulae, Praenestis arces, gemmarum in morem in ipso montium Sabinorum sinu quasi per seriem suspensas; sinistra uero coruscantes Albanas undas, in lacu uiridi depressas; Iouis Latiaris sublime fastigium; Aricinas quercus pinusque Laurentinas; ipsum denique mare, et omnium gentium uela ad litus Ostiense properantia.

J. E. S.

O MIRAM atque fallacem hominum sortem! Leoni iam in uilla Malliana rusticanti nuntiatum est suos Mediolanum occupare. Quibus auditis eo animo esse quo solent uictores. Hilari

to the exultation arising naturally from the successful completion of an important enterprise, and looked cheerfully on at the festivities his people were preparing on the occasion. He paced backwards and forwards till deep in the night, between the window and a blazing hearth —it was the month of November. Somewhat exhausted, but still in high spirits, he arrived at Rome, and the rejoicings there celebrated for his triumph were not yet concluded when he was attacked by a mortal disease. 'Pray for me,' said he to his servants, 'that I may yet make you all happy.' We see that he loved life; but his hour was come, he had not time to receive the viaticum nor extreme unction. So suddenly, so prematurely, and surrounded by hopes so bright, he died—as the poppy fadeth.

[No. 198.]   *Ranke.*

ANOTHER of the king's chief men, approving of his words and exhortations, presently added: 'The present life of man, O king, seems to me, in comparison of that time which is unknown to us, like to the swift flight of a sparrow through the room wherein you sit at

uultu populum spectare foris ouantem ; huc illuc
ad multam noctem obambulare inter fenestram
focique ignem, quippe mense Nouembri. Quibus
rebus haud indefessus Romam uenit, ubi eum uix
finita ouatione mortifer corripuit morbus. 'Orate
pro me,' adsistentibus inquit, 'ut per me etiam
nunc sitis felices.' Itaque quamuis auenti uitam
tamen aderat fatalis dies. Ne ad Eucharistiam
quidem uncturamque supremam excipiendam
suppetebat tempus. Adeo inopinato et intempes-
tiue mortuus est inter summas spes, uelut falce
occisum languet papauer.

T. S. E.

TVM alius quidam e principibus qui iis quae
dicta erant assentiebatur, illud mox insuper
addidit : 'Mihi quidem, O rex,' inquit, 'uidetur
haec aetas nostra, si cum ante acto omni tempore
quod nobis ignotum est comparetur, ita esse quasi
cum brumali tempore, dum horrida foris omnia

supper in winter with your commanders and
ministers, and a good fire in the midst, whilst the
storms of rain and snow prevail abroad ; the
sparrow, I say, flying in at one door, and immediately out at another, whilst he is within, is safe
from the wintry storm ; but after a short space of
fair weather, he immediately vanishes out of your
sight, into the dark winter from which he had
emerged.   So this life of man appears for a short
space, but of what went before, or what is to
follow, we are utterly ignorant.   If, therefore, this
new doctrine contains something more certain, it
seems justly to deserve to be followed.'   The
other elders and king's counsellors, by Divine
inspiration, spoke to the same effect.

    [No. 209.]   *J. R. Green.*

IT would be difficult to describe the eagerness
with which the American throws himself upon
the vast prize, thus offered him by fortune.   In
pursuit of it, he braves without fear the arrow
of the Indian and the diseases of the wilderness.
The silence of the forests does not awe him;
the attacks of wild beasts do not alarm him.
Passion, stronger than the love of life, is for
ever goading him on.   Before him there is

saeuiunt tempestate, tu cum principibus ministris-
que tuis prope focum cenes ardentem, tum forte
celeri uolatu passer per alteram intret ianuam,
mox effugiat per alteram: quippe omnia ille
intus tuta habeat et tranquilla, mox paullulum
moratus in hiemem atram e conspectu euolet:
non aliter et aetas nostra parumper se conspi-
ciendam praebet, at quae ante fuerint, quae mox
futura sint, omnino ignoramus.   Hanc igitur philo-
sophiam, si forte quid certius de his rebus habeat,
iure nobis amplectendam arbitror.'   Cui talia
suadenti ceteri qui aderant assensi, uelut diuino
quodam afflatu moti in eandem sententiam locuti
sunt.

G. G. R.

VIX enarraueris quanto ardore in ingentem
praedam a fortuna ita oblatam Americanus
inuolet.   Quam quominus arripiat, neque Indorum
sagittae, neque ortae paludibus pestes retinent;
nulla siluarum solitudo, ne ferarum quidem impetus terrorem iniciunt, quippe quem cupiditas,
etiam uitae amore acrior, ingredientem semper
stimulet.   Licet enim ante oculos paene infinita
planities pateat, dixeris tamen eum etiam nunc

H 2

spread out an almost boundless continent, and it might be said that fearing even now that there will not be room in it, he is hastening lest he should arrive too late. Sometimes the emigrants advance so fast, that the wilderness reappears behind them. The forest has but bent beneath their feet: the moment they are passed by, it rises again. It is not uncommon to meet with dwellings abandoned in the midst of woods. The ruins of a hut are often discovered in the very heart of a wilderness, and we are surprised at many attempts at clearing the ground, which attest at once the power and the fickleness of man. On these ruins of a day the ancient forest soon throws out new suckers, and Nature comes with a smile to cover with flowers and leaves the traces of man, and to do away with every vestige of his brief occupation.

  [F. C. 278.]   *Robertson.*

PERHAPS there is no more impressive scene on earth than the solitary extent of the Campagna of Rome under evening light. Let the reader imagine himself for a moment withdrawn from the sounds and motions of the living world, and sent forth alone into this wild

festinare, ne serior aduenerit, nullumque sibi in tanta regione locum inuenerit relictum. Non nunquam coloni tam celeriter prouecti sunt, ut post praeteruectos solitudo iterum recrudescat, et oppressa modo pedibus silua a tergo statim resultet. Mediis in saltibus haud raro deserta occurrunt tecta, multosque agri purgandi conatus intuens tum uires cum inconstantiam hominum miraberis. Emissis uero in has fugaces ruinas ex uetusta silua plantariis, natura uelut sub-ridens foliis floribusque omnia uestigia hominum ita obruit ut ne signum quidem breuissimae dominationis relinquatur.

E. A.

NIHIL in orbe terrarum mirabilius, nihil augustius noui uasto illo campo, Romam adiacente, si sero quis et in uespertina luce con-templetur. Immo istuc se fingat lector uel mini-mum temporis, in spatium aridum et desertum, relicto Romae strepitu, silentio solo comitante,

and wasted plain. The earth yields and crumbles beneath his foot, tread he never so lightly, for its substance is white, hollow and carious, like the dusty wreck of the bones of men. The long knotted grass waves and tosses feebly in the evening wind, and the shadows of its motion shake feverishly along the banks of ruin that lift themselves to the sunlight. Hillocks of mouldering earth heave around him, as if the dead beneath were struggling in their sleep ; scattered blocks of black stone, foursquare, remnants of mighty edifices, not one left upon another, lie upon them to keep them down. A dull, purple, poisonous haze stretches level along the desert, veiling its spectral wrecks of mossy ruins, on whose rents the red light rests like dying fire on defiled altars. The blue ridge of the Alban Mount lifts itself against a solemn space of green, clear, quiet sky. Watch-towers of dark clouds stand steadfastly along the promontories of the Apennines. From the plain to the mountains, the shattered aqueducts, pier beyond pier, melt into the darkness, like shadowy and countless troops of funeral mourners, passing from a nation's grave.

[No. 246.]   *Ruskin.*

decessisse. Ibi uel leuissimo incedenti gradu cedit et putris dissoluitur humus, caua scilicet et cariosa et pallida, quasi puluis confusaeque humanorum ossium relliquiae. Vespertina quatiente aura, incerto motu arundines geniculatae uibrantur; quarum tremulae umbrae, uelut aegrorum somnia, fluitant errantque passim per lapsa et ruinosa fragmenta adhuc in lucem exstantia. Vndique putris intumescit terra : diceres ipsos sepultos infra agitari et mortis somnum excutere : imposita uero deprimere et retinere marmoris atri fragmenta quadrata, lautorum relliquiae disiectae et separatae aedificiorum. Ibi deserto adaequata campo incumbit caligo lurida, spiratu noxia : ea paulatim absconduntur immanes et formidolosae moles, musco illitae ; quarum in rimis et foraminibus, ceu direptis moritura altaribus flamma, haeret adhuc et moratur caduci solis rubor. Mons insuper Albanus iam purpurascens in profundum et purum caeli glauci et sereni spatium erigitur; et nigrae nubium formae, immotae, specularum instar, promontoriis Appennini insident : per uastam usque ad montes planitiem, dilapsi aquarum ductus alii alios tamquam lugentium caterua obscura et innumera, ipsius Romae exsequias prosequentium, in tenebras sese abscondere uidentur.

E. D. A. M.

A S early as the time of Cicero and Varro it was the opinion of the Roman augurs that the twelve vultures which Romulus had seen represented the twelve centuries assigned for the fatal period of his city. This prophecy, disregarded perhaps in the season of health and prosperity, inspired the people with gloomy apprehensions when the twelfth century, clouded with disgrace and misfortune, was almost elapsed ; and even posterity must acknowledge with some surprise that the arbitrary interpretation of an accidental or fabulous circumstance has been seriously verified in the downfall of the Western Empire. But its fall was announced by a clearer omen than the flight of vultures : the Roman Government appeared every day less formidable to its enemies, more odious and oppressive to its subjects. The taxes were multiplied with the public distress ; economy was neglected in proportion as it became necessary ; and the injustice of the rich shifted the unequal burden from themselves to the people, whom they defrauded of the indulgences that might sometimes have alleviated their misery. The severe inquisition, which confiscated their goods and tortured their persons, compelled the subjects of Valentinian to prefer the more simple tyranny of the barbarians, to fly

AVGVRIBVS antiquis, Ciceronis et Varronis aequalibus, duodecim Romuli uultures duodecim saecula portendebant urbi fato attributa. Quod praesagium saluis ac prosperis rebus fortasse neglectum tum demum metus ac tristitiam populo incutiebat cum duodecimum saeculum dedecore ac luctu deformatum ad finem uergebat. Et mirandum uidebitur etiam posteris, quod imperii Occidentalis casus rei fortuitae uel fictae cupidam interpretationem probauit. Erant tamen auguria quae multo manifestius ruinam imperii monstrabant: in dies enim Romani minus formidolosi fiebant hostibus, inuisi magis ac grauiores. Crescente miseria multiplicabantur tributa, posci magis ac neglegi parsimonia. Et quamuis potuerint indulgentiae interdum miserias pauperum leuare, ita tamen iis diuites fraudabant populum, ut iniquum onus a se ad tenuiores transferrent. Tandem saeua inquisitione bonis spoliati, cruciati corpora, a Valentiniano ad barbaros, simpliciores scilicet dominos, in siluas montesque confugiebant, aut mercennariorum condicionem uilem atque abiectam amplectebantur. Ciuium Romanorum nomen, omnium quondam gentium studiis exoptatum, abiurabant

to the woods and mountains, or to embrace the
vile and abject condition of mercenary servants.
They abjured and abhorred the name of Roman
citizen, which had formerly excited the ambition
of mankind. . . . If all the barbarian conquerors
had been annihilated in the same hour, their total
destruction would not have restored the empire of
the West ; and if Rome still survived, she survived
the loss of freedom, of virtue, and of honour.

   [No. 257.]   *Gibbon.*

THE tidings of despair created a terrible
commotion in the starving city.   There
was no hope either in submission or resistance.
Massacre or starvation were the only alter-
native. But if there was no hope within the
walls, without there was still a soldier's death.
For a moment the garrison and the able-bodied
citizens resolved to advance from the gates in
a solid column, to cut their way through the
enemy's camp, or to perish on the field. It was
thought that the helpless and the infirm, who
would alone be left in the city, might be treated
with indulgence after the fighting men had all
been slain. At any rate, by remaining, the strong

et detestabantur; nec si barbaros uictores una dies cunctos abstulisset, potuit imperium Romanum recreari; superstes quippe Roma libertati suae, uirtuti, honestati supererat.

H. N.

HIS auditis, statim inter confectos inedia ciues terrore omnia tumultuque misceri. Scilicet, siue dederent se siue resisterent, nihil iam relictum, nisi ut aut ferro aut fame interfice-rentur. At desperatis in urbe rebus licere exeuntibus perire fortiter. Placebat igitur ali-quamdiu, ut conglobati milites cum integerrimo quoque ciuium, et e portis egressi, aut per castra et hostes ui perrumperent, aut pugnantes ilico trucidarentur. Fieri enim posse, ut occisis qui ad pugnandum ualerent, relictae intra moenia inutili infirmaeque multitudini parceretur; sin in urbe contra manerent, neque salutem his neque solatium esse allaturos. Verum, peruulgato consilio, statim

could neither protect nor comfort them. As soon, however, as this resolve was known, there was such wailing and outcry of women and children as pierced the hearts of the soldiers and burghers, and caused them to forego the project. They felt that it was cowardly not to die in their presence. It was then determined to form all the females, the sick, the aged, and the children, into a square, to surround them with all the able-bodied men who still remained, and thus arrayed to fight their way forth from the gates, and to conquer by the strength of despair, or at least to perish all together.

[No. 230.]   *Motley.*

THESE papers were asserted to be equivalent to a second witness, and even to many witnesses. The prisoner replied, that there was no other reason for ascribing these papers to him as the author, besides a similitude of hand; a proof which was never admitted in criminal prosecutions: That allowing him to be the author, he had composed them solely for his private amusement, and had never published them to the world, or even communicated them to any

mulierum puerorumque gemitus tantus fit, ut uersi
in misericordiam milites ciuesque rem omiserint,
illud scilicet metuentes, ne ignaui uiderentur, si
praesentibus his perire nollent. Statuunt igitur
collectis in unum mulieribus ceterisque aetate siue
morbo inualidis quicquid integrum adhuc haberent
uirium circumdare : dein e portis egressi uiam sibi
pugnando efficere, propter ipsam desperationem
uicturi, aut una saltem omnes perituri.

F. D. M.

QVOS commentariolos alterius testis, immo
plurium testium instar esse dictitabant.
Contra reus arguebat nulla alia de causa libellos
illos sibi adscribi, quam quod simili manu exarati
essent ; chirographorum autem testimonium numquam contra capitis reos proferri. Quod si se
scriptorem esse confiteretur, scripsisse tamen
animi causa ; neque edidisse umquam neque
coram alio legisse ; inspecto autem atramenti
colore manifestum fore eos multis abhinc annis

single person : That, when examined, they appeared, by the colour of the ink, to have been
written many years before, and were in vain
produced as evidence of a present conspiracy
against the government : And that where the law
positively requires two witnesses, one witness,
attended with the most convincing circumstances,
could never suffice ; much less, when supported
by a circumstance so weak and precarious. All
these arguments, though urged by the prisoner
with great courage and pregnancy of reason, had
no influence.

[F. C. 269.]   *Hume.*

BY his skill in astronomy Columbus knew that
there was shortly to be an eclipse of the
moon. He assembled all the principal persons
of the district around him on the day before it
happened, and, after reproaching them for their
fickleness in withdrawing their affection and
assistance from men whom they had lately revered,
he told them that the Spaniards were servants of
the Great Spirit who dwells in heaven, who made
and governs the world ; that he, offended at their
refusing to support men who were the objects

exscriptos esse, ideoque frustra ut recentis in rem publicam coniurationis indicia ostendi. Duo testes adessent, e lege necesse esse; unum uel certissimis indiciis fretum, nedum incertis et disiunctis, non sufficere. Quae omnia, quamquam summa constantia disputata, et grauissimis nixa rationibus, reo nihil profuerunt.

E. A.

COLVMBVS autem, ut astrorum scientia cognouerat lunam mox obscuratum iri, principes omnes finitimos, cum pridie quam id erat euenturum conuocasset, propter leuitatem increpuit, quod quos nuper tantopere coluissent, eos iam neque diligerent neque adiuuarent. Hispanos maximo illi deo seruire qui in caelo habitaret, mundi et opifici et rectori; hunc autem, iratum quod illi subleuare nollent homines quibus ipse praecipue faueret, hoc peccatum poena insigni persequi parare: itaque illa ipsa nocte

of his peculiar favour, was preparing to punish this crime with signal severity, and that very night the moon should withhold her light, and appear of a bloody hue, as a sign of the divine wrath and of the vengeance ready to fall upon them. To this marvellous prediction some · of them listened with the careless indifference peculiar to the people of America ; others, with the credulity natural to barbarians. But when the moon began gradually to be darkened, and at length appeared of a red colour, all were struck with terror. They ran with consternation to their houses, and returning instantly to Columbus loaded with provisions, threw them at his feet, conjuring him to intercede with the Great Spirit to avert the destruction with which they were threatened.

[No. 242.] *Robertson.*

THESE northern people were distinguished by tall stature, blue eyes, red hair and beards. They were indefatigable in war, but indolent in sedentary labours. They endured hunger more patiently than thirst, and cold than the heat of the meridian sun. They disdained

lunam, denegata luce, speciem sanguineam esse sumpturam; quod cum uidissent, intellegerent deum irasci, sibi poenas imminere. Hoc portentum dum praedicit, alii, quae est Americanorum incuria, neglegere, alii solita barbarorum credulitate mirabundi excipere; cum uero luna, luce paullatim obscurata,· tandem in ruborem mutata esset, omnes eodem timore perterriti statim ad sua quisque tecta discurrere, inde ad Columbum redire et commeatus quos secum portabant ei ad pedes proicere, denique obsecrare ut deum illum maximum placatum sibi redderet, et calamitatem iam impendentem deprecaretur.

J. D. D.

SEPTENTRIONALIVM partium gentes magnis corporibus insignes, oculis caeruleis, comis ac barbis rutilis. Militiae ad labores impigri, domi segnes; ceterum inediae quam sitis, frigoris quam solis meridiani patientiores. Vrbes contemptui habere tamquam uel inertibus recepta-

towns as the refuge of a timorous, and the hiding-places of a thievish populace. They burnt them in the countries which they conquered, or suffered them to fall into decay; and centuries elapsed before they surrounded their villages with walls. Their huts, dispersed like those of the Alpine people, were placed on the banks of rivulets, or near fountains, or in woods, or in the midst of fields. Every farm constituted a distinct centre round which the herds of the owner wandered, or where, among agricultural tribes, the women and slaves tilled the land. The Germans used very little clothing, for the habit of enduring cold served them in its stead. The hides of beasts, the spoils of the chase, hung from the shoulders of the warriors; and the women wore woollen coats ornamented with feathers, or with patches of skins which they selected for their splendid and various tints. The use of clothes which, fitting accurately the different parts of the body, covered the whole of it, was introduced many ages after-wards, and was looked upon even then as a signal corruption of manners.

[No. 248.]   *Burke.*

culum uel furibus latebras; has igitur in uictis
regionibus uel incendio delebant uel situ dilap-
suras relinquebant: neque uicos nisi saeculis
demum interpositis moenibus cingendi mos inlatus.
At mapalia, more Alpinarum gentium, temere
passim discreta, ut ripa, ut fons, ut silua, ut campus
singulis placuit. Suam quisque domum certo
spatio circumdabant, qua uel pascerentur armenta,
uel, si quibus agri uictum suppetebant, mulieres et
serui culturam exercerent. Vestitus Germanis,
ut frigorum patientia firmatis, admodum exiguus.
Nempe ex umeris suspendebant iuuenes uenandi
praemia, ferarum exuuias; feminae autem laneos
amictus induebant modo plumis, modo maculis
pellibusque uariatos, quas sibi ob colorum diuersi-
tatem delegerant. Nam multo serius posteri—
quod pessimi uel inter ipsos habebatur exempli—
in strictarum uestium usum delapsi sunt quae
singulos artus exprimendo corpus omnino con·
tegerent.

G. H. R.

J ULIAN disguised the silent anxiety of his own mind with smiles of confidence and joy, and amused the hostile nations with the spectacle of military games, which he insultingly celebrated beneath the walls of Coche. The day was consecrated to pleasure; but as soon as the hour of supper was past, the emperor summoned the generals to his tent, and acquainted them that he had fixed that night for the passage of the Tigris. They stood in silent and respectful astonishment; but when the venerable Sallust assumed the privilege of his age and experience, the rest of the chiefs supported with freedom the weight of his prudent remonstrances. Julian contented himself with observing that conquest and safety depended on the attempt; that, instead of diminishing, the number of their enemies would be increased by successive reinforcements; and that a longer delay would neither contract the breadth of the stream nor level the height of the bank. The signal was instantly given, and obeyed; the most impatient of the legionaries leaped into five vessels that lay nearest to the bank; and as they plied their oars with intrepid diligence, they were lost after a few moments in the darkness of the night.

Gibbon.

IVLIANVS tacitis animi sui curis risum quasi
spem ac laetitiam uolutantis praetendit; simul
hostium nationes munere militarium ludorum
eludit, quos contumeliae causa sub ipsis oppidi
moenibus edit. Totus hic dies uoluptati deditus;
statim tamen ut cenauerant, princeps legatis in
praetorium uocatis nuntiat se noctem insequen-
tem traiciendo amni destinauisse. Inde undique
silentium simul obsequium simul admirationem
testantium. Mox Sallustius, uir aetate grauis,
cum libertatem qua senectuti qua rebus gestis
debitam usurpauisset, tum ceteri ultro iis quae
prudenter admonuerat pondus addidere. Iulianus
nihil ultra respondet nisi salutem et uictoriam in
eo coepto uerti; scilicet non minui hostes, immo
auxiliis in dies augeri; si diutius morarentur, nec
fluminis alueum artiorem fore nec humilius
riparum fastigium. Dat extemplo signum et
ipsi obtemperatur, dum acerrimus quisque militum
v nauiculas quae a ripa stabant escendit; qui
cum audaces et strenui remigarent, cito nocturnis
tenebris obuoluuntur.

J. S. R.

SCIPIO was of the same opinion. He was
fully persuaded of the greatness of the evil,
and with a courage deserving of honour, he
without respect of persons remorselessly assailed
it, and carried his point where he risked himself
alone. But he was also persuaded that the
country could only be relieved at the price of
a revolution similar to that which in the fourth
and fifth centuries had sprung out of the question
of reform, and rightly or wrongly the remedy
seemed worse to him than the disease. So with
the small circle of his friends he held a middle
position between the aristocrats, who never for-
gave him for his advocacy of the Cassian law,
and the democrats whom he neither satisfied nor
wished to satisfy; solitary during his life, praised
after his death by both parties, now as the
champion of the aristocracy, now as the pro-
moter of reform. Down to his time the censors
in laying down their office had called upon the
gods to grant greater power and glory to the
state; the censor Scipio prayed that they might
deign to preserve the state. His whole confession
of faith lies in that painful exclamation.

IN eadem erat Scipio opinione. Quantum sane impenderet periculum ciuitati uiderat, et animo uere uirili, nullius neque uiri neque instituti habito respectu, si quando solus capitis periclitabatur, adeo institit ut rem conficeret. Neque alio tamen ritu sanari iam posse ciuitatem arbitratus est quam quibus ciuilibus dissidiis res nouae, ante annos ducentos trecentosque agitatae, rei publicae stetissent. Quod ille quidem remedium morbo perniciosius, recte an secus aestimauit. Itaque perpaucis acceptus amicis, medius optimatium, qui legis Cassiae suasori numquam ignoscebant, et popularium, quibus nec satisfecit nec placere quidem studuerat, uitam quasi solitarius egit; post funera ab utrisque partibus collaudatus est, siue patriciorum uindex siue rerum nouandarum auctor audiebat. Ante hunc uirum quotienscumque censores se munere abdicauerant deos immortales implorare soliti erant ut Populum Romanum imperio ac nomine augerent; Scipio ut seruare dignarentur precatus est. O uocem grauissimam! quae testata est quam paene de re publica desperauerit.

E. W. B.

SOMERS was equally eminent as a jurist and as a politician, as an orator and as a writer. In the great place to which he had been recently promoted, he had so borne himself that, after a very few months, even faction and envy had ceased to murmur at his elevation. In truth, he united all the qualities of a great judge: an intellect comprehensive, quick, and acute, diligence, integrity, patience, and suavity. In council the calm wisdom, which he possessed in a measure rarely found among men of parts so quick and of opinions so decided as his, acquired for him the authority of an oracle. The superiority of his powers appeared not less clearly in private circles. The charm of his conversation was heightened by the frankness with which he poured out his thoughts. His good temper and his good breeding never failed. His gesture, his look, his tones were expressive of benevolence. His humanity was the more remarkable; because he had received from nature a body such as is generally found united with a peevish and irritable mind.

Macaulay.

SOMERS pari iuris et rei publicae prudentia dicendi laudes scriptis aequiperauerat. Summum in honorem cum nuper euectus esset, talem se in eo praebuerat ut paucos post menses ne factiosi quidem atque inuidi praelatum ceteris iam indignarentur. Enimuero quaecumque egregii sunt iudicis omnia unus habebat, mentem amplam acrem uegetam, industriam idem et fidem, lenitatem[1] et comitatem. De re publica cum deliberaretur, placida quadam sapientia, qualem in illa animi celeritate consiliisque tam paratis rarius inueneris, quasi oraculi fidem sibi conciliauerat. Priuatim quoque non minus ceteris antecellebat. Sermonis uenustatem augebat simplicitas hominis quidquid sentiebat effundentis. Numquam suauitatem in eo, numquam humanitatem requireres. Benignum se gestu uoltu uoce significabat, clementia eo admirabiliore quod corporis illam naturam acceperat cuius comes plerumque sit animi morositas et iracundia.

J. P. P.

---

[1] Cf. Cic. *Muren.* 41 ' praetor...beneuolentiam adiungit lenitate audiendi.'

STILL, notwithstanding these unprecedented marks of favour, and the symptoms they revealed of the emperor's infirmity and blindness, Sejanus could not fail to see, in the recent elevation of Drusus, how far his master yet was from contemplating the transfer of the empire from his son to a stranger. To remove the rival whom he despaired of supplanting was become necessary for his own security, for Drusus was instinctively hostile to him; he had murmured at his pretensions, unveiled his intrigues, and even in the petulance of power had raised his hand against him. The prince had complained that his father, though having a son of his own, had in fact devolved no small portion of the Government upon a mere alien. Sejanus, he muttered, was regarded by the people as the emperor's actual colleague : the camp of the Praetorians was the creation of his caprice for the advancement of his authority : the soldiers had transferred to him their military allegiance, and his image had been openly exhibited as an object of popular interest in the theatre of Pompeius.

Merivale.

SINGVLARIA haec et fauoris erga se ipsum et ut in principe infirmitatis indicia ; uerumtamen Druso honoribus nuper elato non potuit non intellegere Seianus quam longe ab eo abesset princeps ut de imperio a filio suo ad alienum transferendo cogitaret. Quem igitur gratia deicere plane nequibat, illum e medio tollendum ut ipse saluus esset putabat. Quippe quasi natura sibi inimicum Drusum cognouerat, qui arrogantiae suae admurmurauisset, artes patefecisset, etiam potestatis petulantia elatus manum ipsi intendisset. Aegre enim tulit iuuenis patrem filium habentem maiorem imperii partem cum alieno communicauisse : Seianum a populo pro uero collega imperatoris duci : castra praetoriana illius arbitrio quo auctoritatem suam adaugeret exstructa : illi milites studere quasi in eius scilicet uerba iurauissent, illius effigiem in theatro Pompeiano populo propositam esse.

E. C. W.

NOTHING in the political conduct of Essex entitles him to esteem ; and the pity with which we regard his early and terrible end is diminished by the consideration that he put to hazard the lives and fortunes of his most attached friends, and endeavoured to throw the whole country into confusion, for objects purely personal. Still it is impossible not to be deeply interested for a man so brave, high spirited, and generous ; for a man who, while he conducted himself towards his Sovereign with a boldness such as was then found in no other subject, conducted himself towards his dependents with a delicacy such as has been rarely found in any other patron. Unlike the vulgar herd of benefactors, he desired to inspire not gratitude, but affection. He tried to make those whom he befriended feel towards him as an equal. His mind—ardent, susceptible, naturally disposed to admiration of all that is great and beautiful—was fascinated by the genius and accomplishments of Bacon. A close friend-ship was soon formed between them, a friendship destined to have a dark, a mournful, a shameful end.

[No. 313.]   *Macaulay.*

QVOD ad rem publicam attinet, nihil hic admiratione dignum habet : ipsa autem mors
tam immatura, tam atrox, eo minus misericordiam
mouet, quod suae ille utilitatis causa uitam fortu-
namque coniunctissimorum amicorum in aleam
dedit, uniuersae ciuitati turbas concitauit. Virum
tamen tam forti ingenio, tam alacri, tam mag-
nanimo, qui erga reginam ferox praeter ciuilem
qui tum erat modum, erga clientes patronus erat
si quis alius uerecundus, ecquis non cupide
intuetur ? Neque enim, sicut solet multitudo,
gratum in se animum sed amorem bene merendo
conciliare uoluit ; neque alio pacto beneficia
collocabat quam ut par cum pari consociaretur.
Hominem uiuido mollique animo praeditum, quicquid excellentius, quicquid uenustius, eius admiratione facile captum, mirum quantum delectabat
Baconi ingenium et elegantia : unde mox summa
illa orta est amicitia in euentum aliquando tristem,
infaustum, flagitiosum peruentura.

S. H. B.

I MUCH question whether an impartial character of this man will or ever can be trans-
mitted to posterity ; for he governed this kingdom
so long, that the various passions of mankind
mingled with every thing that was said or written
concerning him. Never was man more flattered,
nor more abused; and his long power was
probably the chief cause of both. I was much
acquainted with him both in his public and his
private life, I mean to do impartial justice to his
character; and therefore my picture of him will
perhaps be more like him than it will be like any
of the other pictures drawn of him. In private
life he was good-natured, cheerful, social. He
had a coarse, strong wit, which he was too free of
for a man in his station, as it is always inconsistent with dignity. He was very able as a
minister, but without a certain elevation of mind
necessary for great good or great mischief. Pro-
fuse and appetent, his ambition was subservient
to the desire of making a great fortune. He would
do mean things for profit, and never thought of
doing great ones for glory.

` [F. C. 360.]   *Lord Chesterfield.*

HVIVSCE uero uiri haud scio an nullo modo fieri possit ut iudicium de moribus integro animo factum ad memoriam prodatur; qui enim rem publicam tam diu administrauerit, necesse est quidquid de eo aut dictum sit aut scriptum uariis hominum cupiditatibus imbutum et quasi coloratum esse. Nemo umquam tot adulationibus, nemo tot conuiciis oneratus est; quorum utriusque in primis causae arbitror fuisse tam longinquam potestatem. Equidem, ut qui et eum optime nouerim cum publice tum priuatim agentem, et in ingenio aestimando summam aequitatem seruare decreuerim, eam fortasse hominis effigiem expressurus sum quae magis ipsum referat quam alias si quae fuerint effigies. Domi facilis festiuus communis, dicacitate utebatur crassiore, cui cum parum grauitati consentanea sit liberius indulgendo male suae amplitudini consulebat. Idem in publicis rebus ut omnia tractabat ui ingenii praestantissima, ita quadam animi altitudine carebat sine qua nemo magnum aliquid siue boni siue mali efficere potest. Alieni appetens, sui profusus, diuitiarum studio ambitionem posthabebat; et multa sane lucri causa sordida, nihil umquam magnum propter gloriam ausus est,

H. B.

PERHAPS, while no preacher ever had a more massive influence than Savonarola, no preacher ever had more heterogeneous materials to work upon. And one secret of the massive influence lay in the highly mixed character of his preaching. Baldassarre, wrought into an ecstasy of self-mastering revenge, was only an extreme case among the partial and narrow sympathies of that audience. In Savonarola's preaching there were strains that appealed to the very finest susceptibilities of men's natures, and there were elements that gratified low egoism, tickled gossiping curiosity, and fascinated timorous superstition. His need of personal predominance, his labyrinthine allegorical interpretations of the Scriptures, his enigmatic visions, and his false certitude about the Divine intentions, never ceased, in his own large soul, to be ennobled by that fervid piety, that passionate sense of the infinite, that active sympathy, that clear-sighted demand for the subjection of selfish interests to the general good, which he had in common with the greatest of mankind. But for the mass of his audience all the pregnancy of his preaching lay in his strong assertion of supernatural claims, in his denunciatory visions, in the false certitude which gave his sermons the interest of a political bulletin ; and

HAVD scio an alius nemo, qui sacerdos populum adhortatus est, tantum inter se statu ac uoluntate discrepantes tam uehementer unus homo commouerit. Cuius rei si rationem quaerimus, summae sermonis uarietati multum est adscribendum. Nam quod multi ex audientibus, in proprios singillatim affectus intenti, idem acerrime sensit Baldassarius, sui scilicet ulciscendi cupiditate usque ad impotentiam efferatus. Hieronymus enim, ut uiris ad nobilissima procliuibus stimulos interdum admouebat, ita in suas res defixos uel noua ad sermonem quaerentes quasi titillare poterat, timidosque ac superstitiosos sub suam plane ditionem subiungere: qui cum secundas partes uitio naturae nusquam ageret, scripta sacra tortuosissima imaginum ratione explicaret, ambigua uisorum specie certissimam diuinae mentis scientiam falso profiteretur, idem tamen uir amplissima, si quis alius, indole, feruida, ut ita dicam, erga Deos pietate insignis, in infinitatem ipsam ardenti animo peregrinabatur; quod si aliorum commodis acriter decebat interesse, uel singulorum bona rei publicae posthabenda praecipere, prudentia omnium qui uixerunt ne illustrissimo quidem concedebat. Apud plerosque uero ita eloquens, ita grauis erat, ut qui diuini aliquid confidenter sibi adrogaret, uisis suis in populum uates inueheretur, decreta

having once held that audience in his mastery, it was necessary to his nature—it was necessary for their welfare — that he should *keep* the mastery.

[No. 305.]   *George Eliot.*

THOUGH her own security had been the first object, and her ambition the second, the inspirer of so many licentious passions was at last enslaved herself. She might disdain the fear of a rival potentate, and defy the indignation of Octavius, but her anxiety about his sister was the instinct of the woman, rather than of the queen. She could not forget that a wife's legitimate influence had once detained her lover from her side for more than two whole years: she might still apprehend the awakening of his reason, and his renunciation of an alliance which at times he felt, she well knew, to be bitterly degrading. To retain her grasp of her admirer, as well as her seat upon the throne of the Ptolemies, she must drown his scruples in voluptuous oblivion, and invent new charms to revive and amuse his jaded passion.

[No. 301.]   *Merivale.*

plus quam senatoria ficta fiducia e rostris pro-
nuntiaret. Et iniectos semel multitudini frenos
remittere neque ipsius ingenio neque eorum
consentaneum erat saluti.

M. J. R.

QVAMQVAM cetera omnia imperio, imperium saluti posthabuerat, quae tot
ardores excitauerat ipsa tandem irretiebatur.
Poterat aemulos reges, poterat Octauium indig-
nantem contemnere, tamen huius sororis muliebri
magis quam regio metu angebatur. Meminerat
sane amatorem sibi amplius biennium apud
uxorem optimo iure abfuisse; atque etiamnum
uerebatur ne ueternum aliquando excuteret, atque eam repudiaret necessitudinem qua ut nimis
inhonesta nonnunquam illum torqueri uideret.
Itaque ne amores sibi una cum Ptolemaeorum
principatu deficerent, uiri religionem uoluptate
opprimendam, animumque libidinis iam diu satiatum
nouis deliciis reparandum credidit.

E. W. B.

HE was a man of personage proper, inclined
to tallness, in his youth valiant and active,
towards his latter age full and corpulent, of a full
face and clear complexion, with an erected fore-
head, and a large grey eye bright and quick.
Sound and sure he was of his words, true and
faithful to his friends, somewhat choleric, yet apt
to forgive, cheerful in his journeys or at his meals,
of a sound and deep judgement, with a strong
memory, both which were much beautified with
his well-composed language and graceful delivery.
He was somewhat prodigally inclined in his youth,
and generously thrifty in his age, giving good
example to his greatest neighbours by his constant
hospitality. Earnest he was and sincere in the
rightful cause of his client, pitiful in the relief of
the distressed, and merciful to the poor.

[No. 297.]   *James Howel.*

IT is creditable to Charles's temper that, ill as
he thought of his species, he never became a
misanthrope. He saw little in man but what was
hateful. Yet he did not hate them. Nay, he was
so far humane that it was highly disagreeable to him
to see their sufferings, or to hear their complaints.
This, however, is a sort of humanity which, though

STATVRA fuit iusta, sed procerior: in adulescentia fortis et uelox, postquam se aetas flexit, pingui corpore et obeso; spatioso uultu, in quo color translucebat, fronte elata, oculis magnis glaucisque ac uegetum quiddam splendentibus. Certus et tenax erat promissi, in amicos uerax fidelisque; iracundior, sed ut facile ignosceret: hilaris in itinere uel cum cenaret, iudicii nec peruersus nec futtilis, ualidus memoria: quae utraque ut sermone commodo, ita decora pro-nuntiatione commendabat. Adulescens in sumptus effusior, parcus in senectute, citra sordes tamen, ut exemplo liberalitatis esset propter hospitia etiam maximis uicinorum. Clientum ubi iusta causa fuit, diligens nec qui praeuaricaretur, inopes sub-leuabat, pauperum miserebatur.

R. E.

ID Carolo laudi est, quod cum homines tanto opere contempsisset, nunquam euasit cynicus, neque oderat eos quos ex omni parte odiosos putaret; ita scilicet humanus ut nec dolentes uidere posset nec querentes audire. Quod in homine priuato, cui angusti fines bene et male faciendi circumdati sunt, gratum est et laudabile;

amiable and laudable in a private man, whose power to help or hurt is bounded by a narrow circle, had in princes often been rather a vice than a virtue. More than one well-disposed ruler has given up whole provinces to rapine and oppression, merely from a wish to see none but happy faces round his own board and his own walks. No man is fit to govern great societies who hesitates about disobliging the few who have access to him for the sake of the many whom he will never see. The facility of Charles was such as perhaps has never been found in any man of equal sense. He was a slave without being a dupe. Worthless men and women, to the very bottom of whose hearts he saw, and whom he knew to be destitute of affection for him and undeserving of his confidence, could easily wheedle him out of titles, places, domains, state secrets, and pardons. He bestowed much; yet he neither enjoyed the pleasure nor acquired the fame of beneficence. He never gave spontaneously; but it was painful to him to refuse. The consequence was that his bounty generally went, not to those who deserved it best, nor even to those whom he liked best, but to the most shameless and importunate suitor who could obtain an audience.

[No. 300.]   *Macaulay.*

in regibus nocuit saepius rei publicae quam pro-
fuit. Principes sane exstiterunt non mali, qui
ne conuiuarum et familiarium tristitiam uiderent,
totas prouincias ui ac latrocinio tradiderunt. Sed
magnam ciuitatem nunquam bene rexeris, si times
multorum causa, quos nunquam uideris, paucos
praesentes offendere. Facilitatem profecto Caroli
nemo fere pari prudentia aequauit. Facile ei
imperares, imponeres nunquam. Immo uirorum
mulierumque leuissimi, quorum animos penitus
habuit perspectos, quorum studia erga se ac merita
nulla esse nouerat, eblandiebantur insignia, honores, uillas, uenias, arcana imperii. Cum multa
largiretur, beneuolentiae nec fructum nec famam
adeptus est. Nec sponte dabat quicquam, nec
nisi aegre recusabat. Igitur benignitate eius
fruebantur homines neque optime meriti neque
ipsi gratissimi, sed ut quisque impudentissimus
importunissimusque aditus eius occupauerat.

H. N.

HE had that general curiosity to which no
kind of knowledge is indifferent or super-
fluous ; and that general benevolence by which no
order of men is hated or despised. His principles
both of thought and action were great and comprehensive. By a solicitous examination of ob-
jections and judicious comparison of opposite
arguments, he attained what inquiry never gives
but to industry and perspicuity, a firm and
unshaken settlement of conviction. But his
firmness was without asperity; for knowing with
how much difficulty truth is sometimes found, he
did not wonder that many missed it. His delivery,
though unconstrained, was not negligent, and,
though forcible, was not turbulent ; disdaining
anxious nicety of emphasis, and laboured artifice
of action, it captivated the hearer by its natural
dignity; it roused the sluggish and fixed the
volatile, and detained the mind upon the subject
without directing it to the speaker.

[No. 304.]   *S. Johnson.*

HE was pronounced guilty of the act of which
he had in the most solemn manner protested he was innocent ; he was sent to the

OMNIA scire auenti nulla pars doctrinae superuacua aut neglegenda uidebatur: omnes beneuolentia complexo nullum genus hominum odio nec contemptui. Quae cogitabat, quae agebat, a magno proficiscebantur animo largoque pectore. Exceptionibus accurate pensatis, quaeque in utramque partem dicebantur subtiliter comparatis, praemium industriae atque intellegentiae assequebatur ut sententia immotus constaret. Sed constantia huius carebat asperitate: quam aegre enim nonnumquam reperiatur uerum expertus, non mirabatur multos fallere. Actio parum astricta nec soluta, et sine uiolentia uehemens; spreta sollicitudine contentionis gestusque operosis artificiis natiua dignitate audientes capiebat; excitabat pigros, detinebat leues, ut oratio oratore fallente animos occuparet.

D. S. M.

HVNC ergo eius sceleris damnatum, quod maximo opere infitiabatur, in Tullianum demissum, honoribus exutum, motum senatu,

Tower: he was turned out of all his places, and his name was struck out of the Council Book. It might well have been thought that the ruin of his fame and of his fortunes was irreparable. But there was about his nature an elasticity which nothing could subdue. In his prison, indeed, he was as violent as a falcon just caged, and would, if he had been long detained, have died of mere impatience. His only solace was to contrive wild and romantic schemes for extricating himself from his difficulties and avenging himself on his enemies. When he regained his liberty, he stood alone in the world, a dishonoured man, more hated by the Whigs than any Tory, and by the Tories than any Whig, and reduced to such poverty that he talked of retiring to the country, living like a farmer and putting his Countess into the dairy to churn and to make cheeses. Yet, even after this fall, that mounting spirit rose again, and rose higher than ever. When he next appeared before the world, he had inherited the earldom of the head of his family; he had ceased to be called by the tarnished name of Monmouth; and he soon added new lustre to the name of Peterborough.

[No. 294.]   *Macaulay.*

omnem sane famam ac fortunam funditus crederes perdidisse. At feroci uir animo nulla aegritudine erat opprimendus. Primo quidem tamquam aquila recens captus saeuire, ut carceris impatientia moriturus uideretur. Id tantum habere solatii, ut incredibili arte audacia excogitaret consilia, quibus effugeret periclis, inimicos ulcisceretur. At cum tandem esset liberatus, quo se uerteret? Amicis orbatus, infamis, primoribus infimo popularium infensior, popularibus primorum, paupertate tam desperata ut se rus iturum dictitaret, agros culturum, uxori nobili lactis caseique curam permissurum. Tamen ne tanta quidem mala tam forti obstabant, quin uel sublimiora quam antea adsequeretur. Cum iterum in re publica uersaretur, patria nobilitate exornatus, prioris nominis dedecus exuerat, antiquam gentem maiore gloria insignicbat.

A. S.

A MIND like Scipio's, working its way under the peculiar influences of his time and country, cannot but move irregularly; it cannot but be full of contradictions. Two hundred years later, the mind of the dictator Caesar acquiesced contentedly in Epicureanism: he retained no more of enthusiasm than was inseparable from the intensity of his intellectual power, and the fervour of his courage, even amidst his utter moral degradation. But Scipio could not be like Caesar. His mind rose above the state of things around him; his spirit was solitary and kingly; he was cramped by living among those as his equals whom he felt fitted to guide as from some higher sphere; and he retired at last to Liternum to breathe freely, to enjoy the simplicity of childhood, since he could not fulfil his natural calling to be a hero king. So far he stood apart from his countrymen, admired, reverenced, but not loved. But he could not shake off all the influences of his time; the virtue, public and private, which still existed at Rome, the reverence paid by the wisest and best men to the religion of their fathers, were elements too congenial to his nature not to retain their hold on it: they cherished that nobleness of soul in him, and that faith in the invisible and divine, which two cen-

ANIMVS qualis fuit Scipionis, uariis cum loci tum temporis momentis obnoxius, tantum abest ut uno aliquo eodemque tenore promoueatur, ut nonnumquam quam longissime secum discrepet. Ducentos post annos C. Caesar in Epicuri placitis ita acquieuit, ut nihil omnino altioris disciplinae retinuerit, nisi quo prae maxima ingeni ui et uirtute feruidissima etiam in summa morum turpitudine carere non potuerit. Quod idem ut pateretur Scipioni haudquaquam licuit. Inerat ei animus rebus suis maior, inerat ingenium singulare et uere regium; neque non indignabatur quod inter istos ciuiliter uiuendum esset, quibus tamquam e loco superiore imperare debuerit. Itaque Liternum concessit, ut liberius respiraret, et puerili saltem simplicitate frueretur, cui negatum esset, id quod sibi destinasset natura, heroicum imperium exercere. Hactenus a suis semotus uixit, ea condicione ut reuerentiam admirationemque omnium conciliaret, amorem repelleret. Neque tamen saeculi mores omnino exuere potuit. Quippe uirtus, tum publica tum priuata, quae Romae etiamnum florebat, et reuerentia qua optimus quisque et sapientissimus patriam religionem persequebantur, magis ingenio eius congruebant, quam ut inde facile diuellerentur: immo fouebant illam animi magnitudinem, illam

turies of growing unbelief rendered almost impossible in the days of Caesar.   Yet how strange
must the conflict be, when faith is combined with
the highest intellectual power, and its appointed
object is no better than Paganism! Longing to
believe, yet repelled by palpable falsehood, crossed
inevitably with snatches of unbelief, in which
hypocrisy is ever close at the door, it breaks
out desperately, as it may seem, into the region
of dreams and visions and mysterious commun-
ings with the invisible, as if longing to find that
food in its own creations, which no outward
objective truth offers to it. The proportions of
belief and unbelief in the human mind in such
cases, no human judgement can determine : they
are the wonders of history : characters inevitably
misrepresented by the vulgar, and viewed even
by those who in some sense have the key to
them as a mystery, not fully to be comprehended,
and still less explained to others. The genius
which conceived the incomprehensible character
of Hamlet, would alone be able to describe with
intuitive truth the character of Scipio or of
Cromwell.

Dr. Arnold.

rerum diuinarum arcanarumque persuasam opi-
nionem, quibus apud C. Caesaris aequales, glis-
cente per ducentos annos magis atque magis
impietate, nullus fcre relictus est locus. Quam
mirum uero illud certamen, quando fides cum
summo mentis acumine coniuncta nihil melius
sibi propositum habeat quam prauam supersti-
tionem ! Quippe animus, credendi auidus, apertis
mendaciis repulsus, prae dubitatione sui deceptor,
tandem quasi spe abiecta prorumpit in somnia
et uisa et arcana quaedam deorum commercia,
tamquam id pabuli e suis ipsius commentis percepturus, quod res extrinsecus oblatae sufficere
nequeant. Quis fuerit ingeniis huius modi credendi, quis diffidendi modus, non hominum est
diiudicare: immo ea ceu miracula posteris tradit
historia, quae uulgus fato quodam semper per-
peram interpretetur, aliquanto peritiores uix ipsi
intellegant, nedum aliis explicare possint. Ille
demum qui Hamletti personam captu humano
maiorem excogitauit, Scipionis aut Cromuelli
indolem qualis re uera foret, ceu mero mentis
intuitu assecutus, fortasse adumbrauisset.

J. C.

THERE is no person in that age about whom historians have been more divided, or whose character has been drawn in such opposite colours. Personal intrepidity, military skill, sagacity, and vigour in the administration of civil affairs, are virtues which even his enemies allow him to have possessed in an eminent degree. His moral qualities are more dubious, and ought neither to be praised nor censured without great reserve, and many distinctions. In a fierce age he was capable of using victory with humanity, and of treating the vanquished with moderation ; a patron of learning, which, among martial nobles, was either unknown or despised ; zealous for religion, to a degree which distinguished him, even at a time when professions of that kind were not uncommon. His confidence in his friends was extreme, and inferior only to his liberality towards them, which knew no bounds. A distinguished passion for the liberty of his country prompted him to oppose the pernicious system which the Princes of Lorraine had obliged the Queen-mother to pursue. On Mary's return into Scotland, he served her with a zeal and affection to which he sacrificed the friendship of those who were most attached to his person. But, on the other hand, his ambition was immoderate ; and events happened that

NEMO id aetatis exstitit de quo magis discrepat inter scriptores tam in diuersum uitam eius depingentes. Virtute bellica, rei militaris peritia, rei publicae administrandae uigore ac consilio, his artibus magno opere eum conspici ne ipsi quidem inimici infitiantur. De moribus res magis in dubio est, quos neque laudari neque reprehendi nisi caute et cum delectu aliquo oportuerit. In atrocitate temporum potuit uictoria clementer uti, et uictis parcere. Litterarum quoque fautor, quae inter nobiles belli auidos aut ignotae erant aut contemptui habitae: idem religionum studiosus ut supra aequales et ipsos idem studium prae se ferentes enitesceret. Accedebat magna amicorum fiducia, maior tamen munificentia, quae erat infinita. Neque dubium est quin funestis consiliis in quae Lorronenses regis matrem impulere incorrupto libertatis patriae amore adductus se opposuerit: nec minus constat Mariae in Caledoniam reuersae eo studio et caritate inseruisse cui amicitiam sui amantissimorum posthabuerit. Contra cupiditas gloriae erat infinita: quaeque intercesserunt negotia ingenti spe proposita eo usque auidum ingenium allexerunt, ut plus quam ciuilia agitaret. Nam in reginam et sororem, et optime de se meritam, contra quám fratrem et beneficiorum memorem decet sese gerebat.

L

opened to him vast projects which allured his enterprising genius, and led him to actions inconsistent with the duty of a subject. His treatment of the Queen, to whose bounty he was so much indebted, was unbrotherly and ungrateful. The dependence on Elizabeth, under which he brought Scotland, was disgraceful to the nation. He deceived and betrayed Norfolk with a baseness unworthy of a man of honour.

[No. 314.]	*Robertson.*

L ITERATURE was a neutral ground on which he could approach his political enemy without too open discredit, and he courted eagerly the approval of a critic whose literary genius he esteemed as highly as his own. Men of genuine ability are rarely vain of what they can do really well. Cicero admired himself as a statesman with the most unbounded enthusiasm. He was proud of his verses, which were hopelessly commonplace. In the art in which he was without a rival he was modest and diffident. He sent his various writings for Caesar's judgement. 'Like the traveller who has overslept himself,' he said, 'yet

Vtque Caledonia Elissae dedita ciuile erat dedecus, ita deceptus proditusque Norfolciensis
turpem ipsius nomini infamiam intulit.

R. S.

L ITTERAS uero potuit una cum aduersario
salua fama attingere; et cum Caesaris in
tali re iudicium haud minoris quam suum ipsius
aestimaret, ab eo ualde cupiit laudari. Verum ut
perraro fit ut ii qui praestant ingenio in iis sibi
potissimum placeant rebus in quibus excellunt
maxime, ita ipsi Ciceroni quae gesserat in consulatu placebant, placebant inepti quos scripserat
uersiculi: in qua autem arte facile primas tenebat
partes, in ea omnino sobrius fuit atque uerecundus.
Itaque cum scripta sua Caesari misisset iudicanda,
sic ad Quintum fratrem scribit: 'Ego uero,' inquit,
'hoc fortasse efficiam quod saepe uiatoribus, cum

by extraordinary exertions reaches his goal sooner than if he had been earlier on the road, I will follow your advice and court this man. I have been asleep too long. I will correct my slowness with my speed; and as you say he approves my verses, I shall travel not with a common carriage, but with a four-in-hand of poetry.'

[No. 278.]   *Froude.*

HE was born with violent passions and quick sensibilities: but the strength of his emotions was not suspected by the world. From the multitude his joy and his grief, his affection and his resentment, were hidden by a phlegmatic serenity, which made him pass for the most cold-blooded of mankind. Those who brought him good news could seldom detect any sign of pleasure. Those who saw him after a defeat looked in vain for any trace of vexation. He praised and reprimanded, rewarded and punished, with the stern tranquillity of a Mohawk chief; but those who knew him well and saw him near were aware that under all this ice a fierce fire was constantly burning. It was seldom that anger

properant, euenit, ut properando etiam citius eo quo uelint perueniant quam si maturius profecti essent; sic ego te suadente quoniam in isto homine colendo tam indormiui diu, cursu corrigam tarditatem, et quoniam scribis poema ab eo nostrum laudari, non iam equis, ut aiunt, sed poeticis quadrigis uehar[1].'

G. G. R.

[1] Cf. Cic. ad Q. Frat. ii. 15, § 3.

NATVRA quidem flagrantior et affectibus promptior, tamen ciues ardorem ingenii celabat. Ne populo laetitia luctus studium offensio notesceret, obtentui erat frons fixa et composita, qua fretus tamquam rigidi si quis alius animi agebat. Prospera etenim nuntiantibus nullum gaudii signum, irritique aegritudinem explorare qui uicto aderant. Siue quem laude et praemiis seu questu poenisque dignaretur, uultus ei ut Sarmatarum cuidam regulo quietus ac seuerus durabat. Necessarii autem quibuscum uiuebat gnari erant hoc rigore uel acerrimum feruorem tegi. Non saepe impotens ira ruere, quando autem exarserat, impetu metuendus; nec quotiens id, sed raro, acciderat, tutus ad eum aditus.

deprived him of power over himself, but when he was really enraged the first outbreak of his passion was terrible.　It was indeed scarcely safe to approach him.　On these rare occasions, however, as soon as he had regained his self-command, he made such ample reparation to those whom he had wronged as tempted them to wish that he would go into a fury again.　His affection was as impetuous as his wrath.　Where he loved, he loved with the whole energy of his strong mind. When death separated him from what he loved, the few who witnessed his agonies trembled for his reason and his life.　To a very small circle of intimate friends, on whose fidelity and secrecy he could absolutely depend, he was a different man from the reserved and stoical William whom the multitude supposed to be destitute of human feelings.

Macaulay.

IN his private life, he was severe, morose, inexorable, banishing all the softer affections as natural enemies to justice and as suggesting false motives of acting from favour, clemency and compassion.　In public affairs he was the same;

Tamen cum se uicisset, tam prodigus iniurias pen-
sabat ut iterum furere optarent quos incessisset.
Neque ad iracundiam quam caritatem pronior, in
dilectos totis robusti animi uiribus solitus incumbere; quin cum fatum amorem diremisset, qui
pauci praesto erant angoribus, de sanitate atque
etiam de salute eius desperare. Apud potissimos
amicorum (perpaucis enim quos spectatae fidei
cognorat et occulti pectoris se dedit) plurimum ab
illo clauso immotoque uiro distabat quem uulgus
humanitatis expertem rebatur.

J. S. R.

SI priuatum respiceres, seuerus tristis in-
exorabilis erat; beneuolentiae omniumque
quae in hominum natura humaniora sunt, tamquam aequitati obstarent, uanasque agenti causas
gratiam clementiam miserationem subicerent,

he had but one rule of policy—to adhere to what was right, without regard to times or circumstances or even to a force that could control him: for instead of managing the power of the great so as to mitigate the ill or extract any good from it, he was urging it always to acts of violence by a perpetual defiance; so that with the best intentions in the world he often did great harm to the republic.   This was his general behaviour; yet from some particular facts explained above it appears that his strength of mind was not always impregnable, but had its weak places of pride, ambition and party zeal, which, when encouraged and flattered to a certain point, would betray him sometimes into measures contrary to his ordinary rule of right and truth.   The last act of his life was agreeable to his nature and philosophy. When he could no longer be what he had been, and when the ills of life overbalanced the good (which by the principles of his sect was a just cause for dying), he put an end to his life with a spirit and resolution which would make one imagine that he was glad to have found an occasion of dying in his proper character.   On the whole, his life was rather admirable than amiable, fit to be praised rather than imitated.

contemptor; idem si in publicis rebus uersaretur, nihil nisi quod rectum esset spectare, eo
omnia referre; ita temporum incuriosus, ut ne
potentiorum quidem rationem haberet: quorum
auctoritatem cum ita temperare posset, ut uel
prodessent rei publicae, uel certe minus nocerent,
obstando semper in superbiam uiolentiamque
agebat; ita ut quamuis inseruire rei publicae uellet,
grauissimo eam damno plerumque afficeret. Hoc
fere ingenio praeditus erat: is tamen cuius
egregios mores posset nonnumquam expugnare,
ut ante diximus, superbia, studium, nimia in
honoribus capessendis cupiditas; quibus qui
tempestiuo obsequio uterentur, impulere interdum
ut quaedam contra rectum uerumque ageret.
Finem uitae neque ingenio neque philosophiae
alienum habuit; cum enim qualis fuerat, diutius
esse non posset, causam adeptus moriendi, quod
Stoicorum quidem iudicio felicitatis minus quam
miseriarum esset, mortem sibi consciuit, ita forti
animo et obstinato ut libenter occasionem nactus
uideretur qua ut Catonem deceret moreretur.
Ceterum facilius admiratus eum fueris quam
dilexeris; laudes quam imitere.

J. C.

IN Walpole's day the English clergy were the idlest and the most lifeless in the world. In our own time no body of religious ministers surpasses them in piety, in philanthropic energy, or in popular regard. But the movement was far from being limited to the Methodists or the clergy. In the nation at large appeared a new moral enthusiasm, which, rigid and pedantic as it often seemed, was still healthy in its social tone, and whose power showed itself in a gradual disappearance of the profligacy which had disgraced the upper classes, and the foulness which had infested literature ever since the Restoration. A yet nobler result of the religious revival was the steady attempt, which has never ceased from that day to this, to remedy the guilt, the ignorance, the physical suffering, the social degradation of the profligate and the poor. It was not till the Wesleyan impulse had done its work that this philanthropic impulse began. The Sunday schools established by Mr. Raikes of Gloucester, at the close of the century, were the beginnings of popular education. By writings, and by her own personal example, Hannah More drew the sympathy of England to the poverty and crime of the agricultural labourer. A passionate impulse of human sympathy with the wronged and afflicted

VALPOLIO rem publicam tractante, clerus Anglicus ceteros et ignauia et socordia exsuperabat; eosdem hoc saeculo nullum eorum genus qui in rebus diuinis uersantur nec pietate neque erga inopes sedulitate nec fama aequiperat. Sed studium nouum nequaquam clerum solum excitabat uel eos qui se uiuendi normae oboedire sunt professi: uniuersum enim apud populum gliscere amor recti nouus, qui ita tristis in nonnullis est uisus et umbratilis, ut uitiis communibus medelas adhibuerit: qui quantum ualeret indicio erat quod libidines, patriciorum labes, sensim obsoluerunt, et quasi Fescennina locutio obticuit quae post Carolum alterum redditum litteras maculauerat. Maior tamen ex eo laus reuiuiscentis ecclesiae quod multi summa diligentia ex eo tempore enisi sunt perditorum et pauperum ut scelera et ignorantiam minuerent, corporumque dolores et morum contagia malorum leuarent. Cuius initium rei postea erat quam Vesleii disciplina in omnes partes manauit. Ludos instituit sub finem saeculi Racius Glocestriensis in quibus pueri septimo quoque die res diuinas discerent; unde originem traxit ratio uniuersi populi imbuendi. Deinde Anna, Mori filia, et scriptis et factis suis aperuit ciuibus quem ad modum ruricolae miseri, nobilium clientela, paupertate, afflicti ad facinora

raised hospitals, endowed charities, built churches, sent missionaries to the heathen, supported Burke in his plea for the Hindoos, and Clarkson and Wilberforce in their crusade against the iniquity of the slave trade.

J. R. Green.

ALEXANDER rose early; the first moments of the day were consecrated to private devotion, and his domestic chapel was filled with the images of those heroes, who, by improving or reforming human life, had deserved the grateful reverence of posterity. But, as he deemed the service of mankind the most acceptable worship of the gods, the greatest part of his morning hours was employed in his council, where he discussed public affairs, and determined private causes, with a patience and discretion above his years. The dryness of business was relieved by the charms of literature; and a portion of time was always set apart for his favourite studies of poetry, history, and philosophy. The

proni essent. Exarsit amor incitatus et iniuria
laesorum et corporibus debilium, quippe qui ipsi
homines essent: domus exstrui aegrorum sedes:
pecuniae conferri miserorum solamina, fana aedi-
ficari: ad barbaros emitti qui Christi doctrina
instituerent: Burcius pro Indis contionabundus,
Clarsonus et Vilberforcius uociferati contra seruorum commercia cum plausibus excipi.

A. H. C.

PRIMA luce e thalamo Alexander, quasi
cum sole exortus, se deorum obseruantiae
dabat; immo apud se in porticu quadam
simulacra eorum uirorum qui uel commoda uel
noua uirtutis exempla exhibendo ceteris profuerant
et digni qui summa gratia colerentur uisi erant,
plurima posuerat. Cum uero hominum commodis
inseruiendo deos optime coli arbitraretur, quod
temporis antemeridiani supererat, id in consilium
cum suis capiendum insumebat, et causis cum
publicis tum priuatis secandis, mira et maturiore
quam pro aetate patientia et prudentia, operam
dabat. Litterarum etiam studiis rerum molestias
leuabat, tempore aliquantulo iis, quibus ipse
fauebat, poetarum scilicet, et historicorum et

works of Virgil and Horace, the republics of Plato
and Cicero, formed his taste, enlarged his under-
standing, and gave him the noblest ideas of man
and government.   The exercises of the body
succeeded to those of the mind ; and Alexander,
who was tall, active, and robust, surpassed most
of his equals in the gymnastic arts.   His table
was served with the most frugal simplicity ; and
whenever he was at liberty to consult his own
inclination, the company consisted of a few select
friends, men of learning and virtue, amongst whom
Ulpian was constantly invited.

[No. 306.]   *Gibbon.*

TO the religion of his country, he offered, in
the mere wantonness of impiety, insults too
foul to be described.   His mendacity and his
effrontery passed into proverbs.   Of all the liars
of his time he was the most deliberate, the most
inventive, and the most circumstantial.   What
shame meant he did not seem to understand.   No
reproaches, even when pointed and barbed with
the sharpest wit, appeared to give him pain.
Great satirists, animated by deadly personal

sapientium, operibus perlegendis cotidie seposito ;
itaque Maronis et Flacci uersibus, et Platonis et
M. Tulli De Re Publica libris ediscendis, iudicium
subtilius, intelligentiam . probatiorem, summum
denique et nobilissimum erga homines studium
et summam in imperio liberalitatem consecutus est.
Inde mentis disciplinae successit corporis exercitatio ; in qua Alexander, ut qui grandis esset
et agilis et robustus, aequales fere excellebat.
Mensae minime sumptuosae ; quibus, ubi sibi
tantum satisfacere liceret, amicos paucos, doctrinae et uirtutis exempla, et in iis praecipue
Ulpianum, adhibebat.

E. D. A. M.

DEORVM quasi ex mera animi libidine
contemptor patrias religiones foedissimis
atque adeo infandis onerabat iniuriis. Fraudes atque fallaciae, audacia et impudentia in prouerbiis
uersatae sunt ; ut enim ubertate et subtilitate
consulto mentiendi mendacissimum quemque
aetatis suae superabat, ita pudoris ne nomen
quidem audiisse uidebatur. Quippe is erat qui
nullis opprobriis tangi, nullis · contumeliarum
aculeis pungi posset. Inuehebantur in eum uiri in

aversion, exhausted all their strength in attacks upon him.   They assailed him with keen invective : they assailed him with still keener irony : but they found that neither invective nor irony could move him to anything but an unforced smile, and a good humoured curse ; and they at length threw down the lash, acknowledging that it was impossible to make him feel.   That with such vices he should have played a great part in life, should have carried numerous elections against the most formidable opposition by his personal popularity, should have had a large following in Parliament, should have risen to the highest offices in the state, seems extraordinary.   But he lived in times when faction was almost a madness ; and he possessed in an eminent degree the qualities of the leader of a faction.

[F. C. 528.]   *Macaulay.*

SEEING, then, that he has no personal attractions, I may freely say, that in all my acquaintance, which is very large, I never knew any one who was his equal in natural gifts : for he has a quickness of apprehension which is almost

satira acerrimi priuatis insuper odiis uehementis-
sime accensi; iuuabat omnes ingenii facultates
comparare, iuuabat hominem acerbis conuiciis
aperte insectari, cauillatione uel acerbiore oblique
perstringere; haec autem omnia cum nihil illum
mouere possent quominus risu minime arcessito
excepta in malam rem abire animi causa iuberet,
tandem uelut omisso flagello uerbera incassum
effusa esse confessi sunt. Mirum sane dictu qui
tantis uitiis cumulatus esset eum uiri principis
semper personam sustinuisse, comitiis tot grauis-
simos competitores per fauorem populi uicisse, fac-
tionem haudquaquam contemnendam sibi in senatu
conciliasse, honores in re publica amplissimos con-
secutum esse. Atqui cum in illa tempora incidisset
quibus partium studia usque ad amentiam progressa
erant, tum ipse natura atque ingenio ductor erat
partium germanissimus.

H. B.

HIC cum nulla parte corporis formosus sit, non
uereor dicere me ex omnibus familiaribus
meis—sunt autem permulti—pari ingenio alterum
nosse neminem; inest enim uelox et paene
singularis cognitio rerum, estque humanissimus,

M

unrivalled, and he is remarkably gentle, and also the most courageous of men ; there is a union of qualities in him such as I have never seen in any other, and should scarcely have thought that the combination was possible ; for those who, like him, have quick and ready and retentive wits, have generally also quick tempers; they are ships without ballast, which go darting about, and are mad rather than courageous; and the steadier sort, where they have to face study, are stupid and cannot remember. Whereas he moves surely and smoothly and successfully in the path of knowledge and enquiry; and he is full of gentle-ness, and always making progress, like the noise-less flow of a river of oil; at his age, it is wonderful.

Jowett's Theaetetus.

THE men of the eighteenth century knew little of that sort of passion for comfort which is the mother of servitude—a relaxing passion, though it be tenacious and unalterable, which mingles and intertwines itself with many private virtues, such as domestic affections, regularity of life, respect for religion, which favours propriety

idemque fortissimus omnium : quo quidem in uno
tot sunt artes quot nec coniunctas uidi in alio,
nec coniungi credo potuisse ; quibus enim
uegetum, ut huic homini, et erectum ac tenax
suppetit ingenium, his plerumque etiam magis est
in promptu iracundia, unde nauigiorum instar
quibus saburra non est impetu suo huc illuc
feruntur, nec tantum fortes sunt quantum furiosi :
at grauiores, si ad studia se contulerunt,
hebetes sunt nec quidquam queunt reminisci.
Hic uero ad cognoscendas res et inquirendas
motu fertur certo et aequabili et secundo, idemque
abundat comitate, et processus habet constantes,
tam nullo strepitu quam flumen quod aiunt olei :
quod sane mireris, adulescenti tot uirtutes constitisse.

R. E.

PROXIMI uero seculi homines non multum
attigit illa uitae otiosae immodica cupiditas
quae procreatrix quaedam et quasi parens est
seruitutis—nempe eam dico quae licet ipsa
constans pertinaxque sit tamen mentes hominum
uehementer emollire potest, quae pietati fruga-
litati religioni aliisque quae in numero uirtutum

but proscribes heroism, and which excels in making decent livers but base citizens. The men of the eighteenth century were better and they were worse. The French of that age were addicted to joy and passionately fond of amusement; they were perhaps more lax in their habits, and more vehement in their passions and opinions than those of the present day, but they were strangers to the temperate and decorous sensualism that we see about us. In the upper classes men thought more of adorning life than of rendering it comfortable; they sought to be illustrious rather than to be rich. Even in the middle ranks the pursuit of comfort never absorbed every faculty of the mind; that pursuit was often abandoned for higher and more refined enjoyments; every man placed some object beyond the love of money before his eyes. 'I know my countrymen,' said a contemporary writer, in language which, though eccentric, is spirited: 'apt to melt and dissipate the metals, they are not prone to pay them habitual reverence, and they will not be slow to turn again to their former idols, to valour, to glory, and, I will add, to magnanimity.'

[*F. C.* 343.]

earum ponimus quae domesticae habentur implicata et permixta est, quae animi moderationem fouet magnitudinem exterminat, denique quae ciuium priuatim honestorum publice turpium progeniem suppeditat uberrimam. His autem illos et meliores dixeris et peiores. Galli quidem illorum temporum cum in gaudia effusi oblectamenta mirum quantum in deliciis haberent, ut moribus nescio an usi sint solutioribus utque omnia his qui nunc sunt impensius cupere omnia impensius sentire solebant, ita ab hoc studio uoluptatum sobrio, ut ita dicam, ac temperato plane abhorrebant. Nobilitas uero magis studebat uitam exornare quam otiosam reddere, antiquiorque ei fuit gloria quam diuitiae; atque etiam tenuiores tantum afuit ut otium tota mente consectarentur, ut saepe in uoluptates humaniores relictis sordibus incumberent, et sibi quisque aliquid lucro pulcrius proponerent. Audiamus si placet quemdam eiusdem aetatis scriptorem si inusitatius at satis neruose loquentem. 'Noui populares meos,' inquit, 'quos metalla quae totiens liquefacere et dissipare soleant piget nimis constanter adorasse; nec multa hercle mora erit quin ad illa reuertantur quae olim in loco numinum habebant, fortitudinem gloriamque animique, hoc audeo dicere, altitudinem.'

H. B.

AS we familiarize ourselves with the details of this episode, there appears less and less plausibility in the often iterated declamation against Goethe on the charge of his having 'sacrificed his genius to the Court.' It becomes indeed a singularly foolish display of rhetoric. Let us for a moment consider the charge. He had to choose a career. That of poet was then, as it is still, terribly delusive; verses could create fame, but no money ; *fama* and *fames* were then, as now, in terrible contiguity. No sooner is the necessity for a career admitted than much objection falls to the ground; for those who reproach him with having wasted his time on court festivities and the duties of government, which others could have done as well, must ask whether he would have saved that time had he followed the career of jurisprudence, and jostled lawyers through the courts at Frankfort ? Or would they prefer seeing him reduced to the condition of poor Schiller, wasting so much of his precious life in literary 'hackwork', translating French books for a miserable pittance ? *Time*, in any case, would have been claimed; in return for that given to Karl August, he received, as he confesses in the poem addressed to the Duke, 'what the great seldom bestow—affection, leisure, confidence,

QVANTO magis compertum habemus quid Goethius hac in re egerit tanto minus iis est concedendum qui in eum totiens inuecti sunt quod ultro ingenium principi dederet. Rem enim intuenti hoc dictum ineptia singulari effusum esse uidetur. Attendite paullulum quaeso : scilicet aliquod ei negotium proponendum erat. Poetam autem esse, ut etiamnum, tunc specie quidem certe pulcrum, re uera inanissimum erat. Versus enim gloriam non pecuniam gignere poterant, fama a fame minimo interuallo tunc ut etiamnum distante. Quod si ei negotium aliquod esse suscipiendum concesseris, iacet extemplo crimen : qui autem ei uitio uertunt, tempus in publicis muneribus ordinandis temere collocauisse, et in re publica esse uersatum quam alii tam bene administrare possent, secum cogitent quo modo tempore illo fuerit usurus si iuri incubuisset, lictoris ritu aemulos in Francfortensi iudicio summouens. An uero mauis eum ut Schillerum musarum antistitem degisse, qui miser uitam in laboribus cerdonum propriis consumpsit, ut Gallicos libros in Teutonicum uerteret mercedula adductus ? Verum tempus illius utcumque negotiis seruiisset ; fatetur autem in poemate ad principem se pro curis quas Caroli Augusti causa susceperat ei accepta referre,

garden, and house.   No one have I had to thank
but him ; and much have I wanted, who as a poet
ill understood the arts of gain.   If Europe praised
me, what has Europe done for me?   Nothing.
Even my works have been an expense to me.'
  · [No. 307.]   *Lewes.*

'WHAT is there, then, ye will say to me, in
this third ordinance which thou so mis-
likest ? I will answer you in few words. I mislike
the changing of the laws of our fathers, specially
when these laws have respect to the worship of
the gods. Many things, I know, are ordered
wisely for one generation, which notwithstanding,
are by another generation no less wisely ordered
otherwise. There is room in human affairs for
change, there is room also for unchangeableness.
And where shall we seek for that which is un-
changeable, but in those great laws which are the
very foundation of the commonwealth ; most of
all in those which, having to do with the immortal
gods, should be also themselves immortal.'

                                              Dr. Arnold.

quae raro dare principes uidemus,
amorem, otia, cum fide Penates:
huic soli huic mihi gratia est habenda.
nam uates egui inscius lucrandi:
toto si legor orbe, nil dat orbis;
ipsi impensa fuere mi libelli.

A. H. C.

QVIDNAM in hac tertia rogatione insit si uelint sciscitari, quod ipse tantum improbauerit paucis responsurum. Displicere sibi ut maiorum instituta, ea praecipue quae ad deorum immortalium cultum spectent, immutentur. Multa satis scire aliter aliis temporibus instituta esse quae tamen nullo tempore inconsultius ordinentur. Quod si in rebus humanis sint quae mutari, esse etiam quae stare ac manere oporteat. Ecqua autem in re stabile esse quicquam expedire, si non in illis legibus quibus summa res publica innitatur? atque in iis ante alias quae, cum ad deos immortales pertineant, eiusdem immortalitatis esse quodam modo participes debeant.

E. W. B.

THERE is nothing that more betrays a base ungenerous spirit than the giving of secret stabs to a man's reputation. Lampoons and satires, that are written with wit and spirit, are like poisoned darts, which not only inflict a wound, but make it incurable. For this reason I am very much troubled when I see the talents of humour and ridicule in the possession of an ill-natured man. There cannot be a greater gratification to a barbarous and inhuman wit than to stir up sorrow in the heart of a private person, to raise uneasiness among near relations, and to expose whole families to derision, at the same time that he remains unseen and undiscovered. If, besides the accomplishments of being witty and ill-natured, a man is vicious into the bargain, he is one of the most mischievous creatures that can enter into a civil society. His satire will then chiefly fall upon those who ought to be the most exempt from it. Virtue, merit, and every-thing that is praiseworthy, will be made the subject of ridicule and buffoonery.

[No. 386.] *Addison.*

FAMAM alienam calumniis clandestinis lacerare, hoc sane in primis praui est animi parumque liberalis; probrosa carmina satiraeque salsae et aculeatae, sicut tela uenenata, non modo uulnus afferunt, sed etiam eius modi quod medicinam non habeat; quam ob rem ualde stomachor cum maleuolum uideo facetiarum et ad ridiculum omnia detorquendi arte praeditum. Neque enim inhumano homini atque crudeli qui est idem cauillator quicquam magis in deliciis esse potest quam priuatis dolorem concitare, propinquis molestias mouere, domos etiam totas in derisum adducere, dum neque in conspectum ipse neque in cognitionem cadat. Sin autem quispiam et facetus et maleuolus sit, et idem praeterea maleficus, illo nihil fere irrepat in ciuitatem iniuriosius. Contumeliis enim eius plurimum afficiuntur qui plurimum carere debent. Honestas uidelicet et dignitas et quidquid probatissimum est fiet ad iocandum ludificandumque materies.

T. S. E.

BY what has been said of the manners, it will be easy for a reasonable man to judge, whether the characters be truly or falsely drawn in a tragedy: for if there be no manners appearing in the characters, no concernment for the persons can be raised, no pity or honour can be moved but by vice or virtue; therefore without them, no person can have any business in the play. If the inclinations be obscure, it is a sign the poet is in the dark, and knows not what manner of man he presents to you; and consequently you can have no idea, or very imperfect, of that man, nor can judge what resolutions he ought to take, or what words or actions are proper for him. Most comedies, made up of accidents or adventures, are liable to fall into this error, and tragedies with many turns are subject to it; for the manners can never be evident .where the surprises of fortune take up all the business of the stage, and where the poet is more in pain to tell you what happened to such a man than what he was. It is one of the excellencies of Shakespeare that the manners of his persons are generally apparent, and you see their bent and inclination.

[No. 412.]   *Dryden.*

PRVDENTI igitur in promptu erit, si recte de moribus disputauimus, personas tragoediae iudicare num ad ueritatem sint accommodatae. Nisi enim mores distinguuntur, nihil est cur animum quis personis aduertat. Neque enim ad terrorem neque in misericordiam commouemur nisi uitiis ac uirtutibus; quae si absunt, frustra prodeunt personae. Etenim si mores male demon-strantur, uix intellegit sane poeta qualis sit ille quem ostendat: quod ubi fit, ingenium personae aut obscure a spectantibus comprenditur aut omnino ignoratur, ut neque quid talis debeat consulere sciamus, neque quid eam indolem deceat agere uel dicere. In quem errorem incidunt plerumque comoediae, quae in casibus ac periculis uersantur, et quaedam etiam tragoediae, si uariis fortunis res geritur. Nam necesse est mores neglegantur, cum id agit poeta ut res gestas admiremur, et plus in eo laborat ut quid expertus sit quidam discamus, quam quali fuerit ingenio. In quo genere praestat ille noster, quia mores in lucem ita profert ut natura personarum indolesque intellegantur.

A. S.

NOW if Nature should intermit her course and leave altogether, though it were only for a while, the observation of her own laws; if those principal and mother elements of the world, whereof all things in this lower world are made, should lose the qualities which now they have; if the frame of that heavenly arch erected over our heads should loosen and dissolve itself; if celestial spheres should forget their wonted motion, and by irregular volubility turn themselves any way as it might happen; if the prince of the lights of heaven, which now as a giant doth run his unwearied course, should as it were through a languishing faintness begin to stand and to rest himself; if the moon should wander from her beaten way; the times and seasons of the year blend themselves by disordered and confused mixture; the winds breathe out their last gasp, the clouds yield no rain, and the earth be defeated by heavenly influence; the fruits of the earth pine away as children at the withered breasts of their mother, no longer able to give them relief: what would become of man himself, whom these things now do all serve? See we not plainly that the obedience of creatures to the law of nature is the stay of the whole world?

[No. 387.]   *Hooker.*

IAM si intermissa causarum serie natura uel breue per tempus leges suas obseruare omit-teret; si mundi elementa ac materies, terrcstrium origo omnium, uirtutibus caruissent suis, et laxata solutaque caelestis arcus compage, stellae soliti motus oblitae fortuito cursu huc illuc uoluerentur ; si luminum ipse caelestium dux,

>   qui gaudet currere Titan
>   Indefessus iter,

languore quodam stetisset quieturus; si luna, ab orbe uaga suo, tempora uarietatesque anni indistinctas inter se miscuisset, ac uentis aurae, nubibus imbres, terris benignitas caeli deficeret, tabescerentque aruorum fetus ut infantes ex-hausto matris ubere, non iam reddentis alimenta : quid in ipso tandem homine fieret cui haec iam omnia ministrant? Nonne manifestum est naturae legibus obsequendo uniuersum mundum contineri ?

A. T. B.

'I SEE,' cries my friend, 'that you are for a speedy administration of justice; but all the world will grant, that the more time there is taken up in considering any subject, the better will it be understood. Besides, it is the boast of an Englishman, that his property is secure, and all the world will grant that a deliberate administration of justice is the best way to secure his property. Why have we so many lawyers, but to secure our property? Why so many formalities, but to secure our property? Not less than one hundred thousand families live in opulence merely by securing our property.' . . . 'But bless me,' returned I, 'what numbers do I see here—all in black—how is it possible that half this multitude find employment?' 'Nothing so easily conceived,' returned my companion, 'they live by watching each other. For instance, the catch-pole watches the man in debt, the attorney watches the catch-pole, the counsellor watches the attorney, the solicitor the counsellor, and all find sufficient employment.' 'I conceive you,' interrupted I, 'they watch each other: but it is the client that pays them all for watching.'

[No. 359.]   *Goldsmith.*

AT Lentulus 'Moras odisti,' inquit, 'in omni causa iudicum sententias citius reddendas esse putas. Verum constat, ut reor, rem qualemcunque quo diutius, eo melius examinari; etenim Romani est, omnia Romanorum bona in tuto esse dictitare. Estne qui neget, nusquam melius bona in tuto collocari quam ubi lentus iudiciorum processus sit, lenta administratio? Quorsum, nisi ad bona nostra conseruanda, tot causidici? quorsum tot in legibus enuntiandis mysteria? Immo innumeri homines rem nostram nobis confirmando locupletantur.' 'At mehercle,' respondi, 'quot et quales adstare uideo, atratiores quam tristiores! potestne fieri ut uel dimidia tantae multitudinis pars quaestum facere possit?' 'Facile intellexeris,' inquit: 'alter alterum obseruando uictum habet; reciperator scilicet debitorem obseruat, aduocatus reciperatorem, consultus aduocatum, praetor denique consultum; ita unusquisque idoneum uictum, ne dicam opulentiam, adipiscitur.' 'Rem,' inquam, 'manifestam fecisti; cornix cornicis oculos configit, causidicus causidicum obseruat, et locupletatur. At sumptu consultoris inconsultissimi hoc fit; qui, quos patibulo suspendere debebat, iis pecuniam pendit.'

E. D. A. M.

N

IT is noble to be capable of resigning entirely one's own portion of happiness, or chances of it : but after all this self-sacrifice must be for some end ; it is not its own end ; and if we are told that its end is not happiness, but virtue which is better than happiness, I ask, Would the sacrifice be made if the hero or martyr did not believe that it would earn for others immunity from similar sacrifices ? Would it be made if he thought that his renunciation of happiness for himself would produce no fruit for any of his fellow-creatures but to make their lot like his, and place them also in the condition of persons who have renounced happiness ? All honour to those who can abnegate for themselves the personal enjoyment of life, when by such renunciation they contribute worthily to increase the amount of happiness in the world ; but he who does it, or professes to do it, for any other purpose, is no more deserving of admiration than the ascetic mounted on his pillar. He may be an inspiring proof of what men can do, but assuredly is not an example of what they should.

[No. 354.]   *J. S. Mill.*

GENEROSI sane est quod ipse habeat uel speret uoluptatis omnino abicere posse: non tamen ideo solum ut abiciatur, sed fine quodam proposito. At non uoluptas, fortasse quis dixerit, ita expetitur, sed uirtus, uoluptate praestantior. Num quis tamen uel audendo uel patiendo uoluptatem omnem abiceret, ni ita crederet se ceteros eodem dolore erepturum? Num quis hoc faceret, si nihil hominibus se effecturum speraret, nisi ut eadem usi sorte et ipsi carerent uoluptate? Nam maxime sane ii laudandi, qui beata uita ipsi uelint carere, ut digne data opera ceteros faciant beatiores: si quis tamen aliam ob causam hoc uel facit uel facere se simulat, non magis admirandus quam fanaticus ille columnae impositus. Quippe monimento fortasse et exemplo est quid possint homines: quid debeant, non docet omnino.

A. S.

WHAT do we look for in studying the history of a past age ? Is it to learn the political transactions and characters of the leading public men ? Is it to make ourselves acquainted with the life and being of the time ? If we set out with the former grave purpose, where is the truth, and who believes that he has it entire ? As we read in these delightful volumes of the Spectator, the past age returns, the England of our ancestors is revivified. The May-pole rises in the Strand again in London, the churches are thronged with daily worshippers, the beaux are gathering in the coffee-houses, the gentry are going to the drawing-room, the ladies are throng-ing to the toy-shops, the chairmen are jostling in the streets, the footmen are running with links before the chariots or fighting round the theatre. I say the fiction carries a greater amount of truth in solution than the volume which purports to be all true. Out of the fictitious book I get the expression of the life of the time : of the manners, of the movement, the dress, the pleasures, the laughter, the ridicule of society—the old times live again, and I travel in the old country of England.

[No. 393.]   *Thackeray.*

AT, quaeso, quo consilio nobis est antiquitas cognoscenda? Vtrum ut quid fecerint uiri principes, quo modo se in re publica gesserint, exquiramus: an potius ut saecula ipsa antiqua, antiquos ipsos pernoscamus uiros? Quod si grauius illud nobis propositum in animo est, quis est qui se omnia, ut re uera erant, uel inuestigare posse, uel complecti animo arbitretur? At librum illum iucundissimum, cui ' Spectatori ' inditum est nomen, perlegentibus, praeterita illa omnia redire, atque antiqua illa Anglia quasi sub oculis reuiuiscere uidetur. Tum uero festa illa Londinii in uiis attolli arbor, tum a piis iterum celebrari templa, ab elegantibus tabernae: hic ad regiam cernas salutatum properare nobiles, illic emptum crepundia mulieres: hic in uiis obstantes a lecticariis summoueri, illic pedisequos uel praecedere cum funalibus carpenta, uel circum theatra inter se rixari. In talibus profecto fabulis plus merae ueritatis quam in ueris istis annalibus continetur; in iis cernere omnia et quasi praesentia intueri uideor: quo modo se tum gesserint homines, quid fecerint, qua ueste fuerint, quibus deliciis: quid risui habuerint, quid ludibrio: resurgunt mihi iterum ipsa antiqua tempora, atque per priscam illam Angliam peregrinari uideor.

G. G. R.

THERE are wonders in true affection; it is a body of enigmas, mysteries, and riddles, wherein two so become one as they both become two; I love my friend before myself, and yet methinks, I do not love him enough. Some few months hence, my multiplied affection will make me believe I have not loved him at all. When I am from him, I am dead till I be with him; when I am with him, I am not satisfied, but would still be nearer him. United souls are not satisfied with embraces, but desire to be truly each other, which being impossible, these desires are infinite, and must proceed without a possibility of satisfaction. Another misery there is in affection, that whom we truly love like our own selves, we forget their looks, nor can our memory retain the idea of their faces; and it is no wonder, for they are ourselves, and our affections make their looks our own. This noble affection falls not on vulgar and common constitutions, but on such as are marked for virtue. He that can love his friend with this noble ardour will, in a competent degree, affect all.

[No. 338.]   *Sir Thomas Browne.*

MVLTA in uero amore sunt admirabilia, nec quicquam est in quo tot obscuritates, tanta lateant aenigmata, quippe qui ex duobus unum, ex utroque autem duos faciat. Equidem amicis me ipsum semper posthabui, idem tamen amicitiae parum mihi satisfecisse uideor; mox delapsis mensibus cum auctus amor fuerit, ne dilexisse quidem uidebor. Si absens fuerit, paene mortuus ero donec reuisam; si una fuerimus, habebo tamen quod desiderem, quia propius etiam esse uelim. Neque enim amplexibus satiabiles amicorum sunt animi, sed uere alter in alterum quasi immigrare cupiunt; quod cum fieri nequeat, inexplebili tenentur cupidine, neque ullum desiderio finem exspectare possunt. Praeterea illud est in amore miserrimum, quod, quos perinde ac nosmet ipsos diligimus, eorum speciem obliuiscimur, neque in memoria tenere oris lineamenta possumus. Nimirum iidem et hi et ipsi sumus, horum uultum communis nobis affingit amor. Non cadit autem in uulgaris ingenii homines tam praeclara caritas, sed in eos solum quorum eximia eluceat uirtus; qui enim tanto studio amicum prosequi possit, idem ceteros satis poterit diligere.

T. S. E.

ALL things about us do minister (or at least may do so, if we would improve the natural instruments and the opportunities afforded us) to our preservation, ease or delight. The hidden bowels of the earth yield us treasures of metals and minerals; the vilest and most common stones we tread on (even in that we tread on them) are useful, and serve to many good purposes beside: the surface of the earth how it is bespread all over, as a table well furnished, with variety of delicate fruits, herbs and grains to nourish our bodies, to please our tastes, to cheer our spirits, to cure our diseases! How many fragrant and beautiful flowers offer themselves for the comfort of our smell and the delight of our sight! Neither can our ears complain, since every wood breeds a quire of natural musicians, ready to entertain them with easy and unaffected harmony: the woods, I say, which also adorned with stately trees afford us a pleasant view and a refreshing shade, shelter from weather and sun, fuel for our fires, materials for our houses and our shipping, with divers other needful utensils.

[F. C. No. 222.] *I. Barrow.*

INSERVIVNT omnia uel certo inseruire possunt, si modo instrumentis iis atque opportunitatibus quas natura fert recte uti uolumus, conseruationi nostrae, otio, uoluptati. Ex absconditis terrae cauernis effoditur aurum ceterorumque metallorum copia: immo uilissimi quos ubique conculcamus lapides uel ob eam ipsam rem nobis usui sunt, et multos porro utilitatis fructus praebent. Adde huc terram uniuersam mensae in modum lautissimae abundantem incredibili fructuum iucundorum uarietate, herbarum, frumentorum, quae corpora nostra sustentent, gustus oblectent, reficiant animos, aegrotantibus medicinam afferant. Quae uero et quam uaria genera florum fragrantium pulcherrimorumque, qui cum odoratu tum aspectu sensus nostros delectant! Neque minus profecto aurium uoluptati consultum; quarum ad delectationem simplicem quamdam eamque iucundissimam musicorum symphoniam natura ipsa in siluis comparauerit. Iam uero siluae ipsae arboribus proceris exornatae spectaculum otiosis praebent, umbram fatigatis, ab imbre perfugium et a sole; eaedem uero lignum ignibus sufficiunt, domos uel naues aedificantibus materiam, et multa alia ad uictum et ad uitam necessaria.

E. C. W.

T HOUGH I am always serious, I do not know
what it is to be melancholy, and can therefore
take a view of Nature in her deep and solemn
scenes with the same pleasure as in her most
gay and delightful ones. By this means I can
improve myself with those objects which others
consider with terror. When I look upon the
tombs of the great, every emotion of envy dies
in me ; when I read the epitaphs of the beautiful,
every inordinate desire goes out ; when I meet
with the grief of parents upon a tombstone, my
heart melts with compassion : when I see the
tomb of the parents themselves, I consider the
vanity of grieving for those whom we must quickly
follow : when I see kings lying by those who
deposed them, when I consider rival wits placed
side by side, or the holy men that divided the
world with their contests and disputes, I reflect
with sorrow and astonishment on the little competi-
tions, factions and debates of mankind. When
I read the several dates of the tombs, of some
that died yesterday, and some six hundred years
ago, I consider that great day when we shall all
of us be contemporaries, and make our appearance
together.

[F. C. 247.]   *S. Addison.*

COGITANTI mihi seria plerumque obuer-
santur, ita tamen ut animum nunquam
contristent, nunquam deprimant: itaque haud
minus oblectationis adferunt spectanti quae in
rerum natura alta sunt ac seuera, quam quae laeta
et amoeniora. Hinc mihi contingit ut quae ceteris
incutiunt formidinem, ea ipse intuendo lenior fiam
et melior. Clarorum uirorum sepulcra uisenti
tollitur omnis ex animo liuor: formosarum titulos
legenti nulla non libido exarescit: insculptos saxo
parentum dolores cum aspicio, misericordia penitus
perstringor, ipsorum sepulcra spectanti uenit in
mentem quam superuacaneum sit eos lugere quos
mox simus secuturi: cum sedibus uicinis uideo
compositos qui uiui fuerint inimicissimi, cum
regnorum euersoribus reges, cum Lauiniis Teren-
tios, cum Stoicis Epicureos, quorum rixis et
certaminibus omnia nuper strepebant, subit animum
cum maerore admiratio, quantulae sint hominum
lites, iurgia, factiones: tempora uero legenti quo
quisque obierit, hic heri, ille Bruto consule exstinctus, temporis illius suboritur recordatio, cum
de nobis 'splendida Minos fecerit arbitria,' quo
futuri simus omnes omnibus aequales.

W. R. H.

IT is the same with me in politics. In general I care very little about the matter, and from year's end to year's end have scarce a thought connected with them, except to laugh at the fools who think to make themselves great men out of little by swaggering in the rear of a party. But either actually important events, or such as seemed so by their close neighbourhood to me, have always hurried me off my feet, and made me, as I have sometimes afterwards re-gretted, more forward and violent than those who had a regular jog-trot way of busying themselves in public matters. Good luck; for had I lived in troublesome times, and chanced to be on the unhappy side, I had been hanged to a certainty. What I have always remarked has been that many who have hallooed me on at public meetings, and so forth, have quietly left me to the odium which a man known to the public always has more than his own share of; while on the other hand they were easily successful in pressing before me, who never pressed forward at all, when there was a distribution of public favours or the like.

Sir W. Scott.

NEQVE aliter de rei publicae contentionibus sentio; totam enim istam rem plerumque non nauci habeo, neque omnino de ea nisi longis temporum interuallis cogitare soleo; immo stultissimos istos derideo qui se magnos ex pusillis efficere uolunt, dum sese iactant et extremum agmen partium suarum claudunt. Quotiens tamen incidit aliquid uel re uera magnum, uel quod ita mihi uideatur, quia me proxime tangit, tum uero in lubrico uersor, neque queo consistere, et sero non numquam me paenitet quod insolentior exstiti et ardentior quam ii qui uno tenore rem publicam capessunt. O me hominem felicem! Nempe si temporibus ciuitatis turbulentis uixissem, accidissetque mihi ut partes calamitosorum sequerer, certum habeo me laqueo fuisse periturum. Illud enim semper cognoui, eos qui me in contione uel in alio quodam coetu dicentem clamoribus suis inflammarunt, postea delituisse, ut ego solus inuidia defungerer, cuius incendio quisquis in oculis ciuium uersatur semper plus aequo conflagrat. Cum tamen rei publicae beneficia uel alia eius modi commoda in spe essent, idem homines nullo labore me ne currentem quidem praeterierunt.

J. S. R.

THERE is only one cure for the evils which newly-acquired freedom produces; and that cure is freedom. When a prisoner first leaves his cell, he cannot bear the light of day: he is unable to discriminate colours or recognize faces. But the remedy is, not to remand him into his dungeon, but to accustom him to the rays of the sun. The blaze of truth and liberty may at first dazzle and bewilder nations which have become half blind in the house of bondage. But let them gaze on, and they will soon be able to bear it. In a few years men learn to reason. The extreme violence of opinions subsides. Hostile theories correct each other. The scattered elements of truth cease to contend, and begin to coalesce. And at length a system of justice and order is educed out of the chaos. Many politicians of our time are in the habit of laying it down as a self-evident proposition, that no people ought to be free, till they are fit to use their freedom. The maxim is worthy of the fool in the old story, who resolved not to go into the water till he had learnt to swim.

Macaulay.

QVAE e libertate cum primum populo datur proueniunt incommoda eiusmodi sunt quae non nisi per eandem libertatem sanari possint. Quemadmodum enim si quis carcere tenebricoso emissus, uix lucem primo tolerare potest nedum colorum et uoltuum uarietates agnoscere, tantum aberit ut eum in uincula reiciamus quo uidendi facultatem reddamus ut potius oculos lumine paulatim assuefacere conemur : eadem profecto ratione et populo nos mederi oportet; cui quamquam mentis uelut aciem per longum seruitutis tempus hebetem factam ueritatis splendor ac libertatis subito immissus perstringere uidetur et occaecare, diutius tamen contemplanti tolerabilis idem fiet. Tempore enim opus est ut homines discant ratione uti, opiniones quae uehementiores sint temperare, quae inter se oppositae sint comparando corrigere, quicquid autem ueri hic uel illic lateat ita conciliare et in unum contrahere, ut tanquam ex atomorum illo regno et licentia pax ciuilis et communis iustitia enascantur. Quod uero, quasi omnibus constet, dictitare solent aliqui ex iis qui ad rem publicam hodie accedunt, nullum populum liberum fieri debere nisi qui bene libertate uti prius intellexerit, id uel stultissimo illo dignum mihi uidetur qui donec artem nandi didicisset se in aquam descensurum esse negabat.

E. C. W.

I OFTEN consider mankind as wholly inconsistent with itself. Though we seem grieved at the shortness of life in general, we are wishing every period of it at an end. The minor longs to be at age, then to be a man of business, then to make up an estate, then to arrive at honours, then to retire. Thus, although the whole of life is allowed by every one to be short, the several divisions of it appear long and tedious. We are for lengthening our span in general, but would fain contract the parts of which it is composed. The usurer would be very well satisfied to have all the time annihilated that lies between the present moment and next quarter-day. The lover would be glad to strike out of his existence all the moments that are to pass away before the happy meeting. Thus, as fast as our time runs, we should be very glad in most parts of our lives that it ran much faster than it does. Several hours of the day hang upon our hands; nay, we wish away whole years; and travel through time as through a country filled with many wild and empty wastes, which we would fain hurry over, that we may arrive at those several little settlements or imaginary points of rest which are dispersed up and down in it.

[No. 370.]　　　　　　　　　　　*Spectator.*

SAEPE numero mihi cogitanti parum nobis ipsi uidemur homines constare, qui uitam omnino breuem esse questi singula eius quasi spatia finita cupiamus. Gestit puer togam uirilem sumere, mox negotium gerere, deinde patrimonium con-dere, postea honores capessere, postremo otio frui. Totam uitam breuem esse fatentur omnes; singulae particulae longae uidentur taediumque afferunt; et curriculum ipsum quidem producere, quibus uero constat partes corripere cupimus. Libenter tolleret faenerator spatium quo praesens tempus a proximis Kalendis separatur: non inuito peri-rent amatori quot horae ante proximum am-plexum lapsurae sunt. Ergo cum cito ruat uita plerumque etiam celeriorem malimus: tardant cotidie aliquot horae, quin totos annos uotis tollimus; perque uitam tamquam desertis terram haridisque squalentem locis iter facimus, pro-perantes scilicet, quo celerius ad deuersoria illa ac domicilia quae passim sparsa fingimus animo deueniamus.

D. S. M.

' SET speeches,' says Voltaire, 'are a sort of oratorical lie, which the historian used to allow himself in old times. He used to make his heroes say what they might have said... At the present day these fictions are no longer tolerated. If one put into the mouth of a prince a speech which he had never made, the historian would be regarded as a rhetorician.' How did it happen that Thucydides allowed himself this 'oratorical lie,'— Thucydides, whose strongest characteristic is devotion to the truth, impatience of every inroad which fiction makes into the province of history, laborious persistence in the task of separating fact from fable; Thucydides, who was not constrained, like later writers of the old world, by an established literary tradition; who had no Greek predecessors in the field of history, except those chroniclers whom he despised precisely because they sacrificed truth to effect? Thucydides might rather have been expected to express himself on this wise: 'The chroniclers have sometimes pleased their hearers by reporting the very words spoken. But, as I could not give the words, I have been content to give the sub-stance, when I could learn it.'

[No. 401.]   *R. C. Jebb.*

COMPOSITIS autem in orationibus antiquos rerum scriptores licentiam quandam rhetorice mentiendi usurpauisse Voltarius ait, ut quae potuerit quis dicere, ea dixisse fingeretur; illud uero posterioribus non concedi; quorum si quis regem induceret aliquid dicentem quod re uera nunquam dixisset, fore ut non rerum is scriptor esse uideretur uerum rhetor. Qui tamen est factum ut mentiri ita rhetorice uoluerit Thucydides, ueritatis amator unicus, qui neque pati potuerit unquam in historiam ficta irrepere, neque labore ullo deterreri quin a factis fabulas secerneret? Non enim illum, perinde atque recentiorem antiquitatem, scribendi norma quaedam et praescriptio coercebat, quippe qui ad historiam Graecorum omnium primus accederet, exceptis annalium scriptoribus, quos propter id ipsum minoris habebat, quod nitere mallent quam uera scribere. Crederes dicturum potius Thucydidem, illos uerbis ipsis, sicut dicta essent, repraesentandis legentium animos oblectauisse, se autem, cum uerba referre nequiret, illud curauisse tantum, ut dictorum, quae quidem reperiri possent, sententiae litteris mandarentur.

F. D. M.

'THOU sayest, "Men cannot admire the sharpness of thy wits." Be it so; but there are many other things of which thou canst not say, "I am not formed for them by nature." Show those qualities, then, which are altogether in thy power,—sincerity, gravity, endurance of labour, aversion to pleasure, contentment with thy portion and with few things, benevolence, frankness, no love of superfluity, freedom from trifling, magnanimity. Dost thou not see how many qualities thou art at once able to exhibit, as to which there is no excuse of natural incapacity and unfitness, and yet thou still remainest voluntarily below the mark? Or art thou compelled, through being defectively furnished by nature, to murmur, and to be mean, and to flatter, and to find fault with thy poor body, and to try to please men, and to make great display, and to be so restless in thy mind? No, indeed; but thou mightest have been delivered from these things long ago.'

[No. 321.] *M. Arnold.*

IN this crisis I must hold my tongue, or I must speak with freedom. Falsehood and delusion are allowed in no case whatever; but, as in the

NEMPE negas tibi acutum esse ingenium, quod admirentur homines. Esto: at non multa habes ad quae naturam te idoneum finxisse non potes denegare? Quin tu igitur ea praestes quae penes te ipsum sunt: praebe te grauem hominem atque apertum, sorte tua quamuis humili contentum, patientem laboris, a uoluptatibus auersum, beneuolum denique atque magnanimum. Quae omnia cum in tua sint potestate, ita ut si impar tibi sis, neque naturam possis neque ingenium tuum incusare, tu semper ultro inter nullius momenti uiros contemptus iaces? Aut si forte quid natura tibi negauerit, idcirco necesse est sis sordidus atque nugator, ut de corpore semper tuo, quam imbecillum sit, conqueraris, atque iactator tui, blanditor ceterorum, animo semper utaris inquieto? Immo omnibus hisce uitiis iam pridem poteras liberari.

G. G. R.

IAM in hoc tanto rei publicae tempore aut tacendum est mihi aut loquendum libere. Et licet sane aliquando, non quidem fuco fallaciis·

exercise of all the virtues, there is an economy
of truth.   It is a sort of temperance by which
a man speaks truth with measure that he may
speak it the longer.   But as the same rules do not
hold in all cases, what would be right for you, who
may presume on a series of years before you,
would have no sense for me, who cannot, without
absurdity, count on six months of life.   What
I say, I must say at once.   Whatever I write is in
its nature testamentary.   It may have the weakness, but it has the sincerity of a dying declaration.
For the few days I have to linger here, I am
removed completely from the busy scene of the
world ; but I hold myself to be still responsible for
everything that I have done whilst I continued in
the place of action.   If the rawest tyro in politics
has been influenced by the authority of my grey
hairs, and led by anything in my speeches or my
writings to approve this war, he has a right to call
upon me to know why I have changed my opinions,
or why, when those I voted with have adopted
better notions, I persevere in exploded error.

  [No. 445.]

que uti (quod nunquam licet) at certe et ceteras
uirtutes omnes et ueritatem ipsam parcius exercere;
est enim hoc temperare quodam modo ac dispen-
sare potestatem uera dicendi propterea ut diutius
habeamus. Cum tamen leges aliae in alia causa
ualeant, fuerit hoc tibi quidem decorum, cui longam
annorum seriem praecipere adhuc liceat, in me
autem stultissimum, qui ne sex quidem menses,
nisi absurde, expectare possim. Itaque et dicenda
sunt mihi statim, quae dicam ; et si quid scripsero,
erit illud—paene uelut testamentum aliquod uel
morientis uiri 'nouissima uerba'—tenue quidem
fortasse sed sincerum. Dum paucos hosce dies in
uita maneo, careo iam totus rebus curisque
hominum, uerum ita ut reddendam mihi rationem
omnium arbitrer, quae in magistratu meo et in
senatu egerim. Immo si quis uel minime erit
rerum ciuilium usu peritus, tamen si auctoritate
mea et canitie permotus, si dictum aliquod scriptumue meum secutus, bellum hoc probauerit,
debebo huic interroganti causas aperire, uel cur de
sententia destiterim, uel, postquam ceteri omnes
quibus tum sim ego suffragatus consilia iniuerint
meliora, cur in dissipato iam dudum errore solus
permaneam.

F. D. M.

AMONGST too many instances of the great corruption and degeneracy of the age in which we live, the great and general want of sincerity in conversation is not the least. The world is grown so full of dissimulation and compliment, that men's words are hardly any signification of their thoughts; and if any man measure his words by his heart, and speak as he thinks, and do not express more kindness to every man, than men usually have for any man, he can hardly escape the censure of ill breeding. The old English plainness and sincerity, that generous integrity of nature, and honesty of disposition, which always argue true greatness of mind, and are usually accompanied with undaunted courage and resolution, are in a great measure lost amongst us; there has been a long endeavour to transform us into foreign manners and fashions, and to bring us to a servile imitation of none of the best of our neighbours in some of the worst of their qualities. The dialect of conversation is now-a-days so swelled with vanity and compliment, and so surfeited, as I may say, of expressions of kindness and respect, that if a man that lived an age or two ago should return into the world again, he would really want a dictionary to help him to understand his own language, and to know the true intrinsic

QVAM praui ·sint et in deterius corrupti mores huiusce saeculi, ut exempla alia praetermittam quam plurima, id haud quaquam minimum arbitror quod fere in. uniuersum colloquendi ueritas desideratur. Referti enim eo usque iam sumus dissimulatione ac blanditiis, ut uix et ne uix quidem index interpresque cogitationum sit oratio ; quod si quis ex animi sententia uerba proferat, si eadem sentiat, eadem loquatur, neque in omnes plus beneuolentiae, quam qua singuli in singulos fere afficimur, significet, uix fieri potest ut rusticitatis crimen defugiat. Enimuero uetus illa atque aperta nostratium sinceritas, simplex et uere honesta naturae ingenuitas, quae ut animi sane magni indicium praebet, ita fortitudinem et constantiam fere secum solet adportare, magna iam ex parte interiit. Diu iam in eo laboratur ut exterorum mores consuetudinesque imitemur, et a peregrinis, neque iis optimis, pessima quaedam exempla seruiliter mutuemur. Ita blanditiis et adsentationibus sermo cotidianus turget, ita beneuolentiae et obseruantiae significationibus, ut ita dicam, saginatus est, ut si quis abhinc paucis saeculis· mortuus reuiuiscat, ad intellegendam linguam suam interpretem desideret, nec nisi inuitus credat quam uili pretio uerba summam caritatem prae se ferentia in cotidiano usu ac

value of the phrase in fashion, and would hardly at first believe at what a low rate the highest strains and expressions of kindness imaginable do commonly pass in common payment; and when he should come to understand, it would be a great while before he could bring himself with a good countenance and a good conscience to converse with men upon equal terms and in their own way.

[No. 333.]   *Spectator.*

IT is difficult to think too highly of the merits and delights of truth; but there is often in men's minds an exaggerated notion of some bit of truth, which proves a great assistance to falsehood. For instance, the shame of finding that he has in some special case been led into falsehood becomes a bugbear which scares a man into a career of false dealing. He has begun making a furrow a little out of the line, and he ploughs on in it, to try and give some consistency and meaning to it. He wants almost to persuade himself that it was not wrong, and entirely to hide the wrongness from others. This is a tribute to the majesty of truth: also to the world's opinion

commercio aestimentur ; quo perspecto ac cognito,
sero demum id commissurus sit, ut salua fronte ac
conscientia in coetu hominum pari iure et ex
aequo uersetur.

R. S.

VERITAS autem quam et iucunda sit et lauda-
bilis quis nimio possit aestimare? Quamquam partem ueri aliquam ita magnopere nonnumquam animis extollunt homines ut fraudi magno
sit auxilio. Qui enim se falsum in re quadam
fuisse senserit, is interdum eo pudore ita terretur,
ut fraudem non audeat relinquere : sed cum
e recto limite tamquam sulcum diduxerit, in eodem
errore perstat, ut consulto et constanter uideatur
agere.   Nam et sibi paene uolt persuadere se nihil
errasse, et ceteros rem omnino celare. Quod
quidem dum facit, re uera et uenerandam esse
declarat ueritatem, et recte a uolgo laudari : nec
non et in hoc errat, quod inter falsa nihil putat

about truth.   It proceeds, too, upon the notion that all falsehoods are equal, which is not the case, or on some fond craving for a show of perfection, which is sometimes very inimical to the reality.   The practical, as well as the high-minded, view in such cases, is for a man to think how he can be true now.   To attain that, it may, even for this world, be worth while for a man to admit that he has been inconsistent, and even that he has been untrue.   His hearers, did they know anything of themselves, would be fully aware that he was not singular, except in the courage of owning his insincerity.

[No. 350.]　　　　　　　　　　　　　　*Spectator.*

THAT system of morality, even in the times when it was powerful and in many respects beneficial, had made it almost as much a duty to hate foreigners as to love fellow-citizens.   Plato congratulates the Athenians on having shown in their relations to Persia, beyond all the other Greeks, 'a pure and heartfelt hatred of the foreign nature.'   Instead of opposing, it had sanctioned and consecrated the savage instinct which leads us to hate whatever is strange or unintelligible ;

interesse, uel speciem uirtutis stulte exquirit, eoque
difficilius, ut fit, ipsam uirtutem consequitur. Quippe
cum tale quid acciderit, prudentis aeque et generosi
est id agere ut statim ad uerum reuertatur ; quod ut
fiat, uel in hac uita utile fortasse erit confiteri se a
constantia, immo a ueritate declinasse. Qui enim
audiunt, si sese modo norint, nihil in eo sciant
mirandum nisi quod fraudem audeat confiteri.

A. S.

I quibus haec officiorum norma placuit, tum
quoque cum et multum ualebat et proderat
multis, tam fere in odio habendos alienos quam
amandos esse ciues uoluerunt. Et Plato quidem
Athenienses laudat quod illi potissimum Graecorum in Persis ostenderint, penitus insedisse in
animis germanum barbarorum odium. Cum enim
omnes natura eo impellimur ut quicquid ignotum
uel parum intellectum sit pro infesto habeamus,
ut discretis amne nihil confidamus, ut aliena

to distrust those who live on the farther side of a river; to suppose that those whom we hear talking together in a foreign tongue must be plotting some mischief against ourselves. The lapse of time and the fusion of races doubtless diminished this antipathy considerably, but at the utmost it could but be transformed into an icy indifference, for no cause was in operation to convert it into kindness. On the other hand, the closeness of the bond which united fellow-citizens was considerably relaxed. Common interests and common dangers had drawn it close; these in the wide security of the Roman Empire had no longer a place. It had depended upon an imagined blood-relationship; fellow-citizens could now no longer feel themselves to be united by the tie of blood. Every town was full of resident aliens and emancipated slaves, persons between whom and the citizens nature had established no connexion, and whose presence in the city had originally been barely tolerated from motives of expediency. The selfishness of modern times exists in defiance of morality; in ancient times it was approved, sheltered, and even in part enjoined by morality.

[No. 344.]

lingua colloquentes nobis insidias struere pu-
temus,—hanc illi philosophi immanitatem, cum
reclamare oporteret, auctoritate sua sanxerant.
Procedente quidem tempore et commistis inter se
gentibus non nihil de odio remissum est, ita tamen
ut summa inde nata sit ceterorum incuria, defuit
enim unde uerteretur in beneuolentiam. Ciuium
autem illud inter se uinculum, quod commune
periculum utilitasque communis arctius fecerant,
iam laxari coeptum est; nam cum omnia ubique
imperio Romano tuta essent, nihil eius modi erat
cur conuenirent. Ciuitatis quondam uis in con-
sanguinitate quadam posita est, quae iam sublata
esse uidebatur, cum oppida omnia peregrinis
libertinisque essent plena, qui nullam haberent
cum ciuibus naturae societatem, quibus olim,
utilitatis causa, uix domicilium intra muros
patuisset. Hodie, ut uidetur, si quid in alienos
inhumaniter fit, repugnantibus fit philosophis;
apud ueteres comprobabant id philosophi, de-
fendebant, erant etiam qui faciendum praecipie-
bant.

S. H. B.

IT is argued that self-interest will prevent excessive cruelty ; as if self-interest protected our domestic animals, which are far less likely than degraded slaves to stir up the rage of their savage masters. It is an argument long since protested against with noble feeling, and strikingly exemplified, by the ever illustrious Humboldt. It is often attempted to palliate slavery by comparing the state of slaves with our poorer countrymen : if the misery of our poor be caused not by the laws of nature, but by our institutions, great is our sin : but how this bears on slavery, I cannot see ; as well might the use of the thumbscrew be defended in one land by showing that men in another land suffered from some dreadful disease. Those who look tenderly at the slave-owner, and with a cold heart at the slave, never seem to put themselves in the position of the latter : what a cheerless prospect, with not even a hope of change ! picture to yourself the chance, ever hanging over you, of your wife and little children —those objects which nature urges even the slave to call his own—being torn from you and sold like beasts to the first bidder ! And these deeds are done and palliated by men, who profess to love their neighbours as themselves, who believe in God, and pray that his Will may be done on

AT enim quo minus homines nimia crudelitate saeuiant ipsorum utilitas prohibebit. Quasi uero animalibus quae usui domestico inseruiunt utilitas sit praesidio, quae tamen multo minus quam serui consuetudine deprauati truces dominos solent iracundia incendere. Atqui de ista conclusione multos abhinc annos Humboldtius ille, qui sempiterna floret gloria, recusauit, cum multa clarissima exempla promeret, multa ipse splendide sentiret. Qui enim seruitutis patrocinium suscipere uoluerunt, saepe numero seruorum res cum tenuioribus e nostris ciuibus comparauerunt; si autem isti nostris institutis, non quadam quasi naturae rerum lege sunt aerumnosi, nonne prauitate nos uel maxima laboramus? Sed quo modo hoc ad seruitutis disputationem pertineat equidem non inuenio; nam eodem iure confirmes in alia ciuitate homines eculeo recte torqueri, si in alia morbo quodam teterrimo ciuis aegrotare demonstraueris. Scilicet qui dominos benigne, inimice seruos respiciunt, numquam ex horum sorte causam uidentur contemplari. Quam misera istis futuri temporis exspectatio! Quam nulla spes fortunae in melius conuertendae! Vellem etiam cogitatione tibi illud fingeres, uxorem et imbecillos liberos, quos etiam serui non possunt quin suos esse putent et a natura sibi datos,

P

earth ! It makes one's blood boil, yet heart tremble, to think that we Englishmen and our American descendants, with their boastful cry of liberty, have been and are so guilty: but it is a consolation to reflect that we at least have made a greater sacrifice than was ever made by any nation, to expiate our sin.

Charles Darwin.

IT was true then, it is infinitely more true now, that what is called virtue in the common sense of the word, still more, that nobleness, godliness, or heroism of character in any form whatsoever, have nothing to do with this or that man's prosperity or even happiness. The thoroughly vicious man is no doubt wretched enough; but the worldly, prudent, self-restraining man, with his

omnibus posse horis a tuo amplexu diuelli, et
nescio quo emptore digito licente tamquam pecudes
uenire. Talia enimuero flagitia et faciunt et
defendunt qui se uolunt homines secum coniunctos
aeque atque se ipsos amare, qui deos immortalis
credunt esse, qui precantur ut omnes ubique
terrarum diuinis imperiis obtemperent! Ipse
equidem soleo et ira inflammari et animi terrore
perhorrescere, cum reputo nostros ciuis eosque
qui hinc profecti Americanam rem publicam con-
diderunt et de libertate gloriari et eosdem tanta
iam dudum scelera in se admittere. Est tamen mihi
solacio recordari nullam umquam ciuitatem plus
oneris sibi quam nostram imposuisse quo peccatis
defungeretur.

J. S. R.

QVOD uero olim, idem hodie multo magis
re probatum est, ne minime quidem ad
prospere uel etiam beate uiuendum attinere
honestatem illam, qualem plerique interpretantur,
quae in magnitudine animi, quae in pietate, quae
in fortitudine posita est praestantia. Suos sane
cruciatus habet insignis prauitas; qui autem
callidus, prudens, sui continens, omnibus corporis

five senses, which he understands how to gratify with tempered indulgence, with a conscience satisfied with the hack routine of what is called respectability—such a man feels no wretchedness; no inward uneasiness disturbs him, no desires which he cannot gratify; and this though he be the basest and most contemptible slave of his own selfishness. Providence will not interfere to punish him. Let him obey the laws under which prosperity is obtainable, and he will obtain it, let him never fear. He will obtain it, be he base or noble. . . . And again it is not true, as optimists would persuade us, that such prosperity brings no real pleasure. A man with no high aspirations, who thrives and makes money, and envelopes himself in comforts, is as happy as such a nature can be. If unbroken satisfaction be the most blessed state for a man (and this certainly is the practical notion of happiness) he is the happiest of men. Nor are those idle phrases any truer, that the good man's goodness is a never ceasing sunshine; that virtue is its own reward, &c., &c. If men truly virtuous care to be rewarded for it, their virtue is but a poor investment of their moral capital.

[No. 382.]   *Froude.*

appetitibus modicam uoluptatem meditate concedit, praeclare actum esse ratus, si in consuetudine hominum atque aurea, quod aiunt, morum mediocritate manserit, non is animo cruciatur, neque angoribus intus lacessitus neque irritis cupiditatibus; cum tamen ipse sibi emancipatus turpissime deseruiat. Hic ab ultione deorum securus assequendae fortunae rationibus obtemperet; fortunam assequetur; turpisne sit an honestus perinde erit. Neque uero iis qui uolunt optime omnia esse constituta assentiendum est, non cum ista fortuna dictitantibus coniunctam esse ullam, quae quidem uera sit, delectationem. Immo qui nulla animo maiora suscipit, qui opibus pecuniaque augetur uitaeque commoditatibus circumfluit, pro natura sua quam beatissimus est. Si sibi numquam displicere, id est homini exoptatissimum—neque aliter certe in uitae consuetudine beati dicuntur—hic erit omnium beatissimus. Neque plus ualent decantata illa, honestatem esse honestis lucem sempiternam, suam sibi mercedem esse uirtutem, cetera huiusmodi. Honestatis enim mercedem si quis requirit, suo ille damno uirtutem faeneratur.

S. H. B.

WITH every power that we have we can do two things: we can work, and we can play. Every power that we have is at the same time useful to us and delightful to us. Even when we are applying them to the furtherance of our personal objects, the activity of them gives us pleasure; and when we have no useful end to which to apply them, it is still pleasant to us to use them; the activity of them gives us pleasure for its own sake. There is no motion of our body or mind which we use in work, which we do not also use in play or amusement. If we walk in order to arrive at the place where our interest requires us to be, we also walk about the fields for enjoyment. If we apply our combining and analyzing powers to solve the problems of mathematics, we use them sometimes also in solving double acrostics.

[No. 335.]   *M. Arnold.*

THE mere philosopher is a character which is commonly but little acceptable in the world, as being supposed to contribute little either to the advantage or pleasure of society; while he lives remote from communication with mankind, and is wrapped up in principles and notions equally

QVAECVMQVE nobis insunt facultates, eas licet et ad ludum et ad laborem adhibere, quippe quae omnes et utiles nobis sint et iucundae. Nam siue quid commodi nobis in agendo expetitur, habet iucunditatem quandam ipsa illa exercitatio: siue omnino non est, tamen id ipsum aliquid agere delectat. Tum motibus illis omnibus uel animi uel corporis, per quos aliquid in laborando efficimus, iisdem necesse est in ludis oblectamentisque utamur: quippe ambulamus ut eo quo commodi causa uelimus perueniamus; est non nulla etiam per rura uagantibus oblectatio. Quin uis illa mentis peracuta, qua res quasi in membra decerpimus easdemque rursus componimus in unum, eam non ad rationes modo mathematicorum adhibemus explicandas, sed interdum etiam ad perplexa illa acrostichia quae uocant enodanda.

G. G. R.

IPSE per se philosophus partes agit minus acceptas ceteris hominibus, nimirum quod nihil uidetur conferre neque ad commodum neque ad uoluptatem iis quibuscum uersatur, sed a ceterorum commercio abhorrere, totusque esse in sententiis et cogitationibus non minus ab eorum

remote from their comprehension. On the other hand, the mere ignorant is still more despised ; nor is anything deemed a surer sign of an illiberal genius in an age and nation where the sciences flourish, than to be entirely destitute of all relish for those noble entertainments. The most perfect character is supposed to be between those extremes: retaining an equal ability and taste for books, company and business, preserving in conversation that discernment and delicacy which arise from polite letters, and in business that probity and accuracy which are the natural result of a just philosophy. In order to diffuse and cultivate so accomplished a character, nothing can be more useful than compositions of easy style and manner which draw not too much from life, require no deep application or retreat to be comprehended, and send back a student among mankind full of noble sentiments and wise precepts, applicable to every exigence of human life. By means of such compositions virtue becomes amiable, science agreeable, company instructive, and retirement entertaining.

[No. 322.]   *Hume.*

captu abhorrentibus. Contra ipse per se insipiens maiori adhuc contemptui est; neque ulla alia est ingenii infaceti certior significatio, quam et in saeculo et ciuitate doctrinis abundante, nihil quidquam ex hisce lautissimis epulis delibare. Qui perfectus totis numeris et absolutus est, uidetur inter duas personas quas deformauimus medium locum obtinere: qui pari ingenio ac studio ad libros, ad conuictum hominum ac societatem, ad negotia accedit; qui in colloquiis limatam iudicii elegantiam ex litteris humanioribus ortam praestat, idem in negotiis diligentiam et probitatem quam accurata philosophia suopte ingenio progeneret. Quae persona tot dotibus exornata ut excoli et propagari possit, nihil magis solet conducere quam facili stilo et oratione scripta legere; quae cum non ita multum a cotidianis auocent abducantque, neque ut intellegantur assiduitatem et uacationem officiorum postulent, et legentem ab umbratili studio foras regredientem cogitationibus iustis et sapientibus praeceptis instruunt ad qualescunque uitae necessitates accommodatis. Ex huius modi scriptis id usu uenit ut amabilior fiat uirtus, doctrinae iucundiores, a conuictu hominum plus utilitatis et ab otio maiores uoluptatis fructus percipiantur.

R. S.

THE Brahmins assert that the world arose from an infinite spider, who spun this whole complicated mass from his bowels, and annihilates afterwards the whole, or any part of it, by absorbing it again, and resolving it into his own essence.   Here is a theory which appears to us ridiculous ; because a spider is a little contemptible animal, whose operations we are never likely to take for a model of the whole universe.   But still it is in keeping with what goes on in our globe. And were there a world wholly inhabited by spiders (which is very possible) this theory would there appear as natural and irrefragable as that which in our planet ascribes the origin of all things to design and intelligence, as explained by Cleanthes.   Why an orderly system may not be spun from the belly, as well as from the brain, it will be difficult for him to give a satisfactory reason.

[No. 346.]

UNDOUBTEDLY we ought to look at ancient transactions by the light of modern knowledge.   Undoubtedly it is among the first duties of a historian to point out the faults of the eminent

BRAMANI adfirmant mundum ex infinita quadam aranea exortum, quae cum opus tam multiplex e uisceribus contexuerit, postea uel totum uel ex parte qualibet ita destruat ut intus in se ipsum solutum absorbeat. Qua opinione quid nobis uideatur absurdius? quippe paruum animal aranea, indignumque cuius operibus totus hic mundus comparetur. Huic tamen rationi tum ualde consentaneum est quod in nostro orbe geritur, tum sicubi orbis existat (quod potest certe fieri) qui ab araneis solis incolatur, illic non minus certa haec uideantur ac uerisimilia, quam in nostro orbe quod docet Cleanthes, omnia ex unius nasci mente ac consilio. Cur enim rem bene ordinatam minus e uentre quis euoluat quam e cerebro, non facile erit rationem reddere.

A. S.

VETERA recentibus, tenebras antiquorum hodierna luce illustrandas esse satis constat, nec si uitia ista lux patefecerit, tacendum esse annalium scriptori. Immo uero acerrime repre-

men of former generations. There are no errors which are so likely to be drawn into precedent, and therefore none which it is so necessary to expose, as the errors of persons who have a just title to the gratitude and admiration of posterity. In politics, as in religion, there are devotees who show their reverence for a departed saint by converting his tomb into a sanctuary for crime. Receptacles for wickedness are suffered to remain undisturbed in the neighbourhood of the church which glories in the relics of some martyred apostle. Because he was merciful, his bones give security to assassins. Because he was chaste, the precinct of his temple is filled with licensed stews. Privileges of an equally absurd kind have been set up against the jurisdiction of political philosophy. Vile abuses cluster thick round every glorious event, round every venerable name; and this evil assuredly calls for vigorous measures of literary police. But the proper course is to abate the nuisance without defacing the shrine, to drive out the gangs of thieves and prostitutes without doing foul and cowardly wrong to the ashes of the illustrious dead.

[No. 356.]   *Macaulay.*

hendet si quid praue fecerunt qui apud ueteres
laude floruere. Quae enim peccant ii qui bene
de posteris meriti summam auctoritatem consecuti
sunt, idcirco notanda sunt praecipue, quia, si fe-
fellerint, exemplo aliis esse solent. Fit autem in
re publica quod in rebus diuinis: qui caste uixit,
qui deorum fructus est colloquio—Amphiaraum
puta—eius sacellum ἄσυλον ut aiunt constituunt,
efficiuntque ut sicariis, latronibus, ueneficis arx et
perfugium sit. Calchantis ossa uenerantur Colo-
phonii: quid igitur ? Vicina quoque aedi scelera-
torum latibula religio tuetur. Castus fuit Calchas,
nemini nocuit mortalium : confugiunt ad sepulcrum
eius nocentissimi, aedis area lupanaribus, spreta
aedilium potestate, referta est. Haud aliter rationem
hanc nostram, quae de re publica gerenda suscipitur,
deferenda aedilibus uitia spernunt atque eludunt :
nulla res gesta est insignior, nullius nomen
inclaruit, quin plurimae se sordes eo recipiant,
eiusque sub umbra se tueantur. Quid ergo ?
Non ut illic secures lictorum, hic annalium scrip-
toris opem inuocabimus ? Qui tamen ita grassa-
bitur, ut dum submouentur furum greges et scor-
torum, integri tamen sint mortuorum cineres nec
ulla in eos inferatur contumelia.

W. R. H.

ONE of the strongest incitements to excel in such arts and accomplishments as are in the highest esteem among men, is the natural passion for glory which the mind of man has: which, though it may be faulty in the excess of it, ought by no means to be discouraged. Perhaps some moralists are too severe in beating down this principle, which seems to be a spring implanted by nature to give motion to all the latent powers of the soul, and is always observed to exert itself with the greatest force in the most generous dispositions. The men whose characters have shone brightest among the ancient Romans appear to have been strongly animated by this passion. Cicero, whose learning and services to his country are so well known, was inflamed by it to an extravagant degree, and warmly presses Lucceius, who was composing a history of those times, to be very particular and zealous in relating the story of his consulship; and to execute it speedily, that he might have the pleasure of enjoying in his lifetime some part of the honour which he foresaw would be paid to his memory. This was the ambition of a great mind, but he is faulty in the degree of it, and cannot refrain from soliciting the historian, upon this occasion, to neglect the strict laws of history, and in praising

NIHIL fere in maius commouet ut in artibus ornamentisque uulgo apud homines sermoni habitis ipsi aliis praestemus quam illa quae a natura animo ingenerata est gloriae auiditas: quae quamquam si nimia est in uitio fortasse ponitur, haud quaquam idcirco iure excideris. Atque haud scio an non nulli qui de moribus conscripserunt hunc animi affectum aliquando durius reiecerint, quem tamen natura ipsa uidetur intulisse quasi momentum quoddam unde ceteris prius abditis facultatibus mouendi principium trahatur: quo autem quisque excelsiorem se praestat, in eo maxime solet dominari. Inter Romanos quidem clarissima quaeque ingenia hoc stimulo quam maxime concitata uidentur fuisse; qua cupiditate Cicero notus omnibus et doctrina et in patriam beneficiis incredibilem in modum exarsit. Nam a Lucceio, qui aequalium annales conscribebat, uehementer contendit ut in consulatu suo ornando et summam operam diligenter ac studiose collocet, et quam celerrime opus perficiat, ut aliqua saltem parte famae sibi a posteritate debitae uiuus perfruatur. Haec cupiditas magni sane animi erat, nimia tamen eoque culpanda cum sibi temperare non potuerit quominus ab historico flagitaret, ut leges historiae ueras neglegeret, et suis laudibus plusculum etiam quam concederet

him, even to exceed the strict bounds of truth. The younger Pliny appears to have had the same passion for fame, but accompanied with greater chasteness and modesty.

[No. 342.]   *Spectator.* ✓

NOT to lose ourselves in the infinite void of the conjectural world, our business is with what is likely to be affected for the better or the worse, by the wisdom or weakness of our plans. In all speculations upon men and human affairs, it is of no small moment to distinguish things of accident from permanent causes, and from effects that cannot be altered. It is not every irregularity in our movement that is a total deviation from our course. I am not quite of the mind of those speculators, who seem assured, that necessarily, and by the constitution of things, all states have the same periods of infancy, manhood, and decrepitude, that are found in the individuals who compose them. Parallels of this sort rather furnish similitudes to illustrate or to adorn, than supply analogies from whence to reason. The objects which are attempted to be forced into an analogy are not found in the same classes of existence. Individuals are physical beings, subject to laws universal and invariable.

ueritas largiretur. Plinium quoque minorem ita
idem famae appetitus commouit, ut maiore quadam
temperantia et uerecundia moderaretur.

· R. S.

VERVM, ne nubes et inania sectemur deuii, ea
nobis sunt tractanda quae prudenter agentibus meliora fient, peiora imprudenter. Quotiens
autem de hominibus quaeritur rebusue humanis,
magni interest ut fortuita et fluitantia ab iis discer-
namus, quae, siue efficiunt aliquid siue efficiuntur,
mutari nequeunt. Saepe enim ita de uia disceditur,
ut repeti mox orbitam, intermissa rursus uigescere
uideas. Nec mihi quidem prorsus opinio placet
eorum qui eadem ciuitatibus quae singulis hominibus percurrenda esse statuunt aetatis spatia, ut
foedere quodam naturae et necessitate e pueritia
in iuuentutem, e iuuentute in senium uergant.
Quae qui loquitur, exornare potius orationem
putandus est quam uia et ratione grassari. Ita
enim alius rei naturam ex alia colligas, si in
eodem sint genere quae componuntur. Singuli
autem homines eisdem, quibus cetera animantia,
uelut legibus uidentur teneri: in quibus, etsi quid
quaeque effecerit causa parum constat, at quae
plerumque efficiuntur reuocari ad calculos et

The immediate cause acting in these laws may be obscure: the general results are subjects of certain calculation. But commonwealths are not physical but moral essences. They are artificial combinations; and in their proximate efficient cause, the arbitrary productions of the human mind. We are not yet acquainted with the laws which necessarily influence the stability of that kind of work made by that kind of agent. There is not in the physical order (with which they do not appear to hold any assignable connexion) a distinct cause by which any of those fabrics must necessarily grow, flourish or decay; nor, in my opinion, does the moral world produce anything more determinate on that subject, than what may serve as an amusement (liberal indeed, and ingenious, but still only an amusement) for speculative men. I doubt whether the history of mankind is yet complete enough, if ever it can be so, to furnish grounds for a sure theory on the internal causes which necessarily affect the fortune of a State. I am far from denying the operation of such causes: but they are infinitely uncertain, and much more obscure, and much more difficult to trace, than the foreign causes that tend to raise, to depress, and sometimes to overwhelm a community.

[No. 360.]   *Addison.*

praedici possunt. Ciuitates contra non ex uenis, ossibus, uisceribus constant, sed ex hominum ingeniis : conglutinantur enim, non gignuntur : nec si proxima spectes, aliunde ducunt originem quam ex arbitrio hominum et uoluntate. Opus uero eius modi tali ab artifice profectum quibus uel labefactetur causis uel corroboretur, nondum satis compertum habemus. Neque enim in rerum natura, quae quidem in sensus cadit, causa ulla dispici potest qua uel crescant floreantque ciuitates uel marcescant, immo uero ne uinculis quidem ullis cum ea consociari uidentur : neque uitam hominum et mores scrutantibus quicquam mihi certius clariusque adhuc inuentum esse uidetur, quam quod oblectationem tantum, lepidam illam quidem et facetam, praebeat otiosis. Quae enim multis ante saeculis egerint homines, nondum satis cognita habemus—uereor an unquam simus habituri—ut de morbis et affectibus quibus intra se ipsas exortis laborant ciuitates certam aliquam informare rationem queamus. Quod non ita dico ut subesse eius modi causas negem. Sed longe illae incertiores obscurioresque et ad inuestigandum difficiliores sunt quam quibus extrinsecus uenientibus firmari, debilitari, interdum etiam opprimi ciuitates solent.

W. R. H.

Q 2

THE end of a man's life is often compared to the winding-up of a well-written play, where the principal persons still act in character, whatever the fate is they undergo. There is scarce a great person in the Grecian or Roman history, whose death has not been remarked upon by some writer or other, and censured or applauded according to the genius or principles of the person who has descanted upon it. Monsieur de St. Evremond is very particular in setting forth the constancy and courage of Petronius Arbiter during his last moments, and thinks he discovers in them a greater firmness of mind and resolution than in the death of Seneca, Cato, or Socrates. There is no question but this polite author's affectation of appearing singular in his remarks, and making discoveries which had escaped the observation of others, threw him into this course of reflexion. It was Petronius' merit that he died in the same gaiety of temper in which he lived; but as his life was altogether loose and dissolute, the indifference which he showed at the close of it is to be looked upon as a piece of natural carelessness and levity, rather than fortitude. The resolution of Socrates proceeded from very different motives, the consciousness of a well-spent life, and a prospect

SAEPE numero uitae exitus cum fabula bene scripta est comparatus, ubi ad finem quicquid euenerit pro sua quaeque indole partes agant personae. Quid enim? in Graecorum Romanorumque annalibus quis umquam exstitit insignis, quin mortem eius scriptores pro ingenio ac sententia uel reprehenderint uel laudauerint? Nonne Petronii morientis uirtutem miratur Montanus, et constantius fortiusque ait obisse quam Senecam, Catonem, Socratem? Quod uero ita censet uir lepidus, id eius nimirum est qui semper gestit inusitata excogitare, ac quod alii omiserint recludere. Et laudi sane fuit Petronio, quod animo non minus laeto quam uixerat moreretur : cum tamen moribus omnino foedis ac luxuriosis esset, non tam uirtute iudicatur mortem contempsisse, quam insita ingenii leuitate ac socordia. At nihil eius modi in Socrate : qui ideo fortem se praebebat, quod uitam bene actam sibi consciret, aeternam speraret beatitudinem. Quod si faceto isti tam placuit morientis laetitia, quidni Morium nostrum commemorauit? hoc enim longe praeclarius eius fortitudinis exemplum.

A. S.

of a happy eternity. If the ingenious author above-mentioned was so pleased with gaiety of humour in a dying man, he might have found a much nobler instance of it in our countryman Sir Thomas More.

[No. 355.]   *Addison.*

THE sea deserved to be hated by the old aristocracies as it has been the mightiest instrument in the civilization of mankind. In the depth of winter when the sky is covered with clouds, and the land presents one cold and blank and lifeless surface of snows, how refreshing it is to the spirits to walk upon the shore, and to enjoy the eternal freshness and liveliness of ocean. Even so, in the deepest winter of the human race, when the earth was but one chilling expanse of inactivity, life was stirring in the waters. There began that spirit whose genial influence has now reached the land, has broken the chains of winter, and covered the face of the earth with beauty.

[No. 384.]   *Dr. Arnold.*

NEC sine causa apud antiquos mare optimatibus in suspicionem uenit, quippe quod ad
ornandam hominum uitam excolendamque potissimum inseruierit. Nam ut in summa hieme cum
nubibus obtegitur caelum, et per terram undique
sine animalium herbarumque specie torpentes
gelu campi informesque iacent, iuuat in litore
spatiari, perennemque illam Oceani iuuentutem las-
ciuiamque expleri gaudio intuentes: ita in summa
illa quasi generis humani hieme, cum torperent
desidia gentibus, haud mirum erat si Oceanus
uelut anima quadam praeditus et moueri et uigescere uidebatur. Vnde natus ille almus benignus-
que spiritus iam leniter afflauit terris, et quasi
fracta hiemis compede hanc rebus omnibus quam
uidemus speciem induit formosissimam.

G. G. R.

WHEN passion, whether in the political body or in the individual, is once roused, it is vain, during the paroxysm, to combat it with the weapons of reason. A man in love is proverbially inaccessible to argument, and a nation heated in the pursuit of political power is as incapable of listening either to the deductions of the under-standing, or the lessons of experience. The only way in such times of averting the evil is by pre-senting some new object of pursuit which is attractive not only to the thinking few, but to the unthinking many; by counteracting one passion by the growth of another, and summoning to the support of truth not only the armour of reason but the fire of imagination.

   [No. 358.]   *Sir A. Alison.*

THE landed men are the true owners of our political vessel: the moneyed men, as such, are no more than passengers in it. To the first, therefore, all exhortations to assume this spirit of disinterestedness should be addressed. It is their part to set the example: and when they do so, they have a right to expect that the passengers should contribute their proportion to save the

VBI semel exarsit siue in corpore ciuitatis siue in hominis animo libidinis aestus, frustra, dum furit, rationis telis aggrediare. Vt enim amantes surdos esse ferunt, sic libertatis amore percussa gens neque ratione collecta neque usu percepta sibi obici sinit. Vna tunc salus nouam rem ostendere quae tam paucos ac prudentes quam multos atque indoctos ad sequendum alliciat; dum libidinem libidine amoliris, quoque uerum tuearis, non modo argumentis accingeris sed faces spei accendis.

D. S. M.

CETERVM ut a rebus nauticis imaginem ad rem publicam nostram transferamus, cum uectorum tantum in numero habendi sint qui in magno aere suo uersantur, nauiculari uero ipsius locum obtineant agri ac praediorum possessores, hos potissimum hortari debemus ut publico bono priuata commoda posthabeant. Ab his prioribus subueniendum est : quod cum fecerint, tum demum

vessel.   If they should prove refractory, they must
be told that there is a law in behalf of the public,
more sacred and more ancient too, for it is as
ancient as political society, than all those under
the terms of which they would exempt themselves
from any reduction of interest and consequently
from any reimbursement of their principal ; though
this reduction and this reimbursement be absolutely
necessary to restore the prosperity of the nation
and to provide for her security in the meantime.
The law I mean is that which nature and reason
dictate, and which declares the preservation of the
commonwealth to be superior to all other laws.

   [No. 364.]   *Bolingbroke.*

I OFTEN apply this rule to myself; and when
I hear of a satirical speech or writing that
is aimed at me, I examine my own heart, whether
I deserve it or not.   If I bring in a verdict against
myself, I endeavour to rectify my conduct for the
future in those particulars which have drawn the
censure upon me ; but if the whole invective be

a uectoribus iure poterunt exigere ut uelint illi
quoque suam quisque operam in nauem seruandam
conferre. Qui si contumacius restiterint, iam illud
admonendum est esse legem quandam ciuium
causa constitutam quibuslibet aliis legibus sanc-
tiorem et eandem antiquiorem, neque enim ipsa
res publica antiquiorem sibi statum uindicat;
nam quid ineptius quam ad priscas legum prae-
scriptiones decurrere, quibus cautum sit ne qua
liceat umquam condicione aut deminui faenus aut
capitis partem aliquam dissolui, si nullo alio modo
nisi deminuto faenore et soluto capite aut in
futurum prospera aut in praesens salua res publica
fieri possit? Illam enim uero dico et natura
decretam et ratione legem, quae rei publicae saluti
nullas non leges decedere iubet.

G. H. R.

QVA ratione usus, si quid acerbius in me
dictum scriptumue cognoui, me ipse per-
scrutor num iure sim lacessitus. Quo iudicio
si condemnor, ea postea conor emendare, quae
crimini mihi fuerunt: sin ueri nihil obiectum
sentio, rem prorsus omitto, neque magis moueor
nomine palam proposito, quam iis quae a scrip-

grounded upon a falsehood, I trouble myself no further about it, and look upon my name at the head of it to signify no more than one of those fictitious names made use of by an author to introduce an imaginary character. Why should a man be sensible of the sting of a reproach, who is a stranger to the guilt that is implied in it? or subject himself to the penalty, when he knows he has never committed the crime? This is a piece of fortitude, which every one owes to his own innocence, and without which it is impossible for a man of any merit or figure to live at peace with himself in a country that abounds with wit and liberty.

[No. 353.]

THE highest gratification we receive here below is mirth, which at the best is but a fluttering unquiet motion that beats about the breast for a few moments, and after leaves it void and empty. So little is there in the thing we so much talk of, and so much magnify—keeping good company. Even the best is but a less shameful art of losing time. What we call science here, and study, is little better. The greater number of

toribus finguntur nomina, cum personas commen-
ticias inducunt. Cur enim crimine doleat, qui a
scelere quod criminentur abhorreat? Cur poenam
subeat qui facinoris se sciat expertem? Quippe
innocentis est se constantem adeo praebere: quod
ni faciat, quis est homo uirtute uel laude insignis
qui aequum possit animum in hac urbe seruare, ubi
et ingenium tam abundat et quoduis dicendi
libertas?

A. S.

PRAECIPVAM uoluptatum a Dis cepimus
hilaritatem, quae ut summa sit, mentis tantum
trepidatio est, quae cum paulisper nos inquietauit
et intus tumultuata est, inanes mox et uacuos
relinquit. Adeo nihili est id quod tantum iactatur,
tantum extollitur, cum lautis uersari. Qui licet
sint lautissimi, nihil praestant nisi ut honestius
tempus teri possit. Quid ergo? Sapientia quam
hic appellamus ac studia num maioris sunt?

arts to which we apply ourselves are mere groping in the dark; and even the search of our most important concerns in a future being, is but a needless, anxious, and uncertain haste to be knowing sooner than we can, what without all this solicitude we shall know a little after. We are but curious impertinents in the case of futurity. It is not our business to be guessing what the state of souls is, but to be doing what may make our own happy. We cannot be knowing, but we can be virtuous.

[No. 357.]   *Pope.*

IN a word, from the time that Athens was the University of the world, what has Philosophy taught men, but to promise without practising, and to aspire without attaining? What has the deep and lofty thought of its disciples resulted in but eloquent words? Nay, what has its teaching ever meditated, when it was boldest in its remedies for human ill, beyond charming us to sleep by its lessons, that we might feel nothing at all? like some melodious air, or rather like those strong perfumes, which at first spread their sweetness over everything they touch, but in a little while do but offend in propor-

Nempe idem plerique facimus qui in artibus exercemur quod in tenebris micantes: etiam qui grauissimam rerum futura inquirit id tantum properat quod nec prodest nec sine cura ac dubi-tatione fit, ut ante tempus cognouerit ea quae sine omni cura breui post sit cogniturus. Nam de futuris inquirentes ea tantum musinamur quae ad nos nihil. Non enim nobis diuinanda est condicio animorum qualis post mortem futura sit, sed faciendum id quo felices fiamus. Scire non pos-sumus: bonis licet esse.

R. E.

QVID aliud denique, ex quo tempore Athenae illae tamquam una orbis terrarum Academia exstiterunt, praecepit hominibus philosophia, quam ut spem datam frustrarentur metaque sibi pro-posita ipsi deficerent? Qui enim tam incredibili animi subtilitate philosophati sunt, quid praeter copiam uerborum excogitauerunt? Immo uero quid ipsi tandem sibi proposuerunt, quo tempore exquisi-tissima humanorum malorum remedia proferebant, nisi ut doctrinae deliciis sopirent animos, sensum-que nobis plane eriperent? carmina enim uero nescio cuius Orphei haec iure dixeris, nisi graueolentes

tion as they once pleased us. Did Philosophy support Cicero under the disfavour of the fickle populace, or nerve Seneca to oppose an imperial tyrant? It abandoned Brutus, as he sorrowfully confessed, in his greatest need, and it forced Cato, as his panegyrist strangely boasts, into the false position of defying heaven.

[No. 366.]   *J. H. Newman.*

THEY knew nothing of God or the gods, but they had something in themselves which made sensuality nauseating instead of pleasant to them. They had an austere sense of the meaning of the word 'duty.' They could distinguish and reverence the nobler possibilities of their nature. They disdained what was base and effeminate, and, though religion failed them, they constructed out of philosophy a rule which would serve to live by. Stoicism is a not unnatural refuge of thought-ful men in confused and sceptical ages. It adheres rigidly to morality. It offers no easy Epicurean

istos odores potius contuleris, qui principio quidem
omnia uix iam contacta propria dulcedine obducunt,
mox uero non minus fastidio sunt quam nuper
oblectamento. Num Tullium aurae popularis
inconstantia fractum firmauit philosophia? num
Senecae animos addidit, ut nutum principis
contemneret? Quin Brutus ipse se in summo
rerum discrimine ab eadem conqueritur relictum,
Cato autem eo demum depulsus est dementiae,
ut minas—de quo gloriari miror equidem
laudatorem eius—in deos ultro iactauerit.

G. H. R.

DEVM unum siue deos plures cum non
nossent, inerat mentibus eorum cur libido
fastidium non uoluptatem afferret. Vocabulum
officii seuerum in modum interpretabantur; uis
humana quae uirtutes sequitur nec latebat et
colebatur. Contemptores eorum quae turpia sunt,
quae mollia, cum deficeret religio, normam ad
quam uitam agerent a philosophia petebant. Iure
autem prudentissimo cuique turbatis hominum
mentibus fractisque religionum nodis Porticus fit
perfugium, magistra morum non lenis, neque
Epicuria facilitate hominis originem deducens, ex

explanation of the origin of man, which resolves
him into an organization of particles, and dismisses
him again into nothingness. It recognizes only
that men who are the slaves of their passions are
miserable and impotent, and insists that personal
inclinations shall be subordinated to conscience.
It prescribes plainness of life, that the number of
our necessities may be as few as possible ; and in
placing the business of life in intellectual and
moral action it destroys the temptation to sensual
gratifications.   It teaches a contempt of death so
complete that it can be encountered without
a flutter of the pulse ; and while it raises men
above the suffering which makes others miserable,
generates a proud submissiveness to sorrow which
noblest natures feel most keenly, by representing
this huge scene and the shows which it presents
as the work of some unknown but irresistible force,
against which it is vain to struggle and childish to
repine.

[No. 369.]   *Froude.*

THIS writer went through all the usual topics
      of moralists, showing how diminutive, con-
temptible, and helpless an animal was man in his

primordiis scilicet conserti, redituri ad nihilum. Immo hoc sequitur, qui libidinibus seruiant, miseros esse atque impotentes, quod cuique libeat ei quod oporteat esse submittendum. Simplicem imperat uictum ne quis aliorum quam quae necessaria sunt egeat; uitaeque opus dum in iis ponit quae mente uel animo aguntur cur quis sensibus indulgeat superesse non sinit. Docet contemnere mortem eo usque ut cor obeuntis ne palpitet : maioremque factum doloribus quibus reliqui occumbunt, illam quoque aegritudinem qua generosissimus quisque maxime uritur magno animo tolerare facit, dum machinam mundi quaeque ibi tamquam in scena aguntur numinis cuiusdam ignoti inuicti opus esse docet, cui resistere nefas, succensere est puerorum.

D. S. M.

TRACTAT notissimos philosophantibus locos, ostenditque hominem sua natura quam pusillum, quam abiectum, quam debile sit animal,

own nature ; how unable to defend himself from the inclemencies of the air or the fury of wild beasts ; how much he was excelled by one creature in strength, by another in speed, by a third in foresight, by a fourth in industry. He added that Nature was degenerated in these latter declining ages of the world, and would now produce only small abortive births in comparison of those in ancient times. He said it was very reasonable to think not only that the species of men were originally much larger, but also that there must have been giants in former ages ; which as it is asserted by history and tradition, so it hath been confirmed by huge bones and skulls, casually dug up in several parts of the kingdom, far exceeding the common dwindled race of man in our days. He argued that the very laws of nature absolutely required we should have been made in the beginning of a size more large and robust, not so liable to destruction from every little accident of a tile falling from a house, or a stone cast from the hand of a boy, or being drowned in a little brook. From this way of reasoning the author drew several moral applications useful in the conduct of life, but needless here to repeat.

Swift.

contra caeli inclementiam et beluarum iras indefensum, quarum alia uiribus, alia pernicitate, alia prouidentia, alia industria longe eum antecellat. Degenerasse enim senescentis mundi uires et tantum pusillos irritosque partus prae antiquis edere, ac simile ueri esse non modo homines ipsos fuisse olim grandiores, sed et gigantes exstitisse, quod et historia et fama traditum demonstrare uideri procera ossa et caluarias hic illic fortuito exaratas, homunculis uero aetatis nostrae multo maiores. Porro ipsius naturae leges postulare ut grandiores et robustiores ab initio creati fuerimus, nec mortiferis casibus ita obnoxii per deiectam tegulam uel missum a puero quodam lapidem, uel in transitu amnis lapso pede. Quo usus disserendi more nonnulla ad uitam praecepta utilissima ille quidem duxit, quae tamen ut hic repetam superuacaneum est.

A. T. B.

THE town of L. represented the earth, with its sorrows and its graves left behind, yet not out of sight, nor wholly forgotten. The ocean in everlasting but gentle agitation, and brooded over by a dove-like calm, might not unfitly typify the mind and the mood which then swayed it. For it seemed to me as if then first I stood at a distance and aloof from the uproar of life ; as if the tumult, the fever and the strife were suspended ; or respite granted from the secret burdens of the heart ; a sabbath of repose, a resting from human labours. Here were the hopes which blossom in the paths of life reconciled with the peace which is in the grave ; motions of the intellect as unwearied as the heavens, yet for all anxieties a halcyon calm, a tranquillity that seemed no product of inertia, but as if resulting from mighty and equal antagonisms ; infinite activities, infinite repose. Oh, just, subtle, and mighty opium ! that to the hearts of poor and rich alike for the wounds that will never heal, and for 'the pangs that tempt the spirit to rebel,' bringest an assuaging balm ; eloquent opium ! that with thy potent rhetoric stealest away the purposes of wrath ; and to the guilty man for one night givest back the hopes of his youth and hands washed pure from blood ; . . . that summonest to the chancery of dreams, for the triumphs of

VICVS ille orbem terrarum mihi depinge-
bat, derelictis iam sepulcris omnibus atque
aerumnis, neque tamen e conspectu omnino
amotis neque toti traditis obliuioni. Naturam
urbis et quasi affectionem, qua tum agitabatur,
pontus assiduo lenique motu, qui tamen mirabili
obductus est serenitate, haud inepte expresserit.
Videbar enim mihi tum primum a uocibus et
tumultu uitae longe recessisse; constitisse uidebantur turbae, trepidatio, simultates; requieuisse
paulisper secreta animi tormenta, quasi diuinitus
sanctum quoddam adepta otium laborisque humani cessationem. Illic tandem quae uiget in
uita hominum ambitio cum sepulcri quiete con-
cordiam confirmauerat; illic perpetua, ueluti caeli
ipsius, assiduitate fruebatur animus, curarum
tamen omnium ea tranquillitate, iis, ut ita dicam,
alcedoniis, quae non tam ex inertia ulla orerentur
quam e momentorum ingentium compensatione;
compositae scilicet erant in pacem infinitam
infinitae agitationes. O opium nostrum! Quid
te aequius est, quid exquisitius, quid potentius?
Tu diuitum pariter et pauperum animis eorum uul-
nerum quae sanari nequeunt, eorum tormentorum
quae desperationem suadent, almam das conso-
lationem. Quid eloquentius? Tu potenti quadam
suasione iracundo proposita surripis: tu nocenti

suffering innocence, false witnesses; and con-
foundest perjury, and dost reverse the sentences
of unrighteous judges.

[No. 363.]   *De Quincey.*

ALL we see, hear, and touch, the remote
sidereal firmament, as well as our own sea
and land, and the elements which compose them
and the ordinances they obey, are His. The
primary atoms of matter, their properties, their
mutual action, their disposition and collocation,
electricity, magnetism, gravitation, light, and whatever other subtle principles or operations the wit
of man is detecting or shall detect, are the work of
His hands. From Him has been every movement
which has convulsed and refashioned the surface
of the earth. The most insignificant or unsightly
insect is from Him, and good in its kind; the
ever-teeming, inexhaustible swarms of animalculae,
the myriads of living motes invisible to the naked
eye, the restless ever-spreading vegetation which
creeps like a garment over the whole earth, the
lofty cedar, the umbrageous banana are His. His

unam tantum noctem spes pueriles dextramque
restituis incruentam : tu somnianti ad cancellos
quosdam, ne inique plectantur innocentes, falsa
testificatos arcessis ; tu peierantes redarguis, iudi-
cumque iniquorum decreta antiquas.

M. J. R.

QVICQVID denique oculis intueri auribus
percipere manu contingere possumus, siue
per semotum illum stellisque consitum caeli
complexum, siue in hoc nostro terrarum orbe et
marium, omnia pariter illo auctore ex elementis
suis conficta sunt, illius legibus obtemperant.
Statuit porro idem ille prima materiae corpuscula
quales essent ipsa naturas habitura, quemadmodum
inter se uersari, quem inuicem habitum ac situm
seruare deberent: immo uero uis fulminis occulta,
mirabilis illa corporum se inuicem adliciendi
facultas, ponderum inclinatio, natura lucis, uel si
quam aliam his ipsis tenuiorem in rerum natura
uim inesse et uersari aut iam inuenit aut inuen-
turum est humanum ingenium, haec omnia illo
exstiterunt auctore. Nullus profecto absque illo
motus terrarum orbem quassatum in nouam faciem
redegit : eidem porro tribuendum est quod adeo

are the tribes and families of birds and beasts, their graceful forms, their wild gestures, and their passionate cries.

[No. 365.]   *J. H. Newman.*

ANOTHER consideration which may check our presumption in putting such a construction upon a misfortune is this, that it is impossible for us to know what are calamities and what are blessings. How many accidents have passed for misfortunes, which have turned to the wealth and prosperity of the persons to whose lot they have fallen ?   How many disappointments have in their consequences saved a man from

praeclare suis usibus conueniunt animalia quam tenuissima quam uisu foedissima. Respice praeterea quam infinita in singula momenta gignatur bestiolarum multitudo, quam incredibilis exsistat animantium uarietas qualia ne perspicere quidem possit oculorum acies, quam importuna se passim effundat herbarum ubertas et uestis ritu toti telluri obducatur; respice quantam ille cedro proceritatem, quam opacam platano umbram addiderit. Immo etiam uolucres et feras in genera sua ac tribus discriptas alias formae uenustate illustrauit, aliis motuum incitationem, aliis uim uocis inexplebilem adiunxit.

G. H. R.

ILLVD quoque confidentiam nostram refrenare oportet, quominus ita clades interpretemur: scilicet omnino non possumus bona a malis dignoscere. Quot enim res, pro miseriis ab iis quibus acciderunt habitae, tum demum in eorundem amplificationem ac bonam fortunam euaserunt! Quotiens autem homines etiam decepta exspectatione euentum pro exitiali felicem nanciscuntur! Sane si omnium rerum exitus cogitatione

ruin?   If we could look into the effects of every-thing we might be allowed to pronounce boldly upon blessings and judgements: but for a man to give his opinion of what he sees but in part and in its beginnings is an unjustifiable piece of rashness and folly.   The story of Biton and Cleobis, which was in great reputation among the heathens (for we see it quoted by all the ancient authors, both Greek and Latin, who have written upon the immortality of the soul) may teach us a caution in this matter.   These two brothers, being sons of a a lady who was priestess to Juno, drew their mother's chariot to the temple at the time of a great solemnity, the persons being absent who by their office were to have drawn the chariot on that occasion.   The mother was so transported with this instance of filial duty that she petitioned her goddess to bestow upon them the greatest gift that could be given to men: upon which they were both cast into a deep sleep and the next morning found dead in the temple.   This was such an event as would have been construed into a judge-ment had it happened to the two brothers after an act of disobedience, and would doubtless have been represented as such by any ancient authority who had given us an account of it.

Spectator.

praesumere possemus, fas esset fortasse de bonis
aut poenis a dis immortalibus immissis fidenter
iudicare, sed contra quae imperfecta tantum ac
nascentia uidemus, de iis sententiam ferre teme-
rarii ineptique hominis uidetur esse. Quod ut
caueamus documento sit illa de Bitone et Cleobi
fabula, ita ab antiquis celebrata, ut omnium qui de
animorum immortalitate conscripserunt, nemo eam
praeterierit. Hi forte fratres e nobili muliere
Iunonis sacerdote nati, cum ii abessent quorum
erat officium carpentum illius trahere, ipsi iugum
subeunt matremque sollenni quodam festo ad fana
deducunt. Ea igitur tam praeclaro pietatis argu-
mento elata deam exorat ut quod maximum donum
hominibus conferri possit, id natis suis contingat.
Continuo autem ambo alto sopore capti postera
luce in templo mortui inueniuntur. Is certe casus
erat ut si eisdem spreto erga parentem officio
superuenisset, omnes in ultionis speciem tracturi
fuerint; nec dubie, si quis ex antiquis rerum scriptoribus id narrasset, haud alio more depinxisset.

J. S. R.

KNOWING within myself the manner in which this poem has been produced, it is not without a feeling of regret that I make it public. What manner I mean will be quite clear to the reader, who must soon perceive great inexperience, immaturity, and every error denoting a feverish attempt, rather than a deed accomplished. The two first books, and indeed the two last, I feel sensible are not of such completion as to warrant their passing the press; nor should they, if I thought a year's castigation would do them any good;—it will not: the foundations are too sandy. It is just that the youngster should die away: a sad thought for me, if I had not some hope that while it is dwindling I may be plotting and fitting myself for verses fit to live. This may be speaking too presumptuously and may deserve a punishment: but no feeling man would be forward to inflict it: he will leave me alone with the conviction that there is no fiercer torment than the failure in a great object. This is not written with the least atom of purpose to forestall criticisms, but from the desire I have to conciliate men who are competent to look, and who do look, with a jealous eye to the honour of English literature. The imagination of a boy is healthy, and the mature imagination of a man is healthy, but there is a space

PIGET non nihil libellum emittere : adeo mihi sum conscius quo confecerim pacto. Quod cuius modi sit, ne ipse doceam, facile sibi perspicient lectores, multa imperite scripta esse, multa iuueniliter, omnia denique patefacere potius ambitiosam impotentiam quam compotes consilii uires. Nam quattuor carminis partium priores duas itemque, fateor, posteriores uix satis expolitas esse sentio ut audacter e librariis prodeant, nec dimitterem egomet si uel in annum corrigendo aliquid me profecturum opinarer, quod non opinor in his tenuissimae materiae principiis. Itaque intercidant deliciolae meae censeo ; acerbum id quidem, illas exolescere, sed tamen spes me interea alia moliri posse ad aliosque accingi uersiculos sed mansuros. Quam ob uocem fortasse iactantiorem uereor ne non iniuria plectar : quamquam castigandi partes adripiet sibi nemo qui modo sit paulo humanior, sed potius me omittet nihil quicquam ratus tam acribus animum exagitare stimulis quam pulcherrimi incepti uanos inritosque euentus. Neque haec eo scripsi ut iudicantium acerbitatem praeoccupem, quo consilio nihil a me alienius, sed aueo eos exorare qui litterarum apud nos patrocinium et uindicare suo iure possint et non indiligenter exerceant. Sanum enim pueri ingenium, sanum etiam confirmati iam uiri et

of life between, in which the soul is in a ferment, the character undecided, the way of life uncertain, the ambition thicksighted ; thence proceeds maw-kishness, and all the thousand bitters which those men I speak of must necessarily taste in going over the following pages.

[No. 398.]   *Keats.*

THERE is a society of men among us, bred up from their youth in the art of proving, by words multiplied for the purpose, that white is black, and black is white, according as they are paid.   To this society all the rest of the people are slaves.   For example, if my neighbour has a mind to my cow, he has a lawyer to prove that he ought to have my cow from me.   I must then hire another to defend my right, it being against all rules of law that any man should be allowed to speak for himself.   Now, in this case, I who am the right owner, lie under two great disadvantages: first, my lawyer, being practised almost from his cradle in defending falsehood, is quite out of his element when he would be an advocate for justice, which is an unnatural office he always attempts with great awkwardness, if not with ill

conroborati, interpositae autem aetatis spatio aestuat animus, uacillant mores, ambiguae uitae rationes, spes uotumque in obscuro : hinc insulsa illa, hinc inepta, et sescenta quae necessario amaram facient lectionem iis saltem quos significaui hominibus.

W. W.

EXSTAT in nostra ciuitate hominum quaedam societas, a pueris in ea arte erudita, ut uerbis quam plurimis alba nigra, nigra alba, prout mercedem habeant, demonstrent. Quibus sane ceteri inseruiunt omnes. Si enim uicinus uaccam meam adfectat, consultum pretio adducit qui dedendam arguat. Quam ob rem et mihi conducendus alter, qui ius meum defendat, cum nulla lege liceat ut quisquam pro se dicat. Cum autem ita fiat, ego (cuius iure est uacca) duobus laboro incommodis : primo enim aduocatus meus, a matris paene gremio falsa defendendi peritus, cum ius cupit tueri, ut in noua atque insolita re, causam inepte uel etiam morose suscipit. Deinde cautissime est ei agendum ne a iudicibus culpetur, odioque sit consultis tamquam litium numerum imminuat. Si igitur uacca mihi seruanda est,

will.   The second disadvantage is, that my lawyer must proceed with great caution, or else he will be reprimanded by the judges, and abhorred by his brethren, as one that would lessen the practice of the law.   And therefore I have but two methods to preserve my cow.   The first is, to gain over my adversary's lawyer with a double fee, who will then betray his client, by insinuating that he has justice on his side.   The second way is, for my lawyer to make my cause appear as unjust as he can, by allowing the cow to belong to my adversary, and this, if it be skilfully done will certainly bespeak the favour of the bench.

[No. 389.]   *Swift.*

OF this final baseness of the false ideal, its miserable waste of the time, strength, and available intellect of man, by turning, as I have said above, innocence of pastime into seriousness of occupation, it is of course hardly possible to sketch out even so much as the leading manifestations.   The vain and haughty projects of youth for future life; the giddy reveries of insatiable self-exaltation ; the discontented dreams of what might have been or should be, instead of the thankful understanding of what is ; the casting

quid faciam? Aut mihi aduersarii aduocatus
duplici pretio corrumpendus, ut se ius habere
clam indicet, ideoque praeuaricetur; aut meum
oportebit causam iniustam fateri, uaccamque
illius re uera esse: quod si sollertius fecerit,
iudicum certe gratiam conciliabit.

A. S.

SED quid dicam de eorum turpitudine qui falsa
sibi expetenda proposuerunt, qui, quod supra
dixi, neque lasciua seriis, neque studiis oblectamenta distinguunt? quid de absumpto tempore,
dissipatis uiribus, disperdito, quodcunque suppeditat, ingenio? Liceat tandem, quae plenam
uix admittunt explicationem, ea breuiter et summatim attingam. Adulescentes uana et uentosa in
futurum alucinantur: arrogantia inexplebili elati
quos spiritus, quae somnia non concipiunt! Ita
non quae sunt grato animo indagant, ut quid fieri

about for sources of interest–in senseless fiction,
instead of the real human histories of the people
round us; the prolongation from age to age of
romantic historical deception instead of sifted
truth; the pleasures taken in fanciful portraits of
rural or romantic life in poetry and on the stage,
without the smallest effort to rescue the living
rural population of the world from its ignorance
or misery; the excitement of the feelings by
laboured imagination of spirits, fairies, monsters,
and demons, issuing in total blindness of heart
and sight to the true presences of beneficent or
destructive spiritual powers around us; in fine, the
constant abandonment of all the straightforward
paths of sense and duty, for fear of losing some of
the enticement of ghostly joys, or trampling somewhat '*sopra lor vanità, che par persona*': all these
forms of false idealism have so entangled the
modern mind, often called, I suppose ironically,
practical, that I truly believe there never yet was
idolatry of stock or staff so utterly unholy as this
our idolatry of shadows.

[No. 411.]   *Ruskin.*

potuerit, quid esse debeat, queribundi comminis-
cantur: ita non uicinorum et re uera uiuentium
fortunae condicionique student, unde exquisitam
rerum ac ueritatis rationem posteritati tradant,
ut, cum se ineptis longissimeque petitis fabulis
delectauerint, fictos quosdam commenticiosque
annales confirment atque perpetuent. Idem inani-
bus uel poetarum uel histrionum ruris et nescio
quarum futilium personarum descriptionibus
quasi titillantur: ipsos homines, ipsos agricolas
miseriis ac stultitia nihil omnino agunt ut liberent
aut expediant. Quid? cum animum lemures,
nymphas, portenta, genios commentando inflamma-
uerint, restat ut numina ipsa, quibus circumdamur,
siue maleuola sunt siue benigna, mente penitus
occaecati non comprehendant: quod denique
prudenti, quod integro homini quasi ante oculos
positum est, illud idcirco uitant ut arcanis quibus-
dam deliciis ne priuentur, ut suas ipsi ineptias,
quas graues esse credunt, ne proterant atque con-
culcent. His et horum similibus erroribus ita
irretiti sunt nostri, quorum prudentiam, inuersis,
credo, uerbis comprobare solemus, ut haud scio an
ne impurissimus quidem eorum qui ligna uel
baculos uenerati sunt cum nostris his umbrarum,
non deorum, cultoribus pari sit odio detestandus.

M. J. R.

I T is common to hear remarks on the frequent divorce between culture and character, and to infer from this that culture is a mere varnish, and that character only deserves any serious attention. No error can be more fatal. Culture without character is, no doubt, something frivolous, vain and weak; but character without culture is on the other hand, something raw, blind, and dangerous. The most interesting, the most truly glorious peoples, are those in which the alliance of the two has been effected most successfully, and its result spread most widely. This is why the spectacle of ancient Athens has such profound interest for a rational man, that it is the spectacle of the culture of a people. It is not an aristocracy, leavening with its own high spirit the multitude which it wields, but leaving it the unformed multitude still; it is not a democracy, acute and energetic, but tasteless, narrow-minded, and ignoble: it is the middle and lower classes in the highest development of their humanity that these classes have yet reached. It was the many who relished those arts, who were not satisfied with less than those monuments. In the conversations recorded by Plato, or even 'by the matter-of-fact Xenophon, which for the free yet refined discussion of ideas have set the tone for the

CVM saepe animaduertatur doctrinam a bonis moribus seiunctam esse, colligere solent quasi fucum quendam esse doctrinam, et bonis tantum moribus incumbendum esse. Quo nihil prauius cogitari potest. Vt enim sine bonis moribus leuis res doctrina est, inanis, infirma, ita uirtus sine doctrina crudum aliquid, temerarium, periculosum est. Itaque illi populi maxima studia hominum conciliauerunt et clarissima gloria effulserunt, apud quos doctrina cum uirtute felicissime coniuncta plurimos ciues adfecit. Neque alia de causa rerum Atheniensium memoria prudentissimo cuique praedulcis est, quam quod totam ciuitatem exhibent excultam. Non enim optimates rem tenebant, animo suo populum imbuentes subiectum, quem tamen rudem, ut acceperunt, relinquerent; non populus, acer ille quidem et strenuus, animo autem hebeti, angusto, inliberali; sed medii homines et inferiores, ad humanitatem ultra omnem memoriam instituti. Multitudini illae artes cordi erant, nihil satis erat quod illa monumenta non adaequaret. Sermonibus enim Socratis, qui liberae et elegantis disceptationis rerum doctis omnium temporum hominibus exemplum dederunt, siue Plato eos siue propius ad ueritatem Xenophon expressit, tabernarii intersunt et mercatores; neque alia, nisi antiquario, ratio apparet, cur pauculi qui ante

whole cultivated world, shopkeepers and trades-men of Athens mingle.   For any one but a pedant, this is why a handful of Athenians of two thousand years ago are more interesting than the millions of most nations our contemporaries.

[No. 406.] *M. Arnold.*

AMONG the different kinds of representation, statuary is the most natural, and shows us something likest the object that is represented. To make use of a common instance, let one who is born blind take an image in his hands, and trace out with his fingers the different furrows and impressions of the chisel, and he will easily conceive how the shape of a man or beast may be represented by it; but should he draw his hand over a picture where all is smooth and uniform, he would never be able to imagine how the several prominences and depressions of a human body could be shown on a plain piece of canvas, that

duo milia annorum uixerunt Athenienses studia
hominum in sese conuerterint, non innumerae
nostrorum temporum multitudines.

H. N.

VT autem rerum figurae multis modis adumbrari possunt, ita sculptores imprimis et
naturam magistram habent, et simulacra nobis
exhibent a rebus ipsis minime distantia. Nam
ut e medio exemplum petam, si natus fuerit aliquis
caecus, is, si sumpta in manus statua sulcos omnes
digitis pertrectet, notasque quibus caelo sit incisa,
facile intellegat, qua ratione possit effigies ea
speciem hominis uel bestiae praebere; sin per-
currat idem manibus picturam, quae res est omni
ex parte plana atque aequabilis, numquam sane
concipere animo possit, quomodo corporis humani
partes, quarum exsurgant aliae, aliae depriman-

has in it no unevenness or irregularity. Description runs yet further from the thing it represents than painting; for a picture bears a real resemblance to its original, which letters and syllables are wholly void of. Colours speak all languages, but words are understood only by such a people or nation. We are told that in America, when the Spaniards first arrived there, expresses were sent to the Emperor of Mexico in paint, and the news of his country delineated by the strokes of a pencil, which was a more natural way than that of writing, though at the same time much more imperfect, because it is impossible to draw the little connexions of speech, or to give the picture of a conjunction or an adverb.

[No. 399.]

THE Rhodians had a story of their island, he said, that when Jupiter, who ruled them, was delivered of Pallas, it rained there gold in abundance; and this, after their fashion, they moralized. Pallas, so born, they held to signify both prowess and policy, martial worth and wisdom: wisdom too, both human and divine, implying not only instruction for the affairs of men but

tur, tabella mera referat, in qua nihil asperum
sit usquam, nihil uarium. Verbis autem qui res
aliquas exprimunt, hi uel longius a rebus ipsis
quam pictores recedunt: et possunt praeterea
colores omnibus hominibus significationem aliquam
sui facere, contra uocabula non nisi locorum
certorum incolis. Sic enim est traditum, cum in
Americam Hispani primum uenissent, missas esse
ad regem Mexicanorum pro epistolis picturas, et
fortunas regni penicillo declaratas. Naturalius id
quam scribere, uerum multo minus perfectum;
nequeunt enim adumbrari lineis sermonum arti-
culi, aut distinctiones copulationesque uerborum
pingi.

F. D. M.

RHODIOS dixit olim fabulari, cum Iuppiter
qui tum apud illos regeret Palladem pareret,
aurum in insula pluisse plurimum; quam rem ita
more suo interpretatos esse ut quae ita nasceretur
Pallas ferociam cum consilio, prudentiam cum
uirtute coniunctam significare uideretur; et eam
quidem prudentiam haud minus diuinam quam
humanam, quippe quae non humanarum modo

in the service and worship of the gods. The fable, Eliot thought, might have just application to members of that house, and some instruction for their purpose. Aforetime might their island have been taken for a Rhodes, the proper seat of gods, wherein, when action had been added unto counsel, and counsel joined to action, when religion and resolution had come together, there wanted nothing of the felicity or blessing that wealth and honour could impart. Wisdom and valour singly had availed not ; Apollo had not satisfied, Mars had been too weak ; but both their virtues meeting with religion, and concurring in that centre—as in the person of their Pallas, their Minerva, their last great queen !—never had those failed in their chronicles and stories to give both riches and reputation, the true showers of gold mentioned in the fable.

[No. 440.]   *J. Foster.*

SELF-SATISFACTION at least in some degree is an advantage which equally attends the fool and the wise man ; but it is the only one, nor is there any other circumstance in the conduct of life where they are on an equal

rerum disciplinam in se contineret, sed etiam deorum sacra cultumque respiceret. Sibi quidem uideri fabulam haudquaquam a nostris senatoribus et ab hac relatione alienam: nostram quoque insulam potuisse olim alteram Rhodon, propriam deorum uideri sedem ; in qua cum neque agendi alacritas consilio deesset neque consilium alacritati, con- iuncta pietate cum constantia, ne ulla quidem iam pars abesset faustae eius felicitatis, quae in opibus et dignitate poneretur. Parum quidem ipsam per se sapientiam ualuisse, uirtutem parum: neque enim arte Apollinem satis fecisse, neque ui Martem : cum uero utriusque uirtus cum religione ita coiisset ut in unum caput omnes concurrerent— quod ipsi sua nuper Pallade, sua Minerua, am- plissima sua imperante regina, sensissent—num- quam, si fastis fides haberetur, non illis temporibus simul exstitisse diuitias ac famam, ueriores quam fabulae illius imbres aureos.

G. H. R.

SIBI uero placere commodum est quod aliqua quidem ex parte stultum sapientemque pariter sequatur ; sed hac una in re ex omnibus quae ad uitam attinent, solet hic cum illo exaequari. Stultus enim negotiis studiis sermonibus prorsus

footing. Business, books, conversation, for all of
these a fool is totally incapacitated, and except
condemned by his station to the coarsest drudgery,
remains a useless burthen upon the earth. Accordingly it is found that men are extremely jealous of·
their character in this particular, and many instances are seen of profligacy and treachery the
most avowed and unreserved, none of bearing
patiently the imputation of ignorance and stupidity.
Dicaearchus the Macedonian general, who, as
Polybius tells us, openly erected an altar to
impiety, another to injustice, in order to bid
defiance to mankind; even he, I am well assured,
would have started at the epithet 'fool,' and would
have meditated revenge for so injurious an appella-
tion. Except the affection of parents, the strongest
and most indissoluble in nature, no connexion has
strength sufficient to support the disgust arising
from this character. Love itself, which can subsist
under treachery, ingratitude, malice and infidelity,
is immediately extinguished by it when perceived
and acknowledged, nor are deformity and old age
more fatal to the dominion of that passion; so
dreadful are the ideas of an utter incapacity for any
purpose or undertaking, and of continued error and
misconduct in life.

Hume.

est impar; itaque nisi ipsa nascendi condicione coactus sit asperrimo labore uti, inutile tamquam onus terrae incumbit. Vnde fit ut hanc morum suorum partem eleuari homines uel maxime doleant; exempla quidem flagitiorum perfidiaeque habemus amoto omni inuolucro et dissimulatione, inscitiae tamen et ineptiarum crimen aequo animo ferri numquam uidimus. Velut Dicaearchus Macedonum imperator, quem auctor est Polybius aperte aras, alteram impietati, iniustitiae alteram statuisse, ut toti humano generi bellum denuntiaret; at ipse tamen, credo, stulti appellatione commoueretur, et pro tam graui crimine quo modo poenas posset sumere deliberaret. Nulla sane nisi parentum cum liberis coniunctio, quam maxime omnium stabilem et ad soluendum difficilem natura ipsa effecit, fastidia his moribus enata sustinuerit. Amor quoque, qui in fallaces ingratos malignos infidos remanere potest, si modo haec culpa nobis cognita fuerit atque innotuerit, extemplo interit; cui animi affectui neque deformitas neque senectus tam est exitiosa. Ita deterrentur qui sibi proposuerunt cum facultates ad consilia uel coepta suscipienda plane inualidas, tum infinitos errores et in agenda uita imbecillitatem.

J. S. R.

BENEDICK.　O, she misused me past the endurance of a block ! an oak with but one green leaf on it would have answered her; my very visor began to assume life and scold with her: she told me, not thinking I had been myself, that I was the prince's jester; that I was duller than a great thaw; huddling jest upon jest with such impossible conveyance upon me, that I stood like a man at a mark, with a whole army shooting at me; she speaks poniards, and every word stabs; if her breath were as terrible as her terminations there were no living near her, she would infect to the north star.　I would not marry her, though she were endowed with all Adam had left him before he transgressed; she would have made Hercules have turned spit; yea, and have cleft his club to make the fire too.　Come, talk not of her; you shall find her the infernal Ate in good apparel. I would to God some scholar would conjure her; for certainly while she is here a man may live as quiet in hell as in a sanctuary; and people sin upon purpose, because they would go thither: so indeed all disquiet, horror, and perturbation follow her.

[No. 410.]　　　　　　　　　　　　　　*Shakespeare.*

HEUS, illamne mihi irasci? quem ita laces-
siuit ut uel stipes conuiciis restiturus fuerit;
ut caduca quercus, quae uel unam aleret frondem, in
iurgia stimulata esset: immo ipsa haec mea persona uitam sumere et cum ea altercari uoluit:
Etenim me alium esse interpretata scurram me
principis esse coram affirmauit, et niue lutulenta,
Idibus Februariis, crassiorem: tamquam praestigiis
linguae ludibria ludibriis accumulabat, ut ipse, uiro
similis in quem sagittas intendat tota· Parthorum
caterua, attonitus constarem; ita uerbis uerberat
ista, et ubi aliquid ioculatur, iaculatur. Si pariter.
ac sermo spiritus infensus esset, cauerent omnes,
refugerent, infortunium uitarent; immo Hyper-
boreis periculo essent istius linguae contagia. Quae
si uel Croesi diuitias et aurea Saturni regna doti
referret, ego non ducerem: in culinam Herculem
coegisset ad ueru uersandum, et clauam ipsam pro
fomite diffissam igni imposuisset. Tace, ne nomi-
nando eam euoces: Alecto enim, Alecto, lauta ueste
et apparatu, prodibit. Vtinam Thessalus modo
magus adsit qui carmine eam remittat! quae si
longius in terris morabitur, tranquillius apud
Furias uiuendum erit quam apud Vestam, et a
multis consulto peccabitur, ne Tartaro diutius
careant: ita eam tamquam familiares comitantur
Terror Perturbatio Discordia.

E. D. A. M.

T

‘THE lady Beatrice hath a quarrel to you; the gentleman, that danced with her told her she is much wronged by you.’   ‘O, she mis-used me past the endurance of a block! an oak, but with one green leaf on it, would have answered her: my very visor began to assume life and scold with her: she told me, not thinking I had been myself, that I was the prince’s jester; that I was duller than a great thaw; huddling jest upon jest with such impossible conveyance upon me, that I stood like a man at a mark, with a whole army shooting at me; she speaks poniards, and every word stabs; if her breath were as terrible as her terminations, there were no living near her, she would infect to the north star. I would not marry her, though she were endowed with all that Adam had left him before he transgressed; she would have made Hercules have turned spit; yea, and have cleft his club to make the fire too. Come, talk not of her; you shall find her the infernal Ate in good apparel. I would to God some scholar would conjure her; for certainly, while she is here, a man may live as quiet in hell, as in a sanctuary; and people sin upon purpose, because they would go thither: so, indeed, all disquiet, horror, and perturbation follow her.’

[*F. C.* 318.]   *Shakespeare.*

'DRVSILLA nostra habet quod de te quera-
tur; is enim, quocum saltauit, dictitabat te
pessume de ea mereri.' ' Nimirum me peius habuit
quam pro ligni cuiusuis patientia ; ne quercus quidem, cui una tantum frons superesset, tacuisset;
ipsa buccula mea, sumpta anima, obiurgatricem
agebat. Dictitabat enim, quendam alium adesse
opinata, me principis esse scurram, me niue
tabescente insulsiorem ; dicta dictis ingerebat,
celeritate tam incredibili, ut, tamquam qui sagittis
petendus esset, consisterem, toto exercitu inten-
dente. Pugiones loquitur et uoce quaque transfigit ;
quod si halitus eius, ut dicteria, teter esset, uix cum
ea esset uiuendum ; auras enim ad ipsam Arcton
impleret. Illam sane uxorem non ducerem etiamsi
tanta dos esset, quanta Adamo nondum nocenti ;
immo efficeret ut Hercules ipse bucca foculum
excitaret, adeoque clauam diffissam flammis sug-
gereret. Quin illam missam facis? Est enim tibi
Erinys, Iunonis induta ueste. Vtinam per deos
mathematicus quis eam carminibus ad Tartarum
depellat ; ea enim inter uiuos manente, tam secure
apud Tartarum quam in ipsis deum sedibus uiuitur;
homines quidem de industria peccent, ut eo liceat
abire. Tanta perturbatio, tanta animi aegritudo,
tanta molestia eam subsequuntur.'

W. H. B.

THE temper, therefore, by which right taste is formed, is characteristically patient. It dwells upon what is submitted to it. It does not trample upon it, lest it should be pearls, even though it look like husks. It is a good ground, soft, penetrable, retentive; it does not send up thorns of unkind thoughts, to choke the weak seed; it is hungry and thirsty too, and drinks all the dew that falls on it. It is an honest and good heart, that shows no too ready springing before the sun be up, but fails not afterwards; it is distrustful of itself, so as to be ready to believe and to try all things, and yet so trustful of itself that it will neither quit what it has tried, nor take anything without trying. And the pleasure which it has in things that it finds true and good is so great, that it cannot possibly be led aside by any tricks of fashion, or diseases of vanity; it cannot be cramped in its conclusions by partialities and hypocrisies; its visions and its delights are too penetrating, too living, for any whitewashed object or shallow fountain long to endure or supply. ... The conclusions of this disposition are sure to be eventually right; more and more right according to the general maturity of all the powers; but it is sure to come right at last, because its operation is in analogy to, and in harmony with,

ILLVD igitur ingenium unice docile est, unde uerum nascitur iudicium. Immoratur rei iudicandae, neque ei, quamuis paleae speciem praebeat, insultat, ne forte margaritam laedat. Sic enim omnia fouet, sic malis caret cogitationibus, quasi solum bonum, molle, penetrabile, in quo tenerum semen nullis spinis eliditur, quod famem sentit ac sitim, quod rores caducos perbibit. Ex probo scilicet animo atque bono nihil properat ante lucem nasci, exorta autem luce nihil deficit. Ille ita sibi diffidit animus ut paratus sit omnia credere, omnia experiri ; ita fidit, ut nec probata uelit relinquere, nec quicquam accipiat nisi probatum. Adeo iis rebus delectatur, quas ueras ac bonas esse cognouit, ut neque saeculi flosculis pelliciatur, nec ueneno uanitatis. Illud iudicium nec gratia nec falsa species deprauat. Acies illa acerrima et uiuax, illa dulcedo contemplandi, nihil fucati patitur. Sacros amat fontes, riuulos apertos contemnit. Huius modi ingenium quamuis aliquid errauerit, ad summam tamen recte iudicabit, eoque rectius quo magis omnibus partibus maturescit : scilicet quia uniuersae morum rationi, qualis Christianorum est, agit consentanea, et in magnis felicitatis principiis ad ultimum, expleto amore, acquiescit, quae cum omnibus hominibus sint communia, tum in

the whole spirit of the Christian moral system,
and must ultimately love and rest in the great
sources of happiness common to all the human
race, and based on the relations they hold to their
Creator.

[No. 409.]   *Ruskin.*

A GREAT writer is the friend and benefactor
of his readers; and they cannot but judge of
him under the deluding influence of friendship and
gratitude.   We all know how unwilling we are to
admit the truth of any disgraceful story about
a person whose society we like, and from whom
we have received favours; how long we struggle
against evidence; how fondly, when the facts
cannot be disputed, we cling to the hope that there
may be some explanation or extenuating circumstance with which we are unacquainted.   Just such
is the feeling which a man of liberal education
naturally entertains towards the great minds of
former ages.   The debt which he owes to them is
incalculable.   They have guided him to truth.
They have filled his mind with noble and graceful
images.   They have stood by him in all vicissitudes,
comforters in sorrow, nurses in sickness, com-

societate diuinae humanaeque naturae fundata
sunt.

H. N.

PRAECLARI scriptores amici sunt lectorum,
bene de iis meriti; qui rursus amicitia ac
beneuolentia praestricta acie mentium de iis iudi-
cant. Inuiti profecto turpi rumori in eo credimus
quo libenter utamur, qui beneficiis nos affecerit;
diu resistimus testimoniis; cupide ubi de re
constitit spem amplexamur posse restare aliquid
nobis ignotum quod diluat, quod eleuet. Proinde
hunc animum gerit homo libera disciplina usus
erga magna ueterum ingenia. Magnum est
profecto quod iis acceptum refert, qui ad uerum
deduxerunt, qui mentem rebus pulcris ac prae-
claris instruxerunt, per omnes casus fortunae
astitere, consolati tristem, solum comitati, aegro
medici. Quibus alia societatum uincula labefac-
tantur uel soluuntur casibus, huius modi amicitiae
non obnoxiae sunt. Scilicet labenti tempore,
mutabili fortuna, exacerbatis animis, quae non

panions in solitude. These friendships are exposed to no danger from the occurrences by which other attachments are weakened or dissolved. Time glides on; fortune is inconstant; tempers are soured ; bonds which seemed indissoluble are daily sundered by interest, by emulation, or by caprice. But no such cause can affect the silent converse which we hold with the highest of human intellects. That placid intercourse is disturbed by no jealousies or resentments. These are the old friends who are never seen with new faces, who are the same in wealth and in poverty, in glory, and in obscurity.

[No. 408.]   *Macaulay.*

SUCH is the feeling which a man of liberal education naturally entertains towards the great minds of former ages. The debt which he owes to them is incalculable. They have guided him to truth. They have filled his mind with noble and graceful images. They have stood by him in all vicissitudes, comforters in sorrow, nurses in sickness, companions in solitude. These friendships are exposed to no danger from the occurrences by which other attachments are weakened

posse solui uisa erant uincula per utilitatem,
per ambitionem, per libidinem crebro soluuntur.
Tales casus ad tacita illa cum maximis ingeniis
commercia aditum non habent; non turbat
liuor quietos, non irae; una eademque semper
amicorum species, per diuitias ac paupertatem,
splendidis ac sordidis.

D. S. M.

I VRE igitur hoc animo esse solet si quis libera-
liter institutus est in praeclara illa ingenia
quae tulit antiquitas. Quo modo enim iis tanta
uel referri potest gratia quibus ducibus ueri in-
timam naturam cognouerit, qui menti tot splendida
tot uenusta infuderint, qui maerentem solacio,
fomentis aegrotantem, desolatum sodalitate, per
omnes denique fortunae euentus auxilio prae-
stantissimo adiuverint? Scilicet huius modi ami-
citiis nihil ea nocent quae alias familiaritates

or dissolved.   Time glides on ; fortune is inconstant ; tempers are soured ; bonds which seemed
indissoluble are daily sundered by interest, by
emulation, or by caprice.   But no such cause can
affect the silent converse which we hold with the
highest of human intellects.   That placid intercourse is disturbed by no jealousies or resentments.
These are the old friends who are never seen with
new faces, who are the same in wealth and in
poverty, in glory and in obscurity.   With the dead
there is no rivalry.   In the dead there is no change.

    [*F. C.* 534.]   *Macaulay.*

YE pretend to a commonwealth.   How amend
   ye it by killing of gentlemen, by spoiling of
gentlemen, by imprisoning of gentlemen ? A marvellous tanned commonwealth.   Why should ye
hate them for their riches, or for their rule ?   Rule,
they never took so much in hand as ye do now.
They never resisted the king, never withstood
his council, be faithful at this day, when ye be
faithless, not only to the king whose subjects ye
be, but also to your lords whose tenants ye be.

labefactare solent aut euertere. Videmus tempus
praeterlabi, mutari fortunam, morum suauitatem in
amaritudinem abire, firmissima caritatis uincula
spe emolumenti aut ambitione aut ipsa leuitate
saepissime dissolui. His autem ne attingi quidem
potest aequa illa et tranquilla consuetudo, nec
inuidia nec simultatibus turbanda, quam cum ipsis
luminibus humani generis sine uoce coniungimus.
Sis pauper an diues, sis clarus an obscurus, certa
tamen manet fides atque integra, neque umquam
illorum limina frigescunt. Quippe mortuorum
condicio cum aemulatione tum uicissitudinibus
liberata est.

H. B.

SCILICET rem publicam affectatis! Num quid in
ea re proficitis optimatibus trucidatis, optimatibus spoliatis, optimatibus in uincula coniectis?
O miram coriariorum rem publicam! Num igitur
uel quod diuites sunt uel quod imperium capessunt,
illis est inuidendum? Imperium dico? Illi enim
nunquam sibi tantum imperii uindicauerunt quantum uos hodie uindicatis; illi regi nunquam ob-
stiterunt; illi ministris eius nunquam non obtem-
perauerunt; illi etiamnunc fidem seruant: uos

Is this your true duty—in some of homage, in most of fealty, in all of allegiance—to leave your duties, go back from your promises, fall from your faith, and contrary to law and truth, to make unlawful assemblies, ungodly companies, wicked and detestable camps, to disobey your betters, and to obey your tanners, to change your obedience from a king to a Ket, to submit yourselves to traitors, and break your faith to your true king and lords?

If riches offend you, because ye would have the like, then think that to be no commonwealth but envy to the commonwealth. Envy it is to impair another man's estate, without the amendment of your own; and to have no gentlemen, because ye be none yourselves, is to bring down an estate and to mend none. Would ye have all alike rich? That is the overthrow of all labour, and utter decay of work in this realm. For who will labour more, if, when he hath gotten more, the idle shall by lust, without right, take what him list from him under pretence of equality with him? This is the bringing in of idleness which destroyeth the commonwealth, and not the amendment of labour which maintaineth the commonwealth.

[F. C. 75.]   *Sir J. Cheeke.*

autem infidi non modo ipsum erga principem cuius in regno ac dicione estis, sed etiam erga dominos quorum agros colitis. . Num uero sic agentes in officio estis—multi enim iure iurando, plures fide data, omnes lege estis obstricti—ut muneribus relictis, foederibus ruptis, fide uiolata, moribus et innocentia corruptis, coetus iniustos habeatis, contiones scelestas aduocetis, castra iniqua ac de· testanda capiatis, ut bonis hominibus neglectis, coriariis pareatis, ut regem Regulo commutetis, et scelestorum dicto audientes erga regem uerum ac dominos fidem fallatis? Quod si uobis diuitiae sunt inuisae propterea quod uos eadem desideratis, istud uero non est rem publicam constituere, sed potius rei publicae inuidere. Nam inuidorum est alterius rem deterere, nec suam augere, tum uiros liberales expellere propterea quod uos non liberales estis, istud est ciuitatem proruentis nec in melius promouentis. Omnesne uultis paribus frui diuitiis? Ita uero opera omnis interit, ita quaestus in hac re publica pereunt. Quis enim operam quaestui dabit si pluribus congestis diuitiis, ignauissimus quisque, tanquam par sit, libidine et iniuria quaslibet res corripiet? Sic autem infertur ignauia, quae rei publicae damno est, non lex lata est labori quo res publica continetur.

W. H. B.

ONE great cause of our insensibility to the goodness of the Creator is the very extensiveness of his bounty. We prize but little what we share only in common with the rest, or with the generality of our species. When we hear of blessings, we think forthwith of successes, of prosperous fortunes, of honour, riches, preferments, i.e. of those advantages and superiorities over others which we happen either to possess or to be in pursuit of, or to covet. The common benefits of our nature entirely escape us. Yet these are the great things. These constitute what most properly ought to be aecounted blessings of Providence; what alone, if we might so speak, are worthy of its care. Nightly rest and daily bread, the ordinary use of our limbs, and senses, and understandings, are gifts which admit of no comparison with any other. Yet because almost every man we meet possesses these, we leave them out of our enumeration. They raise no sentiment; they move no gratitude. Now, herein is our judgement perverted by our selfishness. A blessing ought in truth to be the more satisfactory, the bounty at least of the donor is rendered more conspicuous, by its very diffusion, its commonness, its cheapness; by its falling to our lot, and forming the happiness, of the great

FACIT ipsa largitas immensa Creatoris ut parum meminerimus quanta sit ille beneficentia. Nam quod commune uel omnium uel plurium est hominum, id minoris aestimamus. Si beneficia quis diuina commemorat, successus aliquis aut prospera fortuna, honores, diuitiae, munera ciuilia animo occurrunt. Quae quidem nihil aliud sunt quam commoda quibus ipsi alios siue superamus, siue superare conamur aut certe uolumus. Quae cum ceteris communia habemus penitus nos fallunt. Atqui haec re uera maxima sunt; haec Dei beneficia aptissime habentur; haec sola, ut ita loquar, digna sunt quae Deus administret. Ecquid enim comparari potest cum somno, cum cibo, cum membrorum, sensuum, rationis usura? Quae quia fere nemo est quin possideat, a nobis praetermitti solent: animum mouere, grates elicere non possunt. Ita nosmet diligimus ut recte in hac re iudicare nequeamus; nam potiora ob hanc ipsam causam beneficia haberi debent, certe auctoris munificentia in eo potissimum elucet—quod late diffluunt, communia fiunt, facile parta sunt, quod non modo nobis sed plerisque hominibus contingunt innumerasque multitudines delectant. Immo etiamsi ea, quibus ceteri fruantur, beneficia ipsi non

bulk and body of our species, as well as of ourselves.   Nay, even when we do not possess it, it
ought to be matter of thankfulness that others do.
  [F. C. 141.]   *W. Paley.*

THE whole course of things being thus entirely
changed between us and the ancients, and the
moderns wisely sensible of it, we of this age have
discovered a shorter and more prudent method to
become scholars and wits, without the fatigue of
reading or of thinking.   The most accomplished
way of using books at present is two-fold : either,
first, to serve them as some men do lords, learn
their titles exactly, and then brag of their acquaintance ; or, secondly, which is indeed the
choicer, the profounder, and politer method, to
get a thorough insight into the index, by which
the whole book is governed and turned, like fishes
by the tail.   For to enter the palace of learning
at the great gate requires an expense of time and
forms ; therefore men of much haste and little
ceremony are content to get in by the back-door.
Thus are the sciences found, like Hercules' oxen,
by tracing them backwards.   Thus are old sciences
unravelled, like old stockings, by beginning at the
foot.   Besides all this, the army of the sciences

percipimus, tamen hoc ipsum, quod fruuntur, gratissimum nobis esse debet.

E. W. B.

NOS autem prudenter agnouimus totam rationem inter nos et antiquos homines mutatam esse. Igitur breuius agitur et sapientius, scilicet ut sine legendi aut cogitandi labore docti fiamus et ingeniosi. Duplex scilicet, ut nunc se res habet, est inter peritos usus librorum ; aut enim nomina eorum, ut quidam in nobilibus amicis faciunt, perdiscenda sunt et consuetudo iactanda, aut (quod altius multo et elegantius est et magis urbanum) indicem oportet bene habere perspectum, quo, sicut cauda pisces, totus liber regitur quodam modo et uersatur. Cum enim ianua domum intrare impendium habet temporis ac religionis, postico contenti sunt qui moras huius modi ac molestias auersantur. Ita, sicut boues Herculis, scientiae auersis uestigiis indagantur, et doctrina uetus, sicut caliga, a pede retexitur. Accedit quod scientiae, multa disciplina quasi ordinibus suis instructae, uno conspectu celerrime lustrari possunt. Quod tantum beneficium indicibus ac summariis totum referemus, acceptum, quibus, quasi cauti feneratores, patres

has been of late, with a world of martial discipline, drawn into its close order, so that a view or muster may be taken of it with abundance of expedition. For this great blessing we are wholly indebted to systems and abstracts, in. which the modern fathers of learning, like prudent usurers, spent their labour for the ease of us their children. For labour is the seed of idleness, and it is the peculiar happiness of our noble age to gather the fruit.

[No. 407.]   *Swift.*

HENCE that unexampled unanimity which distinguishes the present season. In other wars we have been a divided people; the effect of our external operations has been in some measure weakened by intestine dissension. When peace has returned, the breach has widened, while parties have been formed on the merits of particular men, or of particular measures. These have all disappeared : we have buried our mutual animosities in a regard to the common safety. The sentiment of self-preservation, the first law which nature has impressed, has absorbed every other feeling; and the fire of liberty has melted down the discordant sentiments and minds of the British Empire into

nostrae doctrinae nepotum suorum causa laborem impenderunt. Nam labor profecto semen est ignauiae, cuius fructum nobis, saeculo uidelicet nobilissimo, percipere singulari felicitate contingit.

H. N.

HINC uero incredibilis est omnium consensus exortus, qualis post hominúm mcmoriam apud nostros numquam exstitit. Nam in ceteris bellis ita in uarias partes distracta est res publica, ut ciuili dissensione foris imminuerentur uires. Indè autem, pacatis tandem rebus, altius in rem publicam penetrauit discordia, singulìsque tum uiris tum consiliis alii aliis fauebant. Hodie uero praeteriit illa discordia ; nempe restinxit simultates communis salutis cura. Quandoquidem enim natura ipsa nullam prius legem hominibus impressit quam ut se ipsi conseruarent, totus iam animorum impetus ad uitam conseruandam conuersus est, atque ingens libertatis aestus uarias ciuium

one mass, and propelled them in one direction. Partial interests and feelings are suspended, the spirits of the body are collected at the heart, and we are awaiting with anxiety, but without dismay, the discharge of that mighty tempest which hangs upon the skirts of the horizon, and to which the eyes of Europe and of the world are turned in silent and awful expectation. While we feel solicitude, let us not betray dejection, nor be alarmed at the past successes of our enemy, since they have raised him from obscurity to an elevation which has made him giddy, and tempted him to suppose everything within his power. The intoxication of his success is the omen of his fall.

[No. 442.] *Robert Hall.*

IF an honest, and, I may truly affirm, a laborious zeal for the public service, has given me any weight in your esteem, let me exhort and conjure you never to suffer an invasion of your political constitution, however minute the instance may appear, to pass by, without a determined, persevering resistance. One precedent creates another. They soon accumulate, and constitute law. What yesterday was fact, to-day is doctrine. Examples

opiniones, quasi in massam ardentem coactas, omnes simul eodem propulit. Iacent priuata diuersarum partium studia; colliguntur circum praecordia totius corporis uires; nos ipsi denique sollicito quidem animo sed impauido ingentem tempestatis impetum exspectamus quae extremis iam caeli oris ingruit, quamque intentis oculis tristi cum silentio et Europa intuetur et orbis terrarum totus. Instat sane sollicitudo; nolite uero tristi-tiam, nolite metus admittere, quod tot hosti con-tigerint uictoriae: nonne ab obscuro ille loco ad summum rerum fastigium sublatus, tanti animi uertigine corripitur, ut nihil non posse arbitretur? Praebet ipse profecto, fortuna ebrius, certissimum ruinae augurium.

G. H. R.

SI sincera et, quod uerissime dixerim, impensa rei publicae cura aliquid mihi apud uos auctoritatis dederit, oro uos et obsecro ne leges uestras uiolari umquam sinatis, quamuis in pusilla uideatur re, ut non omnes summo studio ac pertinacissime repugnetis. Ex uno exemplo alterum nascitur, cito plura ac mos fit, et quod singulare nuper erat hodie inter praecepta est. Vitiosissimis consiliis auctoritatem adstruunt

are supposed to justify the most dangerous
measures; and where they do not suit exactly,
the defect is supplied by analogy. Be assured
that the laws which protect us in our civil rights,
grow out of the constitution, and they must fall or
flourish with it.   This is not the cause of faction,
or of party, or of any individual, but the common
interest of every man in Britain. Although the
king should continue to support his present
system of government, the period is not very
distant, at which you will have the means of
redress in your own power. It may be nearer,
perhaps, than any of us expect; and I would warn
you to be prepared for it. The king may possibly
be advised to dissolve the present parliament
a year or two before it expires of course, and
precipitate a new election, in hopes of taking the
nation by surprise. If such a measure be in
agitation, this very caution may defeat or prevent it.

Junius.

B UT if I profess all this impolitic stubbornness,
I may chance never to be elected into Parliament. It is certainly not pleasing to be put out of
the public service. But I wish to be a member of

exempla ; quae si parum apta habeas, interpretando
adiuues. Scitote uero leges eas quibus ciuilia
nostra iura continentur ex ipsa re publica nasci,
quacum aut una stent aut una pereant necesse
esse. Nec iam factionis aut partis aut hominis
alicuius priuata defendo commoda, sed communem
unius cuiusque ciuis causam. Nam si princeps
diutius usus erit eo quo nunc utitur regnandi
more, remedia breue intra tempus penes uos ipsos
erunt ; quod quia fortasse ante exspectatum
uenerit, moneo ut exspectetis. Fieri enim potest
ut quidam regi insusurrent senatum dimittendum
esse uno alteroue anno legitimum ante tempus,
quo festinatis comitiis populus capiatur imparatus.
Quod si tale quid re uera agitetur, uos per me
admoniti consilio tali occurrere potestis ac
frustrari.

A. T. B.

AT enim si me in hac tam inconsulta iactabo
peruicacia, est metus ne nullo me honore
populus Romanus ornet. Res iniucunda illa
quidem, demoueri de re publica : honores uero

Parliament to have my share of doing good and resisting evil. It would therefore be absurd to renounce my objects in order to obtain my seat. I deceive myself indeed most grossly if I had not much rather pass the remainder of my life hidden in the recesses of the deepest obscurity, feeding my mind even with the visions and imaginations of such things, than to be placed on the most splendid throne in the universe, tantalized with a denial of the practice of all which can make the greatest situation any other than the greatest curse. Gentlemen, I have had my day. I can never sufficiently express my gratitude to you for having set me in a place wherein I could lend the slightest help to great and laudable designs. If by my vote I have aided in securing to families the best possession, peace; if I have joined in reconciling kings to their subjects and subjects to their prince; if I have thus taken part with the best of men in the best of their actions, I can shut the book. I might wish to read a page or two more; but this is enough for my measure,—I have not lived in vain.

[No. 447.]   *Burke.*

populi Romani quoniam ideo expetiui ut pro mea
parte honesti sim auctor obsistamque improbitati,
quid ineptius quam quo ad curiam facilius perueniam
ab institutis meis desciscere ? Atque adeo—nisi me
uehementer fallo—mallem multo, quidquid reli-
quum sit uitae, obscurissimo loco ignotus delite-
scere ut his consiliis perfruatur animus cogitando
dumtaxat et optando potius quam ad excellentem
aliquam in omni mundo dignitatis praestantiam
attolli, si tamen id unum uotis denegetur, ea colere
et persequi quibus detractis omnis honoris ampli-
ficatio nil nisi acerbiores uideatur adferre cruciatus.
Sed, Quirites, sentio iam me meas partes trans-
egisse. Vobis quam grato sim animo, qua tandem
oratione satis declarare possum, qui me eo
collocaueritis ubi ad magna et inlustria incepta
opis aliquantulum liceret conferre ? Quo in loco si,
quoad mea sententia proficere potui, ciuibus rei
salutarissimae fructum conseruaui, oti atque pacis,
si plebis senatusque animos abalienatos coniungere
studui et conciliare, si denique quas res uiri
honestissimi gesserunt honestissimas, earum ego
socius exstiti, conquiescere non grauabor. Op-
tauerim fortasse longius paullulo procurrere, sed
tamen mihi quidem, quantulocumque sum ingenio,
satis illud, quod non nequiquam uideor uixisse.

W. W.

Οἱ μὲν πολλοὶ τῶν ἐνθάδε εἰρηκότων ἤδη ἐπαινοῦσι τὸν προσθέντα τῷ νόμῳ τὸν λόγον τόνδε, ὡς καλὸν ἐπὶ τοῖς ἐκ τῶν πολέμων θαπτομένοις ἀγορεύεσθαι αὐτόν. ἐμοὶ δ' ἀρκοῦν ἂν ἐδόκει εἶναι ἀνδρῶν ἀγαθῶν ἔργῳ γενομένων ἔργῳ καὶ δηλοῦσθαι τὰς τιμάς, οἷα καὶ νῦν περὶ τὸν τάφον τόνδε δημοσίᾳ παρασκευασθέντα ὁρᾶτε, καὶ μὴ ἐν ἑνὶ ἀνδρὶ πολλῶν ἀρετὰς κινδυνεύεσθαι εὖ τε καὶ χεῖρον εἰπόντι πιστευθῆναι. χαλεπὸν γὰρ τὸ μετρίως εἰπεῖν ἐν ᾧ μόλις καὶ ἡ δόκησις τῆς ἀληθείας βεβαιοῦται. ὅ τε γὰρ ξυνειδὼς καὶ εὔνους ἀκροατὴς τάχ' ἂν τι ἐνδεεστέρως πρὸς ἃ βούλεταί τε καὶ ἐπίσταται νομίσειε δηλοῦσθαι, ὅ τε ἄπειρος ἔστιν ἃ καὶ πλεονάζεσθαι, διὰ φθόνον, εἴ τι ὑπὲρ τὴν ἑαυτοῦ φύσιν ἀκούοι. μέχρι γὰρ τοῦδε ἀνεκτοὶ οἱ ἔπαινοί εἰσι περὶ ἑτέρων λεγόμενοι, ἐς ὅσον ἂν καὶ αὐτὸς ἕκαστος οἴηται ἱκανὸς εἶναι δρᾶσαί τι ὧν ἤκουσεν· τῷ δ' ὑπερβάλλοντι αὐτῶν φθονοῦντες ἤδη καὶ ἀπιστοῦσιν. ἐπειδὴ δὲ τοῖς πάλαι οὕτως ἐδοκιμάσθη ταῦτα καλῶς ἔχειν, χρὴ καὶ ἐμὲ ἑπόμενον τῷ νόμῳ πειρᾶσθαι ὑμῶν τῆς ἑκάστου βουλήσεώς τε καὶ δόξης τυχεῖν ὡς ἐπὶ πλεῖστον.

Thucydides.

IN morem uenit ex hoc loco contionantibus ut eum uirum principio laudarent qui hanc orationem in legibus ascripsisset tamquam idoneam quae in sepeliendis iis qui in bello cecidissent haberetur. Mihimet uero ipsi satis uisum esset eorum qui rebus gestis laude meriti essent re etiam benefacta celebrari; quod quidem publico hoc funeris apparatu praestari uidetis; neque multorum uirtutes in uno aliquo ita periclitari ut perinde ut uel male uel bene orauisset iis quoque fides haberetur. Moderate enim dicere ei difficile est cui uel ueritatis opinio apud auditores uix secura praesto sit. Vsu uenire profecto potest ut qui rerum ipse conscius beneuolentia simul audiat, parcius declaratum aliquid existimet quam ipse et uelit et sciat: qui uero rei ignarus sit exaggerari credet propter inuidiam si quid supra naturam suam audiuerit. Eatenus enim laudes quae aliis tribuuntur tolerabiles uidentur quoad unus quisque se quoque aliquid eorum quae audiuerit facere posse existimet. Quidquid autem ex iis maius uidetur hoc profecto incredulus odisse solet. Quoniam uero maioribus nostris ita placuit, me etiam legi obsecutum operam dare oportet ut quam maxime potero uoluntati uestrae et opinioni satisfaciam.

E. C. W.

BUT again let me ask what are your hearts doing? These millions, 180 millions—for I cannot too often remind you that we have here to answer for about a fifth portion of the earth's inhabitants, men like yourselves—where are your hearts when your eyes fall on them, and see them at the foot of your armies and governed by your own sons, brothers, countrymen? Soldiers flow into the country and give up their lives in war to duty when it calls them, and even in peace to the more terrible demands of a climate which wears them out, and to disease, which occasionally breaks out in fierceness and cuts them off by tens and hundreds in a day. Civilians flow in also, eager for employment, until now the stream is checked because it is superabounding. Merchants and men of business add themselves to the gathering waters, peopling the Presidential towns and directing the whole course of trade, which in remote corners of the land feels everywhere their presiding influence. Barristers and solicitors succeed and reap from a litigious people harvests of gold, which after a few years of strenuous work, they carry back with them to their native soil, there in comfort and in rest to end their days. Engineers and artisans follow, making locomotion easy and distributing with swiftness and precision

SED iterum quaeram, ciues, quid paene frigidi agatis. Respicite illa milies octingenties hominum—nam non possum nimis saepe facere ut illud recordemini, uobis permissam esse quintam eorum partem qui orbem terrarum incolunt, homines uestri simillimos—quos cum oculis respexeritis, nonne animis quoque miseramini homines exercitibus uestris subiectos, filiis fratribus ciuibus denique dicto audientes? nam milites nostri prouinciam inundant, et cum in bello officium praeponunt uitae, tum per pacem ipsam tempestatem Marte atrociorem facile patiuntur, donec ea sunt confecti, et morbos qui saeuo impetu denos uel centenos in singulos dies nonnunquam opprimunt. Magistratus influxerunt homines impigerrimi quorum numerus, cum iam negotiis suppetant, minui est coeptus. His equites et negotiatores commiscentur, urbes praecipuas concelebrant, commerciorum cursum dirigunt, quorum societates loca uel remotissima amplectuntur. Aduocati deinceps et actores secuti auream metunt messem in populo litigioso, quam aliquot annis in maximis laboribus collocatis domum secum asportant, ubi otiosi et securi uitam reliquam degant. Machinatores postremo et opifices sunt, qui cum omnia uiis munitis plana fecerint, et ea quae tellus gignit cum celeritate dispertienda et

the produce which the land yields and the intelligence which interests all nations. We rule the land; upon the whole unselfishly and wisely. We restrain such evil as an honest love of right and truth can put down, by instruments far from perfect, but the best which the land furnishes.

[No. 444.]   *Bishop Douglas of Bombay.*

THESE are maxims so old and so trite, that no man cares to dwell on them, for fear of being told that he is repeating what he learned of his nurse. But they are not the less true for being trite; and when men suffer themselves to be hurried away by a set of new-fangled notions diametrically opposite, they cannot be repeated too often. If we persist in the other course, we must go on increasing our debt till the burden of our taxes becomes intolerable. That boasted constitution, which we are daily impairing, the people will estimate not by what it once has been, or is still asserted to be in the declamations against anarchy, but by its practical effects; and we shall hardly escape

diligentia curauerunt, et artificia quae gentes ex-
teras delectant. Nos autem ita Indis imperamus
ut sapientia plerumque usi nostras fere res non
spectemus; ea enim refrenamus mala quae ueri
rectique amor ingenuus reprimere potest, cuius
quidem rei adminicula si minus sunt absoluta,
optimis tamen utimur quae Indi nobis sufficiunt.

A. H. C.

AT haec tam trita, tam peruulgata sunt, ut
in iis nemo commorari uelit, ne puerorum
quaedam elementa decantare uideatur. Sed ita
trita sunt ut sint tamen uera; cum autem ad
nouas quasdam in re publica rationes, easque his
contrarias, rapiuntur homines, saepius iam dicta
dicenda tamen saepius sunt. Quod si cursum
iam institutum tenebimus, crescente aere alieno
tributorum oneri ferendo impar erit ciuitas. Illa
autem quam et laudamus et magis in dies labe-
factamus rem publicam, talem esse populus iudicabit qualem re ipsa se praestiterit, non ex eo
expendet qualis aut olim fuerit, aut hodie iis esse
uideatur qui in res turbulentas inuehunt: deinde
uereor ne in id ipsum incidamus a quo diligen-

the very extreme we are so anxiously desirous of shunning. The old government of France was surely provided with sufficient checks against the licentiousness of the people; but of what avail were those checks when the ambition and prodigality of the Government had exhausted every resource by which established govern- ments can be supported? Ministers attempt to fix upon others the charge of innovation, while they themselves are, every session, making greater innovations than that which they now call the most dreadful of all, namely, a reform in the representation in parliament. But it is the infatuation of the day that, while fixing all our attention upon France, we almost consider the very name of liberty as odious: nothing of the opposite tendency gives us the least alarm.

[No. 414.]

I THANK you for pointing to me. I really wished much to gain your attention in an early stage of the debate. I have been long very deeply, though perhaps ineffectually, engaged in the preliminary inquiries, which have continued without intermission, for some years. Though

tissime cauemus. Habebat sane Gallorum antiqua
res publica unde populari licentiae resisti posset :
ecquid tamen ista profuerunt cum omnia, quae
rei publicae quasi fundamenta sunt, proiecisset
luxuria principum et cupiditas ? At nostri quidem
principes aliis rei publicae imminuendae crimen
obiciunt; ipsi singulos in annos maius aliquid
in hoc ordine mutant quam illud quod omnium
nocentissimum esse uolunt, ut legibus de senatoribus creandis obrogetur. Sed ea hodie insania
est ut Gallos respicientibus libertatis paene nomen
inuisum sit, a seruitute plane securi simus.

S. H. B.

GRATIAS ago consuli, Patres Conscripti, quod
me praecipue sententiam rogauerit, qui de
hac re uel inter primos quae sentirem dicere
uehementer cuperem. Cum enim inquisitionibus iis
quae huius rogationis causa per plures annos iam
continuatae sunt, diligentiam egomet, si forte in-

x

I have felt with some degree of sensibility the natural and inevitable impressions of the several matters of fact, as they have been successively disclosed, I have not at any time attempted to trouble you on the merits of the subject; and very little on any of the points which incidentally arose in the course of our proceedings. But I should be sorry to be found totally silent upon this day. Our inquiries are now come to a final issue: it is now to be determined whether the three years of laborious parliamentary research, whether the twenty years of patient Indian suffer‐ing, are to produce a substantial reform in our eastern administration, or whether our knowledge of the grievances has abated our zeal for the correction of them, and our very inquiry into the evil was only a pretext to elude the remedy which is demanded from us by humanity, by justice and by every principle of true policy. Depend upon it this business cannot be indifferent to our fame. It will turn out a matter of great disgrace or great glory to the whole British nation. We are on a conspicuous stage and the world marks our demeanour.

Burke.

utilem, attentissimam certe per totum tempus im-
pendi, eorumque grauitatem quae deinceps pate-
facta sunt et necessario percepi et non leuiter tuli,
nulla tamen hora uestro commodo officere uolui ad
senatum de re ipsa referendo, perraro etiam de difficultatibus iis quae identidem in ipsa quaerendi
ratione nobis occurrebant. Hoc uero die, quo inquisitionibus uestris finis tandem impositus est,
omnino tacere noluerim. Iam enim aliquando eo
uentum est ut nobis decernendum sit utrum per
ea quae senatus iussu per triennium ingenti labore
inquisita sunt, quae per uiginti annorum spatium
in Sicilia crudeliter facta, patienter tolerata sunt,
id saltem boni tandem sit euenturum, ut sanctius
posthac et humanius prouinciae nostrae regantur,
an potius iniuriarum cognitio corrigendi uoluntatem
adeo abstulerit, ut uel ea causa mali inquisitionem
tulisse uideamur quo in longius traheremus correc-
tionem illam quam misericordia et fides et ciuilis
prudentia iam dudum postulant. Enimuero ne
ignoraueritis, Patres, non leuem aliquam rem
hodie agi sed eam ex qua pendet aut infamia aut
gloria totius populi Romani. Reputate enim nos
in aliquo orbis terrarum theatro uersari, et omnes
de nobis quomodo partes agamus iudicium esse
facturos.

E. C. W.

THE last cause of this disobedient spirit in the colonies is hardly less powerful than the rest, as it is not merely moral, but laid deep in the natural constitution of things. Three thousand miles of ocean lie between you and them. No contrivance can prevent the effect of this distance in weakening government. Seas roll, and months pass, between the order and the execution; and the want of a speedy explanation of a single point is enough to defeat a whole system. You have, indeed, winged ministers of vengeance, who carry your bolts in their pounces to the remotest verge of the sea. But there a power steps in that limits the arrogance of raging passions and furious elements, and says 'So far shalt thou go and no farther.' Who are you that should fret and rage, and bite the chains of nature? Nothing worse happens to you than does to all nations who have extensive empire; and it happens in all the forms into which empire can be thrown. In large bodies, the circulation of power must be less vigorous at the extremities. Nature has said it. The Turk cannot govern Egypt and Arabia and Kurdistan as he governs Thrace; nor has he the same dominion in Crimea and Algiers which he has at Brusa and Smyrna. Despotism itself is obliged to truck and huckster. The Sultan gets

NEC tantum propter insitam hominibus indolem hoc euenit ut parum obtemperantes
habcamus colonias, sed ipsa quoque natura causae
stetit et uoluntas deorum, interposita maris
immensitate, qua quominus hcbescat uis imperii
nullis artibus effici potest. Sub alio sidere im-
peratur, sub alio patrantur mandata: fluctus in
medio multorumque mensium nauigatio, sublataque
facultate dubitantem legatum edocendi tota fieri
potest ut ratio consiliorum et compages labefactetur.
At enim, sicut fulminis alitem ministrum Iuppiter,
sic nos in extremas terrarum oras naues longas
immittere possumus ultrices. Fateor. Sed est quod
obstet ultionis cupidis, est quo tenus ire detur, est
quod tumescentes animos compescat ac deleniat.
Fingite enim nobiscum loquentes deos. 'Vos,'
inquiunt, 'qui tandem estis qui recalcitretis
frenumque detrectetis quodque ratum est pati
nolitis? Nihil in uos durius constitutum est
quam in ceteros quicunque longinquis imperitarunt
gentibus: ratio autem imperandi nulla potest
excogitari quin huic condicioni sit obnoxia.' Non
uera loquentur? Non sic edixit natura ut et in
pedibus digitisque lentior quam in praecordiis
fluat sanguis, et prouecta in longinquum imperia
languescant? · Alia Persarum regis in Susa et
Ecbatana, alia in Cariam Cyprumque et Aegyptum

such obedience as he can. He governs with a loose rein, that he may govern at all, and the whole of the force and vigour of his authority in the centre is derived from a prudent relaxation in his borders. Spain in her provinces is perhaps not so well obeyed as you are in yours. She complies too, she submits, she watches times. This is the immutable condition, the eternal law of extensive and detached empires.

[No. 446.] *Burke.*

BUT who gave Robespierre the power of being a tyrant? And who were the instruments of his tyranny? The present virtuous constitution-mongers. He was a tyrant, they were his satellites and his hangmen. Their sole merit is in the murder of their colleagues. They have expiated their other murders by a new murder. It has always been the case among this banditti: they

dominatio fuit, nec eadem in Nili ripis quae ad Araxim auctoritas. Adeo ipsum, cuius omni lege soluta potestas est, cauponantem uidemus et obsequia licentiae pretio mercantem parcentemque, ne currus euertatur, habenis, et quicquid in ipso capite imperii uirium habet et auctoritatis, id non aliunde trahentem quam quod in longinquiora leniorem se prudens praebeat. Parthis quoque quis dixerit tam dociles parere populos, quibus imperant, quam uobis prouincias uestras ? Nempe dis se minores fatentur, indictam sibi legem accipiunt, tempora in imperando aucupantur opportuna : aeternum hoc et ineluctabile est, longinquis ac diuersis populis non aliter imperari posse.

W. R. H.

SED ipsam dominationem quisnam Antonio in manus tradidit ? Quis tandem adfuit dominationis administer ? Quis praeter praeclaros hos legum institores ? Esto ille quidem tyrannus, hi uero praesto aderant satellites et carnifices. Vnicam profecto laudem e collegis suis ducunt trucidatis, tot ciuium trucidationes noua trucidatione expiarunt. Nam quid apud huius modi

have always had the knife at each other's throats, after they had almost blunted it at the throat of every honest man. These people thought that in the commerce of murder, he was like to have the better of the bargain if any time was lost; they therefore took one of their short revolutionary methods, and massacred him in a manner so perfidious and cruel as would shock all humanity if the stroke was not struck by the present rulers on one of their associates. But this last act of infidelity and murder is to expiate all the rest, and to qualify them for the amity of a humane and virtuous sovereign and civilized people.

[No. 438.]   *Burke.*

MY Lords, I should be ashamed if at this moment I attempted to use any sort of rhetorical blandishments whatever. Such artifices would neither be suitable to the body that I represent, to the cause which I sustain, or to my own individual disposition upon such an occasion. My Lords, we know very well what these fallacious blandishments too frequently are. We know that they are used to captivate the

latrones usitatius quam sicas optimum quemque
iugulando iam retusas suis inuicem iugulis
intentare? Verebantur, credo, homines nefarii
ne in hoc caedium commercio eundem sibi ille,
modo tempus daretur, quaestum esset praerepturus;
itaque, prout solent rerum nouarum auctores, rem
transigebant, et socium adeo immani perfidia
obtruncauerunt, qua nemo non abhorreret, nisi ille
percussus, hi fuissent percussores. At enim, di
immortales, supremo hoc scelere nefandae caedis
satis iam cetera purgarunt facinora, satis dignos
scilicet se praebuerunt qui in m̄itissimi optimique
regis, et in ciuium humanissimorum societatem
atque amicitiam reciperentur.

G. H. R.

PVDERET me iudices, hoc praesertim tempore, lenocinium aliquod aut illecebras uerborum rationi meae adhibere: quod genus neque
ordini nostro neque huic causae neque meo
ingenio conuenire arbitror. Nempe haec oratoria
pigmenta quid saepissime uelint haud ignoramus.
Etenim scimus ea ad uoluntatem subselliorum
captandam animosque iudicum conciliandos non
erga causam sed erga hominem comparari. Scimus

benevolence of the court, and to conciliate the affections of the tribunal rather to the person than to the cause. We know that they are used to stifle the remonstrances of conscience in the judge and to reconcile it to the violation of his duty, and that thus all parties are induced to separate in a kind of good humour, as if they had nothing more than a verbal dispute to settle, or a slight quarrel over a table to compromise: while nations, whole suffering nations, are left to beat the empty air with cries of suffering and anguish, and to cast forth to an offended heaven the imprecations of disappointment and despair.

[*No.* 452.]

DRIVEN from the accusation upon the subject of pikes, and even from the very colour of accusation, and knowing that nothing was to be done without the proof of arms, we have got this miserable, solitary knife, held up to us as the engine which was to destroy the constitution of this country; and Mr. Groves, an Old Bailey solicitor, employed as a spy upon the occasion, has been selected to give probability to this monstrous absurdity by his respectable evidence. I understand that this same gentleman has carried

id agi ut per illa iudicis conscientia oppressa taceat
et officium ille uiolatum aequo animo ferat, quo
demum omnes perduci ut hilaritate quadam pleni
discedant quasi mera uerborum controuersia aut
rixa nescio qua inter pocula componenda. Attamen interea gentes nationesque oppressae auras
inanes luctu et querimoniis plangere, iratosque
deos uotis inultis et imprecationibus lacessere.

J. C.

AB hac igitur de pilis comparandis non dicam
accusatione, sed specie quoque accusationis
depulsi, cum nisi armorum indicio nihil sibi
profici intelligerent, unum hunc proferunt cultellum, rei publicae, si dis placet, et legum
omnium euersorem: testisque adhibetur Ven-
tidius nescio quis, furum patronus et sicariorum,
quo tum usi sunt exploratore, ut rem ómnium
futilissimam grauissimus scilicet auctor confirmet.
Quem eo usque in arte exploratoria progressum
accepi, ut ne tum quidem, postquam reus hic

his system of spying to such a pitch as to practise it since this unfortunate man has been standing a prisoner before you, professing himself as a friend to the committee preparing his defence, that he might discover to the Crown the materials by which he meant to defend his life. I state this only from report, and I hope in God I am mistaken; for human nature starts back appalled from such atrocity, and shrinks and trembles at the very statement of it. But as to the perjury of this miscreant, it will appear palpable beyond all question, and he shall answer for it in due season. He tells you he attended at Chalk Farm; and that there, forsooth, amongst about seven or eight thousand people he saw two or three persons with knives. He might, I should think, have seen many more, as hardly any man goes without a knife of some sort in his pocket. He asked, however, it seems, where they got these knives, and was directed to Green, a hairdresser, who deals besides in cutlery; and accordingly this notable Mr. Groves went (as he told us) to Green's, and asked to purchase a knife, when Green, ·in answer to him, said, 'Speak low, for my wife is a damned aristocrat.' This answer was sworn to by this wretch, to give you the idea that Green, who had the knives to sell, was

ante uos, iudices, adstitit, eam exercere destiterit,
sed defensionem parantibus amicum se eo consilio
professus sit ut quibus hic caput defensurus esset
rationibus consulibus deferret. Hoc ego auditum,
non compertum refero : quod di faxint ut falsum
sit : scelus enim tam immane uix ferre potest
hominum natura, sed uerbis tantum, non re ipsa
experta, obstupescit horrescitque. Hunc autem
peierasse meridiana luce clarius erit ; dabitque,
dabit, inquam, aliquando poenas. Ait se Gabiis
fuisse : ibi inter septem uel octo milia hominum,
duos tresue se uidisse qui sicas haberent. Potuit,
opinor, et plures uidere. Quotus quisque enim est,
quin cultellum qualemcunque sub ueste habeat ?
Sciscitanti uero, unde paratos eos haberent,
monstratam sibi Naeuii cuiusdam tonstrinam, qui
ferramenta quoque uenditaret. Eo cum uenisset
poposcissetque, qua erat astutia, cultellum—sic
enim narrabat—hunc in modum respondet Naeuius,
'Amabo te, submittas uocem : uxor enim,' inquit,
'quam di perduint, Sullanarum est partium.'
Haec ille homo nequissimus non dixit modo, sed
iure iurando quoque fulcire conatus est ; ideo
scilicet ut uos cultrorum illum uenditorem puta-
retis haud ignarum fuisse quantum in scelus
uenirent cultri, nec eos palam esse uendendos.

W. R. H.

conscious that he kept them for an illegal and
wicked purpose, and that they were not to be sold
in public.

    [No. 448.]   *Lord Erskine.*

I MUST not close my letter without giving you
one principal event of my history; which
was, that (in the course of my late tour) I set
out one morning before five o'clock, the moon
shining through a dark and misty autumnal air,
and got to the sea-coast time enough to be at
the sun's levee. I saw the clouds and dark
vapours open gradually to right and left, rolling
over one another in great smoky wreaths, and
the tide, as it flowed gently in upon the sands,
first whitening, then slightly tinged with gold
and blue; and all at once a little line of insuffer-
able brightness that (before I can write these
five words) was grown to half an orb, and now
to a whole one, too glorious to be distinctly
seen. It is very odd it makes no figure on
paper; yet I shall remember it as long as the
sun, or at least as long as I shall endure.
I wonder whether any body ever saw it before:
I hardly believe it.

    [No. 489.]   *T. Gray.*

NON dandae mihi literae prius quam res
quae mihi inter maximas uisa est, tibi
descripsero. Etenim proximo itinere, sub lucem
profectus, luna per nebulas et caligines, quales
autumno esse solent, perlucente, ad litoris oram
ita perueni ut inter apparitores solis exeuntis
essem. Nubes et uapores hinc et hinc discindi,
aliosque super alios ceu fumi circulos aduolui
uidebam; aestum autem in arenas leniter illa-
bentem primum albescere, mox aureo et caeruleo
colore incandescere. Deinde ex improuiso tenuis
uix tolerandi splendoris linea erumpere, quae
citius quam haec uerba scribere possum, in arcum,
mox in orbem creuit, ita lucidum ut intenta acie
intueri non possem. Rem tantam in scripto tam
pauxillam uideri satis miror, ipse enim memoria
tenebo, quamdiu aut sol lucebit, aut ego certe
uiuam. Alium quemquam mortalium speciem
tam praeclaram uidisse uix crediderim.

E. A.

SIR Clement tells me you will shortly come to town. We begin to want comfort in a few friends around us, while the winds whistle, and the waters roar. The sun gives a parting look, but 'tis but a cold one; we are ready to change those distant favours of a lofty beauty, for a gross material fire that warms and comforts more. I wish you could be here till your family come to town; you'll live more innocently, and kill fewer harmless creatures, nay none, except by your proper deputy, the butcher. It is fit for conscience' sake that you should come to town, and that the duchess should stay in the country, where no innocents of another species may suffer by her. I advise you to make man your game, hunt and beat about here for coxcombs, and truss up rogues in satire: I fancy they'll turn to a good account, if you can produce them fresh, or make them keep: and their relations will come and buy their bodies of you.

[F.C. No. 377.]

SCRIPSERAT mihi quem nosti eques, te Romam breui uenturum: quod lubentibus nobis accidet, amicorum, quot fuerint, societatem nunc desiderantibus, ubi, ut ait Flaccus noster,

Bruma niues Albanis illinit agris.

Sol quidem semel tamquam discessurus nos respicit, uerum frigidius: cui humilem et benigniorem foci ignem, ut nunc est, anteponimus, cum melius sit, quod aiunt, a turpiore amari quam a pulcherrima despici. Velim mecum sis, donec Romam tui etiam uenerint; innocentius enim uiues, nec tot innocua animalium corpora trucidabis, immo nulla nisi per lanium rectius tibi ad id suffectum. Ergo ad istam tuam uirtutem recuperandam, Romam uenias; maneat ruri Tullia tua, ne per illam etiam aliae, sed diuersi generis, insontes animae pereant. At tu nobiliorem expete praedam, me auctore; homines sectator; Nomentanum et Pantolabum excipe et agita; deinde occisos satira tamquam ueru fige et uersa; denique aut recentes pone, aut nigro sale conditos. Accedet inde et a Ioue aliquid fauoris, et a Sosiis: uenient enim, ut decet, in fratris funera fratres, ement libellum quo in stultos inuexeris, eorum simillimi.

E. D. A. M.

AS I ran through your volume of history with
great avidity and impatience, I cannot forbear discovering somewhat of the same impatience in returning you thanks for your agreeable present, and expressing the satisfaction
which the performance has given me. Whether
I consider the dignity of your style, the depth of
your matter, or the extensiveness of your learning,
I must regard the work as equally the object of
esteem ; and I own that if I had not previously
had the happiness of your personal acquaintance,
such a performance from an Englishman in our
age would have given me some surprise. You
may smile at this sentiment ; but as it seems to me
that your countrymen, for almost a whole generation, have given themselves up to barbarous and
absurd faction, and have totally neglected all polite
letters, I no longer expected any valuable pro-
duction to come from them. I know it will give
you pleasure, as it did me, to find that all the men
of letters in this place concur in their admiration
of your work, and in their anxious desire of your
continuing it.

Hume (to Gibbon).

CVM libros tuos historiarum acerrimo studio et mira legendi auiditate euoluerim, non possum quin nunc etiam eiusdem auiditatis non nihil prae me feram, dum pro acceptissimo isto munere gratias tibi refero, et quantum ex tuo opere uoluptatis perceperim demonstro. Siue enim orationis tuae grauitatem, siue rerum ipsarum maiestatem respicio, siue amplissimos istos doctrinarum thesauros, omnibus nominibus laudandum opus agnosco; atque idem confiteor me, nisi iam antea fortuna dedisset ut tua ipsius familiaritate uterer, admirationis aliquid suscepturum fuisse, quod ciuis uester, his praesertim temporibus, litteras tam praeclaras conscripsisset. Forsitan hoc sentiendo risum tibi commouerim; quod tamen mihi uidebantur ciues tui hos uiginti annos prope continuos inmanibus atque ineptis rei publicae contentionibus sese dedidisse, et studia humanitatis ac litterarum prorsus abiecisse, idcirco nihil eos sperabam posse utile in medium proferre. Illud autem certo scio tibi fore pergratum, quod mihi fuit, doctos urbis nostrae homines omnis uno consensu laudes maximas tuis libris tribuere et ut plura scribas cupidissimis uotis exoptare.

J. S. R.

Y 2

M Y DEAR RANDOLPH,—
I must confess it's rather hard on you that after your wholesale slaughter of wild lions (*sic*) in S. Africa, you should have made so little impression on your return upon the tame cats, I mean, of course, y^r constituents at Paddington. On the other hand (pardon a little brag) it's wonderful how popular I've lately become with the Tories. I wish you had heard my speech on the Local Government Bill for Ireland the other night in the House. 'Queen and Constitution,' 'the Emerald Isle,' 'the Union of hearts,' &c., &c. Rounds of applause followed my loyal sentiments. We're on the eve of a dissolution. The G. O. M. is, alas, as fresh as ever. Still I really felt a bit of the old love for him when he harangued the other night on 'Disestablishment of the Welsh and Scotch Churches,' 'One man one vote,' and 'Reconstruction of the House of Lords.' These were once *my* principles, you know.

Are they still? you will ask. Well, to tell you the truth, I hardly know myself.

Yours ever,
JOSEPH.

[No. 482.] *The Granta.*

FATEOR quidem hoc aduersae tuae fortunae fuisse, te, cum feriis Latinis feras plurimas sub sole Aethiope trucidauisses, apud fautores tuos in Carinis apricatos ita refrixisse, ut non feris sed inferis committendus uiderere. Contra, pace tua dixerim, κόμπος πάρεστι κοὐκ ἀπαρνοῦμαι τὸ μή: mirum, quanta gratia ipse apud bonos fiam. Nuper quidem te uehementer desiderabam, de Siculorum municipiis administrandis elocutus; perorantem me solita, scilicet deum Romulum dei filium, et καλλίκαρπον νῆσον, et Romanorum esse idem sentire de re publica, multiplici plausu exceperunt boni. Intra triduum ad suffragia discedendum est. Iam iste, quem nosti, impietate grauissimus, ὀγδωκονταέτης: sed uiridi et impigra senectute esse lacrimabundus fateor: quem nuper contionantem praeferuida ista, scilicet Deorum templa Dis, non aerario, curae esse debere, et tribus praerogatiuae religionem abolendam esse, et senatum fortius purgandum, ἑκών, ut prioris amicitiae memor, ἀέκοντί γε θυμῷ admiratus sum; quippe ista eadem olim ipse contionabar, et fortasse sentiebam. At, inquies, immutatone es animo? Immo in hoc haereo, et diludia postulo. Vale.

E. D. A. M.

HAD it pleased God to continue to me the hopes of succession, I should have been according to my mediocrity, and the mediocrity of the age I live in, a sort of founder of a family : I should have left a son, who, in all the points in which personal merit can be viewed, would not have shown himself inferior to the Duke, or to any of those whom he traces in his line. But a Disposer whose power we are little able to resist, and whose wisdom it behoves us not at all to dispute, has ordained it in another manner, and, whatever my querulous weakness might suggest, a far better. The storm has gone over me. I am stripped of all my honours, I am torn up by the roots, and lie prostrate on the earth ! There, and prostrate there, I most unfeignedly recognize the divine justice, and in some degree submit to it. But whilst I humble myself before God, I do not know that it is forbidden to repel the attacks of unjust and inconsiderate men. The patience of Job is proverbial. After some of the convulsive struggles of our irritable nature, he submitted himself, and repented in dust and ashes. But even so, I do not find him blamed for reprehending, and with a considerable degree of verbal asperity, those ill-natured neighbours of his, who visited his dunghill to read moral, political, and economical

QVOD si dis placuisset haeredis mihi spem confirmare, nouae gentis ut in hac nostra aequaliumque mediocritate, quasi conditor fuissem. Filius enim mihi superfuisset qui in nulla re, qua uirtus aestimatur, aut Consuli nostro aut maiorum cuiquam posthaberetur. Ille tamen rerum Dispensator, cuius nec potentiae obsisti potest, nec sapientiam oportet aspernari, omnia aliter et (quamuis aegre patiar) melius disposuit. Quippe uelut tempestate adorta honoribus exutus, radicitus euolsus, humi prouolutus iaceo, ubi procumbens iuste Deos egisse non sine patientia confiteor. Cum uero Dis me subiecerim, quid obstat quin homines iniquos atque importunos repellam? Quid? Iobus quam patiens fuerit quis ignorat? qui cum paullisper esset reluctatus (ut hominis est aduersa indignari) tandem in paeni-tentiam puluere deformatus se submisit. Nemo tamen quod sciam culpae obiecit, quod in malos illos et uehementius inueheretur, qui in fimo sordibusque iacentem de moribus, re publica, disciplina, longo sermone admonerent. Equidem haud minus desolatus nullum habeo quem hostibus opponam: et ni fallor, amice, in hac saeua tem-pestate ne mucidi quidem frumenti modio uelim

lectures on his misery.   I am alone.   I have none
to meet my enemies in the gate.   Indeed, my lord,
I greatly deceive myself if, in this hard season,
I would give a peck of refuse wheat for all that is
called fame and honour in the world.

[No. 455.]   *Burke.*

MY DEAR WILLIAM,—
      I have just received your kind mes-
sage and melancholy news.   Thank you for
thinking that I'm interested in what concerns
you, and sympathize in what gives you pleasure
or grief.   Well, I don't think there is much more
than this to-day : but I recall what you have said
in our many talks of your father, and remember
the affection and respect with which you always
regarded and spoke of him.   Who would wish
for more than honour, love, obedience, and a
tranquil end to old age ?   And so that generation
which engendered us passes away, and their place
knows them not ; and our turn comes when we
are to say good-bye to our joys, struggles, pains,
affections, and our young ones will grieve and be
consoled for us and so on.   We've lived as much
in forty as your good old father in his four score

omnia coimere, quicquid apud homines fama uel gloria nuncupetur.

A. S.

SCITO me, iucundissime amice, salutem mihi tuis uerbis missam accepisse, doloremque ex tam tristi nuntio subiisse. Scilicet illud mihi pergratum accidit quod reputas nihil tuarum rerum a me esse alienum, omniaque quae tibi uel oblectationem uel maerorem afferant, ad me quoque pertinere. Non equidem uideo quid hodie amplius a me tibi sit scribendum : uerum tamen ista quae in nostris plurimis de patre tuo sermonibus praedicasti recordor, meminique quantum eius amorem, quantam uenerationem et habueris semper et significaris. Quis tandem plura posset sibi optare quam magni aestimari, diligi, suspici, tum integra tranquillitate ad senectutem peruenire? Ad istud quidem exemplum illa quae nos produxit aetas hominum euanescit et in suis sedibus desideratur ; mox nobis quoque eadem erit sors ut gaudia certamina dolores amores missos facia-

years, don't you think so ?—and how awfully tired and lonely we are.   I picture to myself the placid face of the kind old father with all that trouble and doubt over—his life expiring with supreme blessings for you all—for you and Jane and un-conscious little Magdalene prattling and laughing at life's threshold; and know that you will be tenderly cheered and consoled by the good man's blessing for the three of you ; while yet but a minute, but yesterday, but all eternity ago, he was here loving and suffering.   I go on with the paper before me—I know there's nothing to say —but I assure you of my sympathy and that I am yours my dear old friend affectionately,

William Thackeray.

mus; dolebunt itidem uicem nostram minores natu, solaciolumque luctus consequentur; sic enim uiuitur. Nos autem annos quadraginta natos nonne arbitraris plura uiuendo expertos quam quae patri tuo optimo uiro contigerant, summam senectutem adepto? Quam nos taedet rerum, quot amicis destitutos! Equidem benignissimi tui patris mihi cogitatione faciem depingo, in qua nullum istius modi molestiarum, nullum ne dubitationis quidem uestigium supersit, cum animam agens omnibus suis esset fausta deos immortales comprecatus, et tibi et Piliae tuae dilectissimae, Atticulaeque uestrae tanti maeroris insciae, ipsoque in uitae aditu balbutienti ac ridenti. Quae cum considero, illud compertum habeo, tantam humanitatem uotorum ab optimo uiro trium carissimorum capitum causa conceptorum, uobis et gaudio fore et solacio. Vix unus dies, immo uix hora praeteriit, quae tamen quasi instar aeternitatis obtinet, ex quo ille inter os uersatus suam amoris suam laboris partem capiebat. Vides me tabulas manu tenentem scribere perseucrare, quamuis nihili sciam esse quod scribam; tamen uelim tibi persuadeas me et tui luctus participem esse et te uetustate mihi coniunctum facere uel plurimi.

J. S. R.

THE unhappy news I have just received from you equally surprises and afflicts me. I have lost a person I loved very much and have been used to from my infancy; but am much more concerned for your loss, the circumstances of which I forbear to dwell upon, as you must be too sensible of them yourself; and will, I fear, more and more need a consolation which no one can give except He who has preserved her to you so many years, and at last when it was His pleasure has taken her from us to Himself: and perhaps if we reflect upon what she felt in this life, we may look upon this as an instance of His goodness both to her, and to those that loved her. She might have languished many years before our eyes in a continual increase of pain and totally helpless; she might have long wished to end her misery without being able to attain it; or perhaps even lost all sense and yet continued to breathe: a sad spectacle to such as must have felt more for her than she could have done for herself. However you may deplore your own loss, yet think that she is at last easy and happy; and has now more occasion to pity us than we her. I hope and beg you will support yourself with that resignation we owe to Him, who gave us our being for our good, and who deprives us of it for the same

INOPINATVM aeque fuit et luctuosum quod mihi attulisti. Eam enim me amisisse nuntiabas quam ualde amaui et quae toti meae uitae coniunctissima fuerat. Verum magis doleo de tua ipsius calamitate; de qua tamen plura dicere nolim : quanta enim sit iam dudum nimio plus sentis et uereor ne magis in dies solationem eam requisitura sis quam nemo praestare potuerit nisi ille qui sororem tuam cum per tot annos tibi asseruauit, tum idem quando sibi uisum est ad se reuocauit. Quod profecto ipsum, si quae uiuendo passa sit in animo tenemus, haud scio an dei O. M. et erga ipsam et erga nos, qui eam amauimus, bonitatis indicio habere debeamus. Potuit enim per multos annos insanabilis morbi auctis perpetuo cruciatibus fracta in conspectu nostro ita languere ut et ipsa mortem tanquam dolorum finem nequiquam desideraret; uel sensu omni amisso uitam solam producere, quod spectaculum iis sane luctuosissimum fuisset qui magis eius causa quam sua ipsa dolerent. Quam igitur amisisti ita debes lugere ut non obliuiscaris illam otio tandem ac felicitate frui; cui profecto nostri iam misereri potius quam nobis illius iustum sit. Obsecro autem te ut te ipsam soleris, quod et facturam esse spero, res omnes dei O. M. uoluntati permittendo, qui beneuolentiae causa uitam unicuique

reason. I would have come to you directly, but
you do not say whether you desire I should or
not; if you do, I beg I may know it, for there is
nothing to hinder me, and I am in very good
health.

[F. C. 381.]   *T. Gray.*

EVEN your expostulations are pleasing to me;
for though they show you angry, yet they
are not without many expressions of your kindness; and therefore I am proud to be so chidden.
Yet I cannot so far abandon my own defence, as
to confess any idleness or forgetfulness on my
part. What has hindered me from writing to you
was neither ill-health nor a worse thing, ingratitude, but a flood of little businesses, which yet are
necessary to my subsistence, and of which I hoped
to have given you a good account before this time :
but the court rather speaks kindly of me than does
anything for me, though they promise largely ;
and perhaps they think I will advance as they go
backward, in which they will be much deceived ;
for I can never go an inch beyond my conscience
and my honour. If they will consider me as a man
who has done my best to improve the language

nostrum impertierit, et idem a nobis subtrahat.
Ad te continuo uenissem nisi ignorauissem an
uelles. Si uenire me cupis rescribes: nihil enim
est quod me impediat, et bene ualeo.

E. C. W.

ETIAM quod me culpas delector: quamquam
enim te sentio irasci, multa tamen dicis
in me beneuole atque amanter. Placet igitur ita
increpari. Non tamen ita mihi defuerim, ut aut
ignauum me fuisse confitear aut tui immemorem.
Quod enim nihil scripseram, neque ualetudo mea
in causa neque, quod peius, animus ingratus: sed
negotiorum multitudo, quae ut parua sunt ita ad
uiuendum necessaria. Et haec quidem maturius me
speraueram perfecturum; sed primores, permulta
polliciti, uerbis potius collaudant quam re adiuuant.
Qui si eo plus credunt me concessurum quo ipsi
sint tardiores, ualde falluntur; nihil enim ultra
quod uerum atque honestum est potero prouehi.
Si autem me id egisse fatebuntur ut sermonem
patrium et praesertim rem poeticam emendarem,
neque plus de me poscent quam ut omissa censura
quod in ciuitate geritur patiar, hoc et polliceri

and especially the poetry of my country, and will
be content with my acquiescence under the present
government, and forbearing satire on it, that I can
promise, because I can perform it; but I can
neither take the oaths nor forsake my religion. . . .
Truth is but one; and they who have once heard
of it can plead no excuse if they do not embrace
it.　But these are things too serious for a trifling
letter.

[No. 458.]　　　. .　　　　　　　*Pope.*

MY dear Walter,—I know that you are too
reasonable a man to expect anything like
punctuality of correspondence from a translator
of Homer, especially from one who is a doer
also of many other things at the same time; for
I labour hard not only to acquire a little fame
for myself, but to win it also for others, men of
whom I know nothing, not even their names, who
send me their poetry, that, by translating it out
of prose into verse, I may make it more like
poetry than it was.　Having heard all this, you
will feel yourself not only inclined to pardon my
long silence, but to pity me also for the cause
of it.　You may, if you please, believe likewise,

potero et perficere: sed neque iure iurando ob-
stringar neque nouos ritus accipiam. Quippe una
est ueritas: quam qui cognitam nolint amplecti,
non habent quod excusent. Sed grauiora illa
quam quae nugis epistulae conueniant.

A. S.

. .

SCIO equidem, mi Pomponi, non adeo te im-
probum esse ut scribendi diligentiam ab eo
requiras qui cum Homerum Latine uertam, tum
aliis permultis rebus simul intersim. Enitor enim
ut famae aliquantulum non mihi modo com-
parem, sed aliis etiam quorum omnia, et ipsa
quidem nomina ignota sunt, qui tamen ad me
uersiculos suos mittunt ut e soluta oratione in
numerum redacti poemata qualiacumque fiant.
Tu uero cum haec legeris, libenter et ueniam
tam diu tacenti, et si causam respexeris misericordiam adhibebis. Sic quoque tibi uelim persuadeas, posse me etiam intermissis epistolis
meorum esse memorem, nec pilo quidem minus

z

for it is true, that I have a faculty of remembering my friends even when I do not write to them, and of loving them not one jot the less, though I leave them to starve for want of a letter from me.   And now, I think, you have an apology both as to style, matter, and manner, altogether unexception-able.

   [No. 472.]   *W. Cowper.*

MY letter to-day, dear lady, must needs be a very short one, for the post goes in half an hour, and I've been occupied all day with my own business and other people's. At three o'clock, just as I was in full work, comes a letter from a protegée of my mother's, a certain Madame de B., informing me that she, Madame de B., had it in view to commit suicide immediately, unless she could be in some measure relieved (or releived, which is it?) from her present dif-ficulties.   So I have had to post off to this Madame de B., whom I expected to find starving, and instead met a woman a good deal fatter than the most full-fed person need be, and having just had a good dinner; but that didn't prevent her, the confounded old fiend, from abusing the woman

eos amare, etiamsi per me illi littcrarum fame conficiantur. Habes iam defensionem meam; cuius neque in orationis genere neque in re neque in uerbis quicquam, ut opinor, potest desiderari.

S. H. B.

PILIAE salutem dicit plurimam Cicero. Litterae quidem quas tibi hodie scribebam, non poterant quin essent breuissimae, cum intra horam tabellarius esset profecturus, ipse autem totum diem in negotiis cum meis tum alienis consumpsissem. Nona ferme hora, qua iam totus in studia mea incubueram, aduecta est epistula a femina nescio qua, nomine Caerellia, quam mea mater sustentare solita erat, se in animo habere mortem sua sibi manu extemplo consciscere, nisi aliqua ex parte auxilio meo ex aerumnis suis effugisset (an ecfugisset rectius dixerim?) Equidem necessitate coactus ad hanc Caerelliam confestim aduolo, ut qui fame laborantem essem uisurus, quam tamen plus aliquanto carnis habere cognoui quam par est quemuis uel amplissimo uictu saginatum;

who fed her and was good to her, from spoiling the half of a day's work for me, and taking me of a fool's errand. I was quite angry, instead of a corpse perhaps, to find a fat and voluble person who had no more idea of hanging herself to the bed post than you or I have.

W. M. Thackeray.

MR. SPECTATOR,—
The night before I left London I went to see a play called the Humorous Lieutenant. Upon the rising of the curtain I was very much surprised with the great concert of cat-calls which was exhibited that evening, and began to think with myself that I had made a mistake, and gone to a music meeting instead of the playhouse. It appeared indeed a little odd to me, to see so many persons of quality, of both sexes, assembled together at a kind of caterwauling; for I cannot look upon that performance to have been anything

etenim lautioribus epulis modo se ipsa acceperat. Quod quidem uetulam istam, quam pessimam pessime di perdant, minime prohibuit quo minus optimae feminae, quae cibum impertierat beneficiisque cumularat, contumeliosissime malediceret, operamque meam paene dimidii unius diei tolleret, cum me ineptiarum causa aduocasset. Plane eram iratus, qui opinione mea ad mortuam fortasse festinarim, pinguem eandemque loquacissimam inuenerim, cui non magis quam mihi aut ipsi tibi consilium erat in cubiculo suo collum in laqueum inserendi.

J. S. R.

PRIDIE quam ex urbe discessi, ueni uesperi in theatrum. Inducta est ibi togata, quae *miles cerebrosus* inscribitur. Demissis aulaeis statim miratus sum concinere undique pastoricias fistulas; ac uisus sum mihi propter errorem aliquem musicis pro mimis interesse. Tum in illo haerebam, quod uidebantur ad uagitum aliquem tot mundi auditores, cum uiri, tum etiam mulieres, confluxisse. Qui enim concinebant, sibi quidem (credo) placebant satis, mihi autem uisi sunt uagitum germanum edere. De · ea re certior tum fieri nequibam, propterea quod familiarium

better, whatever the musicians themselves might think of it. As I had no acquaintance in the house to ask questions of, and was forced to go out of town early the next morning, I could not learn the secret of this matter. What I would therefore desire of you, is, to give me some account of this strange instrument, which I found the company called a cat-call; and particularly to let me know whether it be a piece of music lately come from Italy. For my own part, to be free with you, I would rather hear an English fiddle : though I durst not show my dislike whilst I was in the playhouse, it being my chance to sit the very next man to one of the performers.

I am, Sir,
Your most affectionate friend and servant,
JOHN SHALLOW, Esq.

[No. 477.]   *Addison.*

I TRUST to the country and that easy indolence you say you enjoy there, to restore you your health and spirits ; and doubt not but, when the sun grows warm enough to tempt you from your fireside, you will (like all other things) be the better for his influence. He is my old friend, and an excellent nurse I assure you. Had it not been for

meorum nemo aderat, ex quo causas sciscitarer, debebam autem mane discedere. Velim igitur tu mihi rescribas, quid sit ὄργανον illud mirum, quod 'pastoriciam fistulam' appellant. Ac rogo primum, num musica sit nuper huc ab Italia aduecta. Pace enim tua, nostratium fides libentius audiuerim: quamquam in theatro tum dolorem meum dissimulaui timide, forte enim fistulatorum illorum unus a meo ipsius latere sedebat proximus. Multum te amamus.

F. D. M.

QVOD ruri es et otiosa ista tranquillitate perfrueris, id maxime confido et corporis et animi doloris medicinae fore. Sol uero si caluerit ut a foco te foras eliciat, apricationem illam persuasum habeo, cum ceteris fere rebus prodesse soleat, tibi certe profuturam. Nam nos quidem sole familiarissime utimur, et est sane in

him, life had often been to me intolerable. Pray
do not imagine that Tacitus, of all authors in the
world, can be tedious. An annalist, you know, is
by no means master of his subject ; and I think
one may venture to say that if those Pannonian
affairs are tedious in his hands, in another's they
would have been insupportable. However, fear
not, they will soon be over, and he will make
ample amends. A man who could join the
brilliant of wit and concise sententiousness
peculiar to that age, with the truth and gravity of
better times, and the deep reflection and good
sense of the best moderns, cannot choose but
have something to strike you. Yet what I admire
in him above all, is his detestation of tyranny,
and the high spirit of liberty that every now and
then breaks out whether he would or no.

Thomas Gray.

YOUR entertaining and pleasant letter, re-
sembling in that respect all that I receive
from you, deserved a more expeditious answer ;
and should have had what it so well deserved,

refouenda ualitudine saluberrimus; quo si caren-
dum fuisset, saepius iam uitae pertaesum esset.
Sed heus tu qui Tacitum, quem minime decebat,
in scribendo molestum esse credis. An fugit te
annalium scriptorem minime suo arbitrio quae
scribat eligere? Illas uero res Pannonicas, si ab
ipso parum commendantur, bona uenia dixerim ab
alio scriptas omnino non fuisse ferendas. Verum
erige te, peractis enim his molestiis breui tibi
cumulate satisfaciet. Nempe in quo uno exstite-
rint non solum quae in illa potissimum aetate
enitebant, sales, argutiae, pressa quaedam dicendi
subtilitas, sed fidei quoque et grauitatis quantum
mutati in melius mores adhibuerint: cum idem
sapientia et iudicio tantum ualeat quantum pauci uel
eorum qui hodie scribunt, nonne hunc admiratione
aliqua esse dignum confitendum est? Mihi uero
cum plurima in illo uiro placent, tum in primis
saeua illa in tyrannos indignatio, et uindex libertatis
animus qui inuito ipso aliquando tamen erumpit.

H. C. G.

TAM lepidae tamque iucundae fuerunt litterae
tuae, quam solent omnes esse quas a te
accipio. Ad eas debebam rescribere citius; et
quod debebam fecissem, nisi ad me tum perue-

had it not reached me at a time when, deeply in debt to all my correspondents, I had letters to write without number. Like 'autumnal leaves that strew the brooks in Vallombrosa,' the unanswered farrago lay before me. If I quote at all, you must expect me henceforth to quote none but Milton, since for a long time to come I shall be occupied with him only.

I was much pleased with the extract you gave me from your sister Eliza's letter; she writes very elegantly, and (if I might say it without seeming to flatter you) I should say much in the manner of her brother. I rejoice that you are so well with the learned Bishop of Sarum, and well remember how he ferreted the vermin Lauder out of all his hidings, when I was a boy at Westminster.

What letter of the 10th of December is that which you say you have not yet answered? Consider, it is April now, and I never remember anything that I write half so long. But perhaps it relates to Calchas, for I do remember that you have not yet furnished me with the secret history of him and his family, which I demanded from you.

Adieu, Yours most sincerely,

W. COWPER.

WESTON, *April* 8.

[No. 478.]

nissent, cum, quasi rationem repetentibus omnibus qui dederant ad me litteras, scribendae mihi essent epistolae innumerae. Iacebant tabellae passim acceptae ac neglectae—

    quam multa in siluis autumni frigore primo
    lapsa cadunt folia, et Tusco glomerantur in amni.

Iam posthac exspectare debes ut aut nullos omnino poetas aut Vergilium unum laudem, in illo enim diu totus ero.

Periucunda mihi fuerunt quae e sororis tuae epistola descripsisti. Est enim in scribendo per-elegans, ac paene dixeram tui similis. Sed cauen-dum est ne adulari uidear. Gaudeo te apud pontificem uirum doctissimum in gratia tanta esse. Ab eo, cum Athenis puer essem, memini beluam illam Lauderium e latebris suis omnibus pulcre exagitari.

Quas, quaeso, me ad te litteras a. d. iv Id. Dec. dedisse scribis, te uero iis nondum respondisse? Mensis enim Aprilis nunc est, et soleo omnium quae scribo multo breuiore tempore obliuisci. Nisi forte de Calchante epistola ea erat. Suc-currit enim me a te postulasse, ut et ipsius et familiae eius secreta omnia narrares, quam tu mihi narrationem non misisti. Vale. Dabam Baiis a. d. vi Id. Apriles.

F. D. M.

MOST sorry I am (as God knows) that being thus surprised by death, I can leave you no better estate.   God is my witness, I meant you all my office of wines, or that I could have purchased by selling it ; half my stuff, and all my jewels, but some one for the boy; but God hath prevented all my resolutions, even that great God that worketh all in all : but if you live free from want, care for no more, for the rest is but vanity; love God, and begin betimes to repose your trust in Him ; therein shall you find true and lasting riches, and endless comfort.   For the rest, when you have travailed and wearied your thoughts over all sorts of worldly cogitation, you shall but sit down by sorrow in the end. . . . Remember your poor child for his father's sake, who chose you and loved you in his happiest time.   Get those letters (if it be possible), which I writ to the lords, wherein I sued for my life.   God is my witness, it was for you and your's that I desired life; but it is true that I disdain myself for begging it, for know (dear wife) that your son is the son of a true man, and one who in his own respect despiseth death, and all his misshapen and ugly forms. I cannot write much, God He knoweth how hardly I steal this time while others sleep ; and it is also high time that I should separate my thoughts

ID mehercule maxime dolco, quod morte praeuentus rem tibi ita imminutam relinquo; tibi enim cellam uinariam omnem, uel quantum uendenda comparare possem, et instrumenti dimidium, omnesque gemmas destinaueram, una aliqua excepta quam seposueram puero; quae omnia ne facerem Deus impediuit Optimus Maximus, cuius omnium rerum perficiendarum arbitrium est. Tu si non egebis, noli quod superest curare, cetera enim profecto inania sunt. Deum ama, huic incipe mature confidere, in quo uerae aeternaeque diuitiae ac sine fine solacium. Quid enim? cum laboraueris teque in omni rerum cogitatione fatigaueris, tamen ad finem tibi cura adsidebit. . . . Memento pueri patris causa, qui te in rebus meis felicissimis duxi uxorem et amaui. Epistolae quibus mortem deprecatus sum cura, si potes, ut tibi a iudicibus reddantur. Deos testor me tui quidem ac tuorum causa cupiisse uitam, tamen me ipse contemno qui ad preces descenderim; scis enim, uxor carissima, scis profecto filii tui patrem esse uirum, qui mortem, quotquot turpes informesque induerit species, ipse contemnat. Plura scribere nequeo; hoc tantulum mehercule temporis aegre, aliis dormientibus, subripio ; tempusque erat me ab huius modi rerum cogitatione absistere. Corpus meum, quod uiuum

from the world. Beg my dead body, which living was denied thee, and either lay it at Sherborne (if the land continue), or in Exeter church by my father and mother; I can say no more, time and death call me away.

[No. 479.]   *Sir W. Raleigh.*

I HAVE already given my landlady orders for an entire reform in the state of my finances. I declaim against hot suppers, drink less sugar in my tea, and check my grate with brick-bats. Instead of hanging my room with pictures I intend to adorn it with maxims of frugality. These will make pretty furniture enough, and wont be a bit too expensive ; for I shall draw them all out with my own hands, and my landlady's daughter shall frame them with the parings of my black waistcoat. Each maxim is to be inscribed on a sheet of clear paper, and wrote with my best pen ; of which the following will serve as a specimen. 'Look sharp ;' 'Mind the main chance ;' 'Money is money now ;' 'If you have a thousand pound, you can put your hands by your sides and say you are worth a thousand pounds every day of the year;' 'Take a farthing from an hundred

tibi dare denegarant, cura ut reddant; redditum uel Sherborniae sepeliri uolo, si agri nostri incolumes fuerint, uel iuxta parentes in ecclesia Exoniensi. Plura dicerem, nisi mors me et tempus auocarent.

H. N.

IAM ut res nostra summa parsimonia administretur, cum illa apud quam cenaculo locato commoror, uehementer egi : scilicet, quas olim amabam, cenas seras idem ego deuoueo, et calida porci tomacula iam iterum ignibus, sed Tartareis, imponenda reor; nec iam Hymettia Falerno mella diluo, nec focum ipsum, nisi lateribus coctilibus interpositis contractum, accendo. Absint etiam cenaculo nostro, quae ceteris placent, pictae tabulae ; sententiis parsimoniae congruentibus parietem potius ornare uolo, munda scilicet supellectile et uili; equidem propriis manibus praecepta describam, quae ne limbo careant, filiola hospitae comminutis togulae atrae nostrae laciniis quadrando decorabit; charta etiam pura eluceat una quaeque sententia, stylorum, quos habeo, optimo descripta : scilicet huius modi praecepta, ut XII Tabulae, dum tacent, clamant.

pound, and it will be an hundred pound no longer.'
Thus, whichever way I turn my eyes, they are sure
to meet one of those friendly monitors ; and as we
are told of an actor who hung his room round with
looking-glasses to correct the defects of his person,
my apartment shall be furnished in a peculiar
manner to correct the errors of my mind.

[No. 485.] *Goldsmith.*

THOUGH there is no use in writing because
there is no post, but *que voulez-vous,
Madame ? On aime à dire un petit bonjour à ses
amis.* I feel almost used to the place already
and begin to be interested about the politics. Some
say there's a revolution ready for to-day. The
town is crammed with soldiers, and one has
a curious feeling of interest and excitement, as in

Quam admirandum illud 'hoc age'; quam Horatio digna illa, 'quocunque modo rem,' et 'O ciues, ciues, quaerenda pecunia primum est ': quin illud recentioris cuiusdam addiderim

'Quadringenta tenes? i, totam ostende per urbem;
  En, quod habes, omni fit noua summa die.'

Denique sapientissimi hoc inscribetur

'Parce tuis nummis : minuas quos asse uel uno,
  Pauper eris, uictus ratione ruentis acerui.'

Quoquo igitur oculos conuertero, correctorem beneuolum intuebor : immo ad exemplum Roscii, qui speculis per cameram dispositis ne se agrestius in scena traduceret studebat, ipse paries mihi mirifice indolis nostrae erroribus et culpis corrigendis inseruiet.

E. D. A. M.

QVAMQVAM non opus erat litteris, quia tabellarios nullos habebam, tamen τί σοὶ διαφέρει, ὦ γύναι; οὐ γὰρ ἅπαντες φιλοῦσιν ὅμως τοὺς φίλους ἀσπάζεσθαι. Equidem hic me hospitem uix iam sentio ; immo res huius populi curae mihi coeperunt esse. Sunt quidem qui opinentur hic hodie orbem rei publicae se conuersurum. Vrbs certe militibus est referta ; et nobis animus est

walking about on ice which is rather dangerous, and may tumble in at any moment. I had three newspapers for my breakfast, which my man (it is rather grand having a *laquais de place*, but I can't do without him and invent all sorts of pretexts to employ him) bought for five pence of your money. The mild papers say we have escaped a great danger, a formidable plot has been crushed, and Paris would have been on fire and fury but for the timely discovery. The Red Republicans say, 'Plot! no such thing, the infernal tyrants at the head of affairs wish to find a pretext for perse-cuting patriots, and the good and the brave are shut up in dungeons.' Plot or no plot, which is it? I think I prefer to believe there has been a direful conspiracy, and that we have escaped a tremendous danger. It makes one feel brave somehow, and as if one had some merit in over-throwing this rascally conspiracy.

W. M. Thackeray.

nescio quo modo intentus et commotus, quasi non
nullo cum periculo in tenui glacie ambulemus,
quae forsitan improuiso sub pedibus corruerit.
Ecce me prandente tres rerum in urbe actarum
nuntii, quos mihi tribus quadrantibus (ut uos istic
appellatis) procurator meus conciliauerat. Videsne
me lautius agere, qui procuratore utar? Quo
quidem carere plane non queo, ideoque ne cesset
semper aliquid negoti comminiscor. Qui mitiora
de re publica censent, nos ingentem quandam
procellam effugisse uolunt; seditionem uidelicet
horrendam reuictam; urbem in eo fuisse ut in-
cendiis atque insaniis periret, nisi indicia essent
opportune facta. Contra ea ardentiores e popularibus clamant nihil coniurationis factum, tyran-
norum esse sceleratissimorum, quos penes summa
rerum sit, optimum quemque quouis crimine
perdere; idcirco egregios ciuis et fortis uiros in
carcerem compegisse. Vtrum igitur horum uerum
dicam? Coniurassene aliquos an neminem omnino?
Videor mihi malle credere nefarios homines
sceleris causa coisse, nosque ex immani quadam
flamma euolasse. Haec enim opinio mihi uirtutis
conscientiam facit, tamquam mea sit aliqua laus,
quod pessimorum hominum consilia sint refutata.

J. S. R.

A a 2

NOTHING else (but ill health) should have detained me so long at Paris, a place which in cold weather I think excessively disagreeable and peculiarly unwholesome. In fine weather, when a stranger can visit the various works of art which the tempest has assembled here from every quarter of the globe, it is highly interesting ; and it is encircled by so many delightful gardens, that one may pass the summer here without feeling one's absence from the country.   Yet I have never seen a spot where I should more grieve at fixing my residence, nor a nation with which I should find it so difficult to coalesce.   A revolution does not seem to be favourable to the morals of a people. In the upper classes I have seen nothing but the most ardent pursuit after sensual or frivolous pleasures, and the most unqualified egotism, with a devotion to the shrines of luxury and vanity unknown at any former period.   The lower ranks are chiefly marked by a total want of probity, and an earnestness for the gain of to-day, though purchased by the sacrifice of that character which might ensure them ten-fold advantage on the morrow.   You must not think me infected with national prejudice.   I speak from the narrow circle of my own observation and that of my friends, and I do not include the suffering parts

NIHIL aliud nisi languor Lutetiae me retinere poterat, in loco frigoribus, ut mihi uidetur, mirum quam inamoeno et insaluberrimo. Nam aprico tempore aduenae, dum artes inuisunt plurimas quas huc ex omni parte orbis ἅρπυιαι ἀνηρείψαντο, multum se oblectare possunt: circumiecti etiam horti plurimi florentissimi ubi ita degere aestatem possis ut rus non desideres. Sed nunquam nec locum uidi ubi sedem habere minus uelim, nec populum quocum difficilius meus coalescat animus. Res profecto nouae moribus eorum qui passi sunt, non uidentur prodesse. Nam apud optimates uoluptarios solos atque ineptos comperi, eosque ardentissimos, qui se tantum diligunt, luxum et iactantiam uenerati tanquam deos sicut nunquam antea: in plebe autem probitas nulla, ut summatim dicam, lucri hodierni summum studium, etsi decemplex cras commodum moribus ita corruptis omittunt. Sed ne me odio gentili infectam haec loqui putaueris: dicebam sane de iis quae et ego et amici animaduerteramus in gyrum exiguum inclusi; mittebam de parte populi laboranti, quae alia inter se societate quam nostra coniuncta exteris minime utitur. Napoleonem et uxorem salutatum ieram: lautissimus apparatus, splendor summus. Ipse est habitu optimo, uultu parum blando.

A. H. C.

of the nation, who have little intercourse with strangers, and who form a society apart. I have been presented to Bonaparte and his wife, who receive with great state, ceremony, and magnificence. His manner is very good, but the expression of his countenance is not attractive.

[No. 480.]   *Mrs. R. Trench.*

I KNOW that the ears of modern verse-writers are delicate to an excess, and their readers are troubled with the same squeamishness as themselves. So that if a line do not run as smooth as quicksilver they are offended. A critic of the present day serves a poem as a cook does a dead turkey, when she fastens the legs of it to a post and draws out all the sinews. For this we may thank Pope; but unless we could imitate him in the closeness and compactness of his expression, as well as in the smoothness of his numbers, we had better drop the imitation, which serves no other purpose than to emasculate and weaken all we write. Give me a manly rough line, with a deal of meaning in it, rather than a whole poem full of musical periods, that have nothing but their oily smoothness to recommend them.

NOVI equidem quam teretes, quam religiosae
poetarum nostrorum sint aures; noui lectores eodem fastidio adeo affectos esse ut uno
quolibet uersu, nisi olei ipsius cursu ac mollitia
profluat, offendantur. Nempe censores hodie ita
tractant poema ut pauonem coqui, cuius cruri-
bus ad palum adligatis neruos omnes euellunt.
Quod cum Papae acceptum sit referendum, tum
nisi eundem non leuitate tantum numerorum sed
pressa etiam uerborum concinnitate imitari possumus, satius est ab exemplo desciscere, quippe
eo modo spectanti ut eneruata et exsanguia reddat
quae scribimus. Malo hercle equidem uersum
unum horridum, uirilem, sententiosum, quam
poema totum iis conclusionibus refertum, quae
canorae sunt illae quidem, sed sola laudabiles
leuitate.

I have said thus much, as I hinted in the beginning, because I have just finished a much longer poem than the last; which our common friend will receive by the same messenger that has the charge of this letter. In that poem there are many lines which an ear so nice as the gentleman's who made the above-mentioned alteration would undoubtedly condemn; and yet (if I may be permitted to say it) they cannot be made smoother without being the worse for it. There is a roughness on a plum, which nobody that understands fruit would rub off, though the plum would be much more polished without it.

[No. 481.]　　　　　　　　　　　　*Cowper.*

Haec scribebam, quod antea significaueram, qui iam longius postremo et modo perfectum carmen eidem tabellario, cui has litteras, ad amicum illum nostrum tradidissem. Nam insunt ibi uersus non nulli quos homo ea iudicii subtilitate ut istud emendarit uitium, sine dubio sit correcturus; qui tamen (ut ne quid molesti dicam) leuiores fieri non possunt quin detrimentum capiant. Ita pruno asperitas quaedam inest, qua certe carens leuius fiat et politius; quam tamen imperiti est abstergere.

M. J. R.

TERCENTENARY

OF

TRINITY COLLEGE, DUBLIN

Vniversitas Dvblinensis
Vniversitati Glasgvensi
S. P. D.

TRIBVS iustis saeculis iam feliciter peractis, postquam hoc Collegium Sacrosanctae et Indiuiduae Trinitatis iuxta Dublinum a regina Elizabetha conditum est, occasionem tam laetam festo ritu celebrare constituimus, atque Vniuersitates orbis terrarum nobilissimas in partem gaudii nostri uocare. Idcirco uos, quos longis maris et uiarum spatiis diuisos uinculum tamen studiorum communium nobis arcte adnectit, pro humanitate uestra impense rogamus ut duos doctos uiros ex uestro illustri coetu adlegetis, quos hospitio libenter accipiamus per dies festos quos indiximus in

quintum usque ad octauum Iulii, MDCCCXCII : oramusque ut certiores nos faciatis quos adlegaueritis.

DABAMVS DVBLINI, *die 7ᵐᵒ Nouembris*, MDCCCXCI.

Scribendo adfuerunt,

ROSSE,
Cancellarius Vniuersitatis Dublinensis.

GEORGIUS SALMON,
*Praepositus Collegii SS. Trinitatis
Dublinensis.*

VNIVERSITATI SACROSANCTAE ET INDIVIDVAE

TRINITATIS IVXTA DVBLINVM

CANCELLARIVS MAGISTRI AC SCHOLARES

VNIVERSITATIS OXONIENSIS

S. P. D.

GRATVLAMVR ex animo uobis Ferias Triseculares hodie concelebrantibus, praesertim cum tanti temporis decursus neque senectutem uestrae Societati neque ueternum neque roboris defectum attulerit, sed contra nouam uirium accessionem et laudabilem doctrinae profectum.

Nos quoque Oxonienses, quibus uobiscum amicissima semper fuit necessitudo ac familiaritas, praesentis laetitiae partem haud paruam capes-

simus, tam honorabilem uirorum insignium con-
cursum uehementer admirati, qui ab omni fere
orbis terrarum regione adsunt, ut debito honore
Vniuersitatem uestram prosequantur.

Quod si longissime liceat respicere et Societatis
uestrae primordia in memoriam reducere, habetis
etiam tunc amicitiae nostrae quasi praerogatiuam ;
si modo fide sit dignum ab eruditissimo uiro Ioanne
Case, amplius CCC abhinc annis, editum esse
Oxonii libellum, noui typographei primitias, in quo
potentissimos rei publicae principes affatus
'feracissima Hibernorum ingenia' extollit ; illud
modo conquestus, 'quod in tam beato solo nullum
Musarum Collegium, nullum philosophiae semina-
rium floreat.' Pergratum est nobis reputantibus
optabile illud consilium, quod tecte innuerat nostrae
Vniuersitatis alumnus, summa munificentia con-
fecisse Elizabetham reginam, cuius singularem
famam in bellando, inperando, doctrinam pro-
mouendo nulla fere regio, nulla nesciat aetas.
Verum enim uero inter tantam hospitum alum-
norumque frequentiam, approbante etiam omnium
uoluntate, superuacaneum uidetur uestrae domus
felicem fortunam fusius referre, quot quantisque
difficultatibus debellatis quam celso se in fastigio
stabiliuerit, quantam in omnibus humanitatis ac
litterarum studiis consecuta sit laudem. Neque

tamen omnino praeterire fas est summorum uirorum nomina quorum ope tam clara lux uestrae Societati affulserit.   Quis enim est qui ignoret Adami Lofti miram   sagacitatem,   aut   Platonicam   Berkeleii subtilitatem ac uim dialecticam?   Cui non nota est Burkii sublimis eloquentia, omnibus numeris absoluta ; aut Congreuii palliatae ; aut benigna Goldsmithii uena ; aut strictus ensis quo secuerit urbem Lucilius alter,

primores populi arripiens populumque tributim?

Adest etiam hodie et ipsis ordinibus uestris tam praeclara alumnorum cohors, theologiae, philo‑ sophiae, scientiae, uniuersis denique litterarum studiis tanto opere pollens, ut non tam ueteri famae quasi incumbere sed optimam spem successus posteritati spondere uideamini.

Quod ut feliciter uortat Vniuersitati uestrae orat obsecratque Academia Oxoniensis.

Datum in domo nostra Conuocationis die septimo mensis Iunii, A. S. MDCCCXCII.

W. W. M.

VNIVERSITAS CANTABRIGIENSIS

VNIVERSITATI DVBLINENSI

S. P. D.

REM nobis periucundam fecistis, uiri doctissimi, quod Vniuersitatis uestrae ludos saeculares

celebraturi, etiam nostram Vniuersitatem gaudii uestri in partem uocare uoluistis. Vt enim cum omnibus doctrinae domiciliis studiorum communium consuetudine sumus consociati, ita uobiscum praesertim eo artiore uinculo sumus coniuncti, quod Vniuersitas illa uestra, quae nunc certe Professorum suorum in ordine tot alumnos suos uaria et multiplici doctrina insignes numerat, tribus abhinc saeculis nostro potissimum e coetu quinque deinceps Praesides eligere dignata est.

Eo libentius igitur uestrae uoluntati obsecuti, e Senatu nostro legatos quattuor delegimus, proximo (ut speramus) in anno uestrum omnium laetitiae non modo testes sed etiam participes futuros. Iuuat legatorum nostrorum nomina ipsa apponere. Ergo primus erit Vniuersitatis nostrae Procancellarius, IOANNES PEILE, Litterarum Doctor, Christi Collegio praepositus; deinde Collegii Sacrosanctae et Indiuiduae Trinitatis Magister, HENRICUS MONTAGU BUTLER, Sacrae Theologiae Professor; deinceps Iuris et Scientiarum Doctor, GEORGIUS GABRIEL STOKES, Baronettus, Scientiae Mathematicae Professor Lucasianus, Collegii Pembrochiani Socius, Vniuersitatis nostrae in nomine Senatui Britannico adscriptus; denique Medicinae Doctor, ALEXANDER MACALISTER, Collegii Diui Ioannis Socius, Anatomiae Professor.

Habetis nomina uirorum et litterarum humaniorum et scientiae non unius amore insignium ;
quos eo benignius sine dubio accipietis, quod uni
ex iis, quondam a uobis honoris causa Iuris
Doctori nominato, ipsa Hibernia patria natalis fuit;
quod alter a Caledonia Hiberniae donatus, a uobis
deinceps. auspiciis optimis Britanniae redditus
est; quod e Collegiorum denique Praefectis uterque
Angliam ipsam patriam esse profitetur, quae
imperii Britannici partem eximiam insulam illam
esse gloriatur, ubi uestra Vniuersitas trium
saeculorum per uices arx et asylum doctrinae, et
libertatis legibus temperatae propugnaculum exstitit.   Valete.

J. E. S.

Datvm Cantabrigiae,
Die xvii° *Decembris,*
A. S. M.DCCC.XCI.

Vniversitas Cantabrigiensis

Vniversitati Dvblinensi

S. P. D.

QVOD uobis, uiri doctissimi, auspiciis optimis
illo die sumus ominati, quo primum nobis
ferias uestras saeculares indixistis, idem hodie
feliciter euenisse uehementer laetamur.   Namque

uestrae Vniuersitatis uocem trans maria lata uocantis plurimae doctrinae sedes procul audi-uerunt, auditae libenter obsecutae sunt. Nostra uero Academia, necessitudinis uinculo artissimo uobiscum olim consociata, per legatos suos uelut ipsa ludis uestris interesse uidebitur; uestra per atria spatiari; uestra templa uenerari; uestras aulas, siue litterarum studiis siue hospitii ob-lectamentis uariis dedicatas, ingredi; uestram eloquentiam admirari; uestro in theatro fabulas lepidas spectare; uestros denique inter hortos, factionum a clamoribus dissonis remotos, quasi inter ipsas Musarum sedes uagari, quasi ipsos Hesperidum susurros audire, ipsi Hesperiae omnia fausta precari.

Quod ad uestram autem Academiam attinet, nihil hodie auspicatius arbitramur, quam doctrinae sedi tam insigni annos iam trecentos feliciter exactos gratulari, atque etiam in posterum per saecula plurima fortunam in dies feliciorem ex-optare. Valete.

J. E. S.

Datvm Cantabrigiae,
Mensis Iunii die xxi°,
A.S. M.DCCC.XCII.

Viris amplissimis ornatissimis
Cancellario Doctoribvs Magistris
totiqve Vniversitati Dvblinensi
S. P. D.
Senatvs Vniversitatis Glasgvensis

GRATVLAMVR uobis animis libentissimis quod tribus uitae academicae felicissime peractis saeculis, has ferias hodie celebrare uoluistis, celebrantibusque bona omnia et fausta et felicia precamur.

Non leuis enim gloriandi uobis, nobis autem gratulandi, causa adest, quod per tot saecula, per tot tantasque rei publicae iactationes, apud populum cuius is ardor animi est ut nullas laudes non attigerit, in nullos non eruperit furores, per Collegium uestrum illustrissimum sacrosanctae et indiuiduae Trinitatis toti orbi patefactum est terrarum quid in litteris posset tenue illud atque exquisitum ingenium Hibernorum, quid in scientia, quid in omnibus denique colendis artibus quibus nostra haec humanitas ornari possit.

Quod propositum a maioribus exemplum uos ipsi, qui nunc estis, diligentissime secuti, artes omnes atque ingenia cum tanto laborum fructu excoluistis, ut hodie iactare liceat taedam uos illam scientiae doctrinaeque quam lucentem a parentibus accepistis, ardentem atque adeo flagrantem posteris

tradituros esse. Quod tantum opus uestrum per tot annos e uicinis admirati regionibus, uelut grauior annis soror sororem laudat iuniorem, sic uestram nos Vniuersitatem, separati mari, amore penitus propinqui, et auximus semper laudibus et nunc augemus, omnibusque iustis honoribus cumulare cupimus.

Quippe non in academicis modo rebus, sed in rebus omnibus et publicis et priuatis, uobis nos ciuibusque uestris et semper fuisse coniunctissimos gaudemus, et semper fore optamus atque augura-mur. Atque in hoc sanctissimae collegio Trini-tatis, hoc ipso die cum in tot urbibus de summa re publica decertatur, illud saltem sine partium studio exoptare licet : posse fieri ut ex iurgiis et factionibus aliquando requiescant animi, atque ex trinitate nostrarum gentium—Scotorum, Anglorum, Hibernorum—noua quaedam et pulcherrima con-iungatur unitas : unitas studii atque animorum, unitas ingenii et litterarum, unitas legum atque imperii : ita ut patria nostra dilectissima, tergeminis unita uiribus, ad nouas usque famae exsurgat altitudines, et nominis nostri splendor usque clarius per terras omnes atque in omne tempus enitescat.

G. G. R.

DABAMVS GLASGVAE,
A.D. III Non. Iul. M.DCCC.XCII.

B b 2

Q. B. F. F. F. S.

Senatvs Academicvs Aberdonensis

Senatvi Academico Dvblinensi

S. D. P.

SOROREM in sororis suae rebus prosperis ipsam quoque laetari consentaneum est. Academiae igitur uestrae Ludos Saeculares tertium celebraturae, rite, ut par est, ex animo gratulamur, eoque impensius, quia gaudio est recordari Hiberniam uestram et Scotiam nostram genere lingua institutisque pristinis esse cognatas, adeo ut utra sit prisca Scotia in dubio relin-quendum sit. Huc quoque accessit uinculum cognationis arctissimum, quasi proprium et pe-culiare, quoniam unum ex Collegiis nostris, scilicet Mariscallanum, uestro Collegio inclito paene gemellum exstitit, quippe quod tantummodo uno anno posterius fundatum sit atque eodem fluctu decumano Religionis Reformatae sub Elizabethae clipeo illustri feliciter prouenerit.

Grandem igitur eximiamque seriem luminum uestrorum quae in litteris humanioribus scientiis-que per tria saecula inclaruerunt, iuuat con-templari, uestraeque Academiae omnia fausta precari. Quapropter Academiam uestram in insulis Britannicis maxime Occidentalem iterum

atque iterum salutat Academia maxime Arctoa.
Valete.

W. D. G.

ABERDONIAE,
Kal. Mart. A. D. M.DCCC.XCII.

SENATVI ACADEMICO DVBLINENSI
S. P. D.
SENATVS ACADEMICVS EDINBVRGENSIS.

QVOD nobis nuper saecularia sacra tertium
agentibus amicissime gratulati estis, pietate
simul atque officio impellimur ne in pari uestrum
laetitia nostra erga uos beneuolentia desideretur.
Qua in re uidemur uel optimo iure posse uobis
gratulari, si quidem inter nostram uestramque
Academiam non modo temporum quibus sunt
conditae congruentia, sed studiorum quoque
consensio haud mediocris intercessit. Quantum
enim in re medica per trecentos hos annos pariter
utraque elaborauerit neque ipsi ignoramus et uos
paulo ante comiter scriptis epistolis in memoriam
reduxistis. Accedit quod mathematicae scientiae
periti multi insignes uiri annales uestros nominibus illustrauerunt. Quorum plerique cum in
manibus et oculis hominum et sint et fuerint non

est quod nominatim enumerentur. Vnum uero Praesulem uestrum Georgium Salmon non possumus hoc loco silentio praeterire, quem propter miram ingeni doctrinaeque praestantiam mathematici simul atque theologi, tam exteri quam nostrates, certatim laudibus efferunt. Iam illud nouissimum decus quod Vniuersitas uestra sicut per tria saecula ceteris quae diximus studiis summa cum laude feliciter incubuit, ita intra hos proximos annos ad proprium litterarum humaniorum patrocinium acrius atque elatius aspirauit. Cuius quidem uoti ut compos fieret Professorum qui hodie uiuunt uigentque doctrina, acumine, sollertia perfectum est.

Decora praeterita recolentibus succurrit quasi saeculorum quoddam augurium futurorum. Placet uota pro incolumitate uestra publice nuncupare, ut quam uiam uobis usque adhuc fortunauerit Deus Optimus Maximus eam faustis ominibus ad immortalitatem gloriae sequamini.

Valete, et nobis, ut facitis, fauete.

Dabamus Edinburgi, mensis Iunii die uicesimo quarto, anno MDCCCXCII.

H. C. G.

Vniversitatem Dvblinensem
Vniversitas Victoria
SALVERE PLVRIMVM IVBET

BIS iam, uiri doctissimi, Britanniae sceptrum reginae ciuibus iure optimo dilectissimae plurimos per annos felicissimis tenuerunt auspiciis: quarum altera, quo melius inuida maris illius dissociabilis claustra refringeret et utriusque insulae populos artiore quodam uinculo cum ingeniorum tum pectorum coniungeret, Academiam uestram exstare iussit; altera autem, imperio mirandum in modum propagato, diuturna pace florentibus ciuibus et in liberalium artium studia magis magisque incumbentibus ita nouam doctrinae lucem et pocula sacra praebere uoluit, ut Collegia, haud secus ac paterna ipsius regna, tria iuncta in uno, nomine suo tamquam insigni Academiae nouae decore honestare dignaretur. Itaque non aliter quam natu minorem adultae iuuat sororis nuptiis adstare, nobis quoque cordi est feriis uestris interesse, et ad natales hosce iam tercentesimos celebrandos qua estis suauitate morum et comitate aduocatis fausta omnia precari. Vos quidem ad eam metam iam diu peruenistis quo nobis uixdum e carceribus emissis decurrendum est. Vobis per tot trium saeculorum uices uersatis nec constantia

defuit nec consilium nec uirtus; nulla non litterarum
et doctrinae certamina feliciter attigistis ; praeclara
ex omnibus partibus scientiae siue diuinae siue
humanae tropaea reportastis ; neque quisquam est
e re publica litterarum quin multum uel maximi
momenti alumnis uestris acceptum referat.   Nobis
quidem laus erit eximia ita uestris insistere
uestigiis ut iis tandem auspiciis aequiparemus,
quibus uos hodie clarissima alumnorum cohorte
stipati inter greges amicorum et ingenti hominum
plausu quartum iam uitae saeculum inire pergitis.

G. H. R.

A. D. III *Non. Iul.* M.DCCC.XCII.

INDEX TO ENGLISH PASSAGES

[The Number prefixed to a Reference is the number of that Passage in Vol. II of ‘Ramsay's Latin Prose Composition.' The Initials following it are those of the Author of the Latin Version.]

FINIS.